Another epic, heart wrenching, fire igniting, earth shattering dark romance written by the fabulous Zoe Blake!
- Maysen M.

Zoe Blake has done it again. This book and this entire series is not one you that want you want to miss!
- Dirty Romance Reviews

Zoe Blake can write some spicy, aggressive, alpha men, there is no question in that, but she also gives them strong willed women to fight them on everything, and I go feral for it!
- BookBirches

Speechless! I devoured this book in less than day! From beginning to end it was everything and more.
From Bianca to Enzo everything was AMAZING.
- More Books To Read

Enzo and Bianca finally get their story and it is heartbreaking and devastating at times, but also hopeful and inspiring. Secrets of the Brother was sensational and spectacular.
- Kelly Reads Books

SECRETS OF THE BROTHER

A DARK ENEMIES TO LOVERS ROMANCE

CAVALIERI BILLIONAIRE LEGACY
BOOK THREE

ZOE BLAKE

Poison Ink Publications

Blake, Zoe

Poison Ink Publications

Secrets of the Brother

Cover Design by Dark City Designs

Model Blaze A.

Photographer Wander Aguiar

CONTENTS

CHAPTER 1

BIANCA

*E*nzo Cavalieri's glare was like a hand wrapped around my throat.

His strong fingers slowly forcing the air from my lungs.

I tilted my chin to the side, hiding my face behind the wide brim of my hat.

It didn't help.

I hadn't seen Enzo in close to seven months... *not since that awful night.*

The night that changed—everything.

He was still as handsome as the devil himself, and if the rumors were to be believed about my sister, just as evil.

I clawed at the sheer black veil draped over the black pearl wheel hat brim and secured around my neck, obscuring my face. Loosening the folds, I inhaled a shaky breath, grateful no one could see the hot flush on my cheeks.

As a uniformed server passed, I plucked at his sleeve, halting him.

His tray carried a small crystal plate of amaretti cookies surrounded by delicate bone china cups of espresso.

I lifted one of the espressos by the saucer.

Raising my veil as high as my nose, I tried to take a sip, but my stomach turned at its bitterness.

The cup clattered against the saucer as my hand trembled putting it back in place. Several heads turned in my direction. I pulled the veil down over my face again and set the cup and saucer on the nearest table.

Risking another glance under the brim, the blood in my veins crystallized into tiny sharp icicles which pierced every nerve ending as I froze in place under Enzo's continued intense, icy scrutiny.

What had I been thinking?

Slapping him like that in front of all those people... and in church, no less.

Everyone knew the Cavalieris were practically a force of nature in Italy.

Their name was synonymous with power and wealth.

It was no coincidence their name meant *knight*.

Their family legacy stretched back to the time of feudal lords, probably even further. I wouldn't be surprised if there were ancient papyrus scrolls buried in the caves of the nearby Apennine mountains with the Cavalieri name attached to some Roman general or forgotten emperor.

They owned half of western Italy, including the village I grew up in which was named after them.

There wasn't a family I knew that didn't somehow owe their livelihoods to the beneficence of the Cavalieris, including my own.

So to freaking slap Enzo, the eldest son, the heir to the Cavalieri throne? In church?

In the middle of my sister's funeral?

Never mind he was my brother-in-law.

Never mind that half the village believed he murdered my sister.

Never mind he had been the man I desperately loved before my sister stole him from me.

Never mind he was the reason why I fled to America.

Never mind the very sight of him brought all those bitter memories flooding back. Weighing down my heart until I thought it would become unmoored from within my body, sending it crashing into my bones, breaking them like a loose anchor splintering weathered wood.

I clenched my jaw and stared straight ahead, willing the threatening tears not to fall. My nose itched. My eyes stung. My eyelids fluttered, the alternating flashes of bright sunlight and pitch-black darkness disorienting me. Swaying, I dug my fingernails into the edge of the table for stability.

I had the dizzying urge to faint.

Dark oblivion would be a blessed relief right now. A salvation from this living hell.

The cloying scent of carnation, bergamot, and amber preceded my mother's approach. My earliest memory of her was the stench of Yves Saint Laurent's Opium perfume, which clung to her like a moth-eaten fur wrap.

It was why I hated the scent, or even the sight, of carnations.

She dug her claws into the soft flesh of my upper arm,

holding me in place to hiss, "Stop making a spectacle of yourself, Bianca," in my ear.

I bit the inside of my cheek, the pain centering me. "My apologies, Claudia." I hadn't been allowed to call her "Mother" in public since I was six years old. "Exactly how should one behave when attending a murdered sister's funeral?"

She tightened her grip.

I winced but resisted the urge to pull away. I wouldn't give her the satisfaction.

"For starters, you don't slap the grieving husband in front of the priest and Don Cavalieri like some common trollop," she snapped, her hot breath wreaking of menthol cigarettes and Amaro liquor. "And stop using that vulgar word."

I lifted one eyebrow. "Trollop?"

"No," she seethed through clenched teeth slightly smeared with crimson lipstick. "You know very well I mean *murdered*," she gritted out. "Your sister's death was a *tragic accident*."

Yes, she *tragically accidentally* tripped into a man's fists several times over until she died, and then she *tragically accidentally* fell over a cliff.

The whole damn village, including my parents, knew who that man was, but no one was brave enough to utter his name out loud... including me.

I lifted my veil, tucking it up on the brim to better survey the sallow pallor of her complexion underneath the layers of contouring makeup, but avoiding her glassy eyes trying to focus on me.

"A bit early for *Mother's Little Helper*, isn't it, Mommy dearest?"

"It's a shame you weren't charming enough to keep a man

like Enzo Cavalieri's attention. Then it would be you moldering in the ground"—she pressed a wrinkled handkerchief to her nose— "instead of my beautiful Renata."

After twenty-three years, knife strikes straight to the heart like that should have stopped hurting. They didn't.

I inhaled deeply through my nose in a vain attempt to control my emotions before responding.

It didn't work.

The corner of my mouth lifted in a smirk. "I'm sorry, Claudia. I don't think he found Renata *charming* as much as he enjoyed my sister's *charms*."

Her eyes widened.

With a huff, she opened her clutch and fumbled for her cigarette case. Tucking a cigarette in her mouth, she let it dangle from her obscenely red lips, vainly trying several times to spark her lighter. "How dare you say such things about your dead sister. And at her funeral!"

I yanked the lighter from her hands and lit the cigarette.

It annoyed me that she was right. It was in poor taste.

There was no love lost between me and Renata.

A lifetime of her cruel behavior toward me, capped off by her ultimate betrayal, put an end to any sisterly affection I may at one time have foolishly harbored. But she was still family and I owed her at least that much respect.

I tossed the lighter back into my mother's purse. "Why are we even here? That man"—I still couldn't say his name— "killed her. Why did you and Father agree to let him and his family host the funeral? Talk about disrespecting Renata. How can you let him play the grieving husband like this?"

My mother blew a cloud of smoke in my face. "Shut your mouth. Someone will hear you."

"Are you serious? Mother—"

"Claudia."

I let out a frustrated sigh. "Claudia, the entire fucking—"

"Don't curse. Only trollops curse."

I looked heavenward and prayed for patience.

Taking a deep breath, I started again, speaking slowly. "Claudia, the entire fu—the entire village is here gossiping about how he's the one who probably killed Renata. Everyone knows it's *always* the husband. Anyone who watches *Dateline* knows that."

"What is *Dateline*?"

"It's an American true crime show, but that's not the point. The point is, he killed your daughter and you're here fawning all over him like he's the suffering son-in-law."

She picked a nonexistent piece of tobacco off her lip before responding.

It was a gesture she'd seen an Italian sex symbol do in an old black-and-white movie once.

Everything about my mother was affectation.

Same with my sister, or at least it had been the same with my sister.

"We never should have agreed to let you study in America. It has given you a smart mouth." After an overly dramatic sigh, she continued. "Bianca, there are sensitive business matters at play here that don't concern you."

Translation—my parents' greed couldn't afford to make an enemy of the Cavalieri billions.

I lowered my veil to cover my face once again. "Well I, for one, want no part of this farce. I'm going home."

I had only taken a few steps when I was wrenched back by my hair.

"Where do you think you're going?"

I turned to face my furious father, Bruno Moretti. His bloated face was a mottled purple.

I pulled my long curls out of his grasp and lowered my voice as I responded. "Home."

"The hell you are. You're going to march up there and pay your respects to Don Cavalieri and offer your brother-in-law a groveling apology for your disgraceful behavior earlier. I have already told them it was a side effect of some tranquilizers an American doctor gave you to handle your grief over your sister's tragic passing."

I wrenched my veil back up to face him. "I will do no such thing."

His beefy fist shot out and grabbed the collar of my dress. "Listen, you spoiled little bitch—"

Before I could respond, an iron band wrapped around my waist and pulled me backward against a solid wall of muscle, breaking my father's hold.

A dark, commanding voice ground out, "Get your hands off her."

I looked up past the brim of my hat to see Enzo Cavalieri's cold, emerald eyes glaring down at me.

CHAPTER 2

ENZO

*N*o one touched her like that and lived.

No one. Not even her father.

I didn't give a fuck if every last person in this room was only here to gawk at the wife killer.

And that this was giving them even more fodder for the gossip mill.

No one touched my girl.

As least, she *had* been mine before I fucked everything up.

My fingers tightened around her waist.

Christ, she felt good pressed against my side.

It felt… right. Except it was wrong. All wrong.

I inhaled the familiar scent of her perfume. I never knew what it was called, but I always associated the scent of spicy jasmine with her. A part of me was glad she hadn't changed it over the last few months. It was a subtle attachment to the past, a nostalgic connection to what had been between us.

Her startled dark eyes stared back at me from under the brim of the hat she had been using as a weapon all morning to shield her face from my gaze.

In their depths, fear and uncertainty swirled.

That one innocent display of raw emotion nearly sent me to my knees like no false show of my own grief for a conniving wife ever could. Those same eyes had once turned to me as her protector, her knight.

Now I was the enemy.

The man who broke her heart in the most brutal and heartless way imaginable.

The man who murdered her sister.

I couldn't even claim to be a tarnished knight in a dark fairy tale.

I was the villain in her nightmare.

Bianca's stiffening body tried to pull away.

I tightened my grasp.

With a look of warning from me, she stilled.

By now, both Cavalieri security and the extra men Sebastian Diamanti had provided in case there was trouble at the funeral had covertly circled us.

Refocusing my attention on Bruno Moretti, I said, "Gentlemen, Signore and Signora Moretti are feeling overwhelmed from the day's events. Please escort them home."

Claudia Moretti choked on a puff of smoke as she opened her mouth to object.

Bruno placed a restraining hand on her arm and glanced over my shoulder before responding, "I think you may be right, *son.*"

I didn't miss the reference to our familial connection because of my ill-fated marriage to his daughter, nor his look over my shoulder. I also didn't have to follow his gaze to know my father and brother were standing behind me, quietly supporting my decision.

Claudia tossed her cigarette into a discarded cup of espresso. "Come, Bianca."

Bianca began to shift her body in obedience to her mother's order.

Using my grasp on her waist, I took advantage of her momentum to push her behind me while I stepped forward. "She stays. It's been months since I've seen my... *sister*. I find her presence...comforting...in my *grief*."

A soft, outraged gasp erupted behind me.

There was going to be hell to pay for what I was doing, but I just couldn't summon up enough fucks to care anymore.

She wasn't leaving with her parents.

Not before I had a chance to speak with her alone.

A chance I had been denied after that night.

The night that ruined everything.

The night I fucked up and destroyed the future I had planned for us.

As if controlled by puppet strings, Bruno and Claudia's heads moved in stiff unison to survey the guests who were covertly hanging on every word of our exchange.

Bruno clutched at Claudia's forearm and whispered something harshly in her ear. The only phrase I caught was "the slap."

Bruno then nodded. "Of course. Of course, *son*."

There it was again.

Shoe leather scuffed against marble as my father moved closer and settled his hand on my shoulder. "*My son* and I once again offer our condolences for your terrible loss."

Bruno and Claudia caught the hint.

Bruno cleared his throat and said loudly enough for anyone listening to hear, "Thank you, Don Cavalieri. I know you loved our beautiful and charming Renata like a daughter and will always cherish her memory as we do."

Bile burned the back of my throat.

Their beautiful and charming daughter, *my wife*, had conspired with one of the most dangerous crime families in Italy, the Agnellos.

She had also tried to kill Milana, my brother's fiancée, in cold blood.

It was still a question whether their baby would survive the ordeal or not.

And all for what? Money?

As my wife, she'd had more money than any one human being could ever need in a lifetime and still, it wasn't enough to satisfy her greed.

It had taken a great deal of that same money and influence to cover up the scandal and rush the funeral.

All so we could honor the *beautiful and charming* Renata, tragic victim of a senseless accident.

A bullshit story *no one* was buying.

I looked over my shoulder in time to see my cousin Matteo wrap his arm over my brother Cesare's shoulders and move him away before he said something to ruin the carefully orchestrated farce we had been performing all morning.

Thank God, at least Milana and Amara were safe at the villa and away from all this poison. Poor Milana attended the funeral of her would-be killer to keep up appearances for the family and for me, not that I deserved such a show of love and support from her. But it was too much to force her to mingle at the after-event.

Fuck, I needed this to be over.

Catching Alfonso's eye, he gave me a nod and gestured to the guards standing by who were dressed in dark suits to blend in with the rest of the mourners. They quickly encircled the Morettis and ushered them out before they could cause any more trouble.

I turned to face Bianca.

She stepped back, breaking my hold on her waist. Placing her fists on her hips, she said, "How dare yo—"

I wrapped my arm back around her and pulled her close. "Not one word."

As I ushered her out of the room, I tossed over my shoulder to the nearest guard, "See that no one follows us."

We crossed the expansive marble entranceway to my private study. The moment we cleared the threshold, Bianca broke free. She stormed several steps away and turned on me.

Ripping her hat and veil off, she held them before her like a shield. "Why have you brought me in here?"

I closed the door and locked it. "We need to talk."

Her eyes widened as she raised her arm and gestured behind me. "Unlock that door this instant."

"No."

God, she was gorgeous. She looked like a Fellini film

suddenly burst into glorious color. She was the living embodiment of Sylvia, my own unattainable woman.

La Dolce Vita.

La Vita Amara.

Thoughts of her over these last few months had tortured me. The idea that I couldn't touch her, hold her, protect her, had been slowly driving me insane.

The only thing worse than being separated from her was the heart-wrenching knowledge that I had no one but myself to blame.

I had caused this beautiful, sweet creature pain and for that I deserved every twisted, tormented moment of madness.

Unable to stop myself, I stepped toward her, my fingers flexing as if already anticipating the soft, warm feel of her skin pressing against my palms once more. The feeling was like a drug, and I craved it more than my next breath.

Bianca backed away, placing a leather chair between us. "Don't come any closer."

Her dark eyes were bright and alert with fear as her gaze darted about the room. The same fear added a warm pink flush to her cheeks. I really had degenerated into a sick bastard for thinking the terror my very presence inspired actually added to her natural beauty.

I ran the tip of my finger over my lower lip, studying her, measuring my next words carefully. "I owe you an apology."

It was thin broth, a meager statement of fact given the magnitude of the destruction I had wrought and yet I hoped against hope that the simplest, most straightforward appeal, unweighted by any self-serving prose, would get her to just...

stay... here... with me, alone in this room, if only for a few minutes more.

I just needed her to stay.

I couldn't let her go, not just yet.

Pressing her lips between her teeth, she stared at the ceiling and blinked rapidly before rasping, "I don't give a damn about your apologies."

I crossed the room until I was within an arm's length of her. "Please, Bianca. I need you to understand."

Her hat slipped from her fingers as she staggered back a step, bracing her palm against the flat surface of my desk.

The tears she was trying so hard to hold back fell down her cheeks, leaving a watery, light-gray stain from her mascara.

"What part do you need me to understand, Enzo? The part where you said you loved me? Or the part where you broke up with me over a *text message* and then *slept with my sister?*"

I raised my arm and swung my fist out to slam it into the side of a nearby bookcase. "Dammit, Bianca. I have told you that it wasn't me who texted you that night. She put something in my drink."

Bianca jumped at my show of violence and skirted around the desk.

"I know that. You think I don't know that? I know what my sister was capable of. I know what she was like. But why? Why did you have to go and marry her?"

I deliberately flexed my fingers, forcing them straight, when all I wanted to do was curl them into fists and rage with my frustration. "You know why."

"You could have waited. Made sure she was really pregnant. Made sure the baby was yours."

I ran my hand through my hair. "She threatened to... you know what she threatened... unless I married her as soon as possible. I couldn't take that chance. I didn't have a fucking choice."

She slowly shook her head as she twisted her fingers in the fabric of her dress. "There's always a choice... and you made yours. You know what, it doesn't matter. None of this matters. It's not like we had been dating that long. We weren't engaged or anything. You said you loved me, but we hadn't even... not like you had with her...so...obviously you and she were better suited. Right?"

The raw pain of betrayal in her voice brought me up short.

It was that final question, the one practically begging me to agree with all the bullshit she just said.

This whole building could crumble into dust around me, and I wouldn't notice.

My entire focus was on Bianca.

Her every breath. The way her lower lip trembled. The barest movement of her eyes. The way her pupils dilated at my approach. The flush on her cheeks. The rapid beat of her pulse at the base of her throat. The pitch of her voice. How her arm lifted as if to reach for me too before it fell to her side while she shook her head and denied me.

She still loved me.

A dangerous, almost feral, possessive heat fired in my chest.

It was hope.

It might just be a small, deeply buried flame she was desperately trying to smother, but it was still there.

Her body betrayed her mind.

In that moment, I didn't give a fuck about the obstacles, or the possible murder charge hanging over my head, or the future.

There was only us, and the rest of the world be damned.

I could survive anything if I knew I hadn't completely lost her love.

I reached for her.

She fell backward until her body slammed against the other bookcase.

"Don't even think about it. *You made your choice!*"

She snatched up a brass letter opener from my desk. Grasping it in her right hand, she held it before her like a dagger.

"I'd say it was one you'd have to live with, but we both know that isn't true, is it, Enzo?"

I looked from her face to the sharp edge of the letter opener and back. Keeping my gaze trained on her, I ripped off my suit coat and tossed it aside then stepped closer until the tip of the letter opener pressed against the flesh over my heart. "Ask me."

I wanted no more lies or betrayals between us.

She wrapped her left hand around her right fist to steady her hold. Before responding, she nervously licked her lips, wetting them. They were now a glossy dark pink.

Her brow furrowed. "What?"

I clenched my stomach to stifle a hungry growl.

My mouth watered as I remembered the taste of those sweet lips.

My gaze focused on her beautiful mouth with her partially open lips, jealously watching each gasping breath entering her body.

"Ask me if I killed your sister."

CHAPTER 3

BIANCA

*M*y body trembled so badly I almost dropped the letter opener.

Enzo's warm hand covered my fists, steadying my hands and actually pressing the edge more firmly against his heart.

I traveled halfway around the world to get over this man.

And still, the chains he had wrapped around my heart were unbroken.

It was like he had some kind of dark power over me.

His very nearness made me quake with awareness.

My lower lip quivered as tears blurred my vision.

"Don't do this to me, Enzo," I whispered.

"Ask me, *tesoro mio.*"

My treasure.

White-hot anger flared inside me, fanning the flames of betrayal, at hearing one of his pet names for me. "Stop it! You don't get to call me that. Not after what you did. Not after what you've done."

My heart couldn't take this.

I thought I was strong.

I thought I was over him.

I thought my bitter hate was enough of a shield, but it wasn't.

My hatred for him had dissipated like smoke the moment his arm wrapped around my waist and I looked up into his vivid green eyes. Eyes that seemed to see deep within my soul and guess all my secrets.

Eyes that seemed to guess my darkest secret of all... that I still loved him.

Despite the betrayal, and the pain.

Defying all reason and sense of self-preservation, I loved him.

And I hate myself for it.

But it didn't matter, I at least had enough self-respect to fight it with every fiber of my being.

I would rather be miserable and alone, clinging to a useless love, than crawl back to him.

He'd made his choice.

He'd chosen her over me.

Now we would both live with the consequences.

Her death hadn't changed anything.

He leaned in closer. The pointed edge of the letter opener pierced the thin linen of his shirt. A tiny droplet of crimson blossomed through the crisp white fabric.

"Ask me, Bianca," he ground out. "Ask me if I murdered Renata."

I couldn't.

I wanted to know.

I needed to know.

But the truth would destroy me.

There was no hope for us.

No future.

I knew that and was determined to stick by my decision to stay away from him... But somehow, the only way I could possibly live with the decision was if I allowed the tiniest bit of light into the darkness, the slimmest, faintest possibility of... maybe.

It was like the option of *maybe* made the decision to stay away *my choice*.

It gave me a weird semblance of power, despite feeling powerless and overwhelmed with sadness at the thought of walking away from him forever.

Forever wasn't truly forever until you made it so.

If I knew with certainty he murdered my sister, it would have to be forever.

If it remained a question, then forever was a construct of my own choosing.

Before I could respond, Enzo growled a curse and wrapped his strong fingers around my slim wrists. "Dammit, Bianca. You're still mine and I'll prove it to you."

I lost my grip on the letter opener.

It clattered to the floor at our feet.

He used his hips to further imprison me as his mouth fell on mine.

His tongue swept inside so forcefully he stole the breath from my body. Releasing my wrists, his hands moved to cup my jaw, tilting my head back as he drove his fingers into my hair. Twisting his fist into my curls, anchoring me.

The sharp edges of my teeth pressed against the soft inner flesh of my lips as he took possession.

I whimpered, trying to turn my head away, overwhelmed by his onslaught, but his grip on my hair prevented it.

His lips moved to the corner of my mouth, the edge of my jawline. The tip of his tongue licked the tears from my cheek. His powerful body towered over me, caging me in.

He pulled back, cupping my face as he stared down at me, piercing me with his intense gaze. "Christ, I've missed the sweet taste of you."

He claimed my mouth again. This time there was an edge of desperation to his kiss, as if he were a man starved. His hand moved down over my throat to cup my breast through my dress.

I moaned, lost in the feel of his touch.

Lost in the past.

His hand slid down to my waist, fingers possessively gripping my hip and sending a shiver up my spine. His teeth nipped at my bottom lip before his tongue teased mine again. He palmed the fabric of my dress, raising the hem.

The hard length of his cock pressed against my stomach. A threat and a promise.

His mouth moved down my throat as he pushed the hem of my dress higher.

He slipped his hand under my knee and lifted my leg high, allowing him to thrust his hips against my core.

I gripped his shoulder and gasped at the intimate contact.

Heat pooled in my stomach, my inner thighs clenching.

His free hand wrapped around my neck as he rasped, "I need to be inside of you. Now, baby," against my lips.

Alone in my bed, an ocean away, I had dreamed a thousand times about what it would feel like to have him finally press his weight between my thighs and push deep inside of me.

For we'd never had a chance to be intimate when we were together.

I had wanted to take it slow.

But each time, the dream turned into the same nightmare.

Each time, I switched places with my sister, and was forced to watch as she fucked the man I loved.

And now my sister is dead.

And the man I love killed her.

It was too much.

I pushed against his chest, wrenching my head to the side. "I can't."

He dropped his grip on my leg and clasped both his hands on either side of my face. "Bianca?"

I curled my shoulders inward and straightened my arms, shoving against his embrace. "I can't do this."

He pressed his palm against the base of my skull as he wrapped his other arm around my waist, forcing my body flush with his chest. "No. Fuck that. I won't lose you again."

I opened my mouth to cry out, but he swallowed my scream with a kiss so violent I tasted the coppery tang of blood.

His arm secured me tightly to him. I didn't know where I ended and he began.

He broke our kiss, and for the barest of moments, pressed his lips to my forehead as he pled, "Please, *tesoro mio*. I need you."

I desperately wanted that to be enough.

I wanted the sound of his voice and the taste of his lips and the feel of his arms and the idea of us together again to be enough… but they weren't.

I had struggled too long and too hard to forget him.

And now there was blood between us.

I broke free. "No. You made your choice."

I stumbled toward the door.

Enzo grabbed me from behind, his hand wrapping around my throat, his arm closing around my ribcage.

Enveloping me in his unyielding embrace, he pushed my head against his shoulder as he snarled in my ear, "You belong to me, Bianca. Nothing has changed that."

Terror seized the air in my lungs.

He was so much bigger and stronger than me.

"You have to let me go, Enzo."

"Never," he said fiercely. "I made that mistake once. I won't do it again."

He spun me around to face him. His eyes were dark with heated purpose.

I backed away. "I'll scream."

He loosened his tie as he stalked toward me. "Scream. Kick. Slap me again. Do whatever you want to me, babygirl. I'm not letting you go."

In a last-ditch effort, I tried to dash past him.

He caught me around my waist with one arm and lifted me off my feet.

I kicked out as he placed me on the edge of the desk and forced my thighs open, stepping between them.

Once again, he wrapped his hand around the back of my neck and pulled me close, claiming my mouth.

This time, I kept my lips tightly closed.

Enzo growled his frustration.

He gripped my jaw. "Open your mouth for me."

Releasing his hold, he pushed his hand between my legs, palming my pussy.

I cried out.

His fingers slipped past the silk edge of my panties to caress me.

He leaned in and bit my earlobe before whispering harshly, "I can feel how wet and ready you are. You were meant for me. It was you who was meant to be my wife, who was meant to bear my child. You, Bianca, not your sister. *You.* You were always meant to be mine."

Over our labored breathing, I heard the metallic clicks of him lowering his zipper.

Oh, God.

A harsh knock at the study door broke the spell. "Enzo?"

It was his father, Don Cavalieri.

Neither of us answered.

After a pause, Don Cavalieri continued to speak through the door. "You're needed. Benito just arrived. He has a coroner's report."

CHAPTER 4

ENZO

My father knocked again. "Enzo?"

I called out over my shoulder, "I'm coming."

I looked down at Bianca's frightened, tearstained face.

I was a fucking monster.

I stepped back and turned. After zipping up my trousers, I faced her and ran a hand through my hair. "Bianca, I—"

She slid off the desk. "Don't."

She pushed her wrinkled dress back into place and leaned down to pick up her discarded hat and veil then moved toward the door.

I blocked her path.

Her body stiffened in response.

Raising my palms, I took a step back to give her space. "I shouldn't have taken it that far. I just—I needed— Fuck! Please, Bianca. I need to see you again. We need to talk. I need to tell you about Rena—"

Her eyes widened as all the color drained from her face.

She staggered backward, slowly shaking her head. "No! I don't want to hear it."

Fresh tears fell down her cheeks. "I just want to forget that I ever knew you. *That I ever loved you.*"

She darted around me, unlocked the door and flung it open, almost colliding with my father as she dashed out of the room.

Papà sent me a questioning look. "Should I send someone to stop her?"

I bent to pick up my discarded suit jacket and shrugged into it. Clearing my throat, I said, "No. I'm sure Alfonso will send a guard to escort her home."

He nodded. "I'm sorry, son."

I swallowed past the lump in my throat. "So am I."

* * *

To AVOID anyone overhearing our conversation, we led Benito down to the wine cellars located below my house. Similar to the rooms underneath the villa, these were essentially man-made caves carved out of rock over a couple thousand years ago.

Ancient soundproofing.

My brother Cesare was already down there, along with my cousin Matteo and his father, my Uncle Benedict.

My father's older brother had traveled down from the family's properties in the north, as a show of support.

Since he was somewhat infamous in our family for being a curmudgeon who hated society and preferred the company of the champion horses he raised, it was a quiet testament to how much trouble I was in that he made an appearance for this sham funeral, especially since he hadn't bothered to attend my sham wedding.

The spitting image of my father, he crossed the room and handed me a glass of Scotch he had poured from a bottle he must have snatched from the bar upstairs. "Drink. I have a feeling you're going to need it," he said as he clapped me on the shoulder.

He then made the rounds, splashing Scotch into everyone's empty glasses.

I took the etched crystal glass and nodded but didn't drink.

I couldn't stop thinking about Bianca.

Christ, she looked even more beautiful in person than I remembered, which was saying a lot since her beauty had reached idolatry proportions in my imagination.

There wasn't a day, an hour, a minute that had gone by that I hadn't thought about her.

Even her most mundane daily activities consumed me.

What was she eating?

What was she reading?

I never looked at a clock without calculating the time difference between Italy and New York and comparing it to what she would be doing in that moment.

Bianca would be sleeping right now.

Bianca would be in her graphic design class right now.

Bianca would be... with another man right now.

The last possibility was what had kept me up at night. It was what had kept me reaching for the bottle more often than

I liked. I was shocked I wasn't a complete raging alcoholic by now.

I probably would be if I hadn't taken *certain measures*.

I wasn't proud of what I'd done.

Hell, fucking Renata and getting her pregnant was just the tip of the iceberg.

If Bianca knew the lengths I'd gone to….

I glanced down at the amber liquid in my glass and raised it to my lips, savoring the burn as it flowed down my throat.

She could never find out.

It was a secret I kept, even from my close family.

Bianca only thought she was angry with me now.

If only she knew….

I really was a monster.

Casting her aside to marry her sister, but then making damn sure no other man would claim what I still considered mine.

That no man touched what was mine.

And I still considered Bianca mine.

It defied all sense of moral decency. It flew in the face of all logic. It made a mockery of the vows I took before God. It damned me for a liar. And it laid bare that I was not the honorable gentleman I once aspired to be.

And I couldn't care less.

She. Was. Mine.

No matter that she was living halfway across the world.

Fortunately, I had the money and the connections to keep tabs on every aspect of her life. I knew what she ate for breakfast. I knew the passwords to her computer. I knew her favorite cafe and the names of all her friends in New York. I had even made sure she was occupied beyond her usual schoolwork with business clients through various shell companies I set up so she would have no time for a social life.

I really was a fucking bastard.

If I hadn't been so distracted with the cover-up of Renata's murder and the rushed funeral, I would have been able to prevent Bianca returning from America before I was ready. I would have cancelled her credit cards or paid to have her passport flagged so she couldn't fly.

Money bought a person all kinds of manipulative ways to get something done.

The first sight of her in the flesh after so much time apart rocked me to my core.

The one line I had refused to cross during these long, torturous months was I had never allowed myself to fly to New York to see her, even from a distance. I knew I would not have the self-control to stay in the shadows, and this afternoon proved it.

The moment I saw her, smelled her perfume, touched her, kissed her—I was like a man possessed.

All my careful planning for our future together had gone up in smoke.

I needed her now. In that moment. I needed to be inside her. I needed to finally claim her as mine. I was done waiting. I was over trying to pay for my mistake. I wanted the future I was supposed to have had with her. I wanted her as my wife. And if I were truly honest with myself, I needed to get her pregnant. I wanted her to bear my child. I wanted a blood tie to her. A bond she could never break.

In my zeal, I had almost fucked her on my goddamn desk

as if she were no better than a whore, instead of the cherished love of my life. Instead of the innocent I knew her to be.

I really was a fucking monster.

And now I had ruined everything.

Fuck.

Benito interrupted my gloomy thoughts.

He tossed a manila folder onto a dusty wine cask and sighed as he put his hands into his uniform pockets as if to distance himself from any ownership of the file. "It arrived today. You have to know, I didn't even know it was being prepared or who ordered it. And I have to warn you, you're not going to like it."

All six of us stood around the barrel in silence, staring at the folder. None of us moved.

Finally, Papà set his drink down and reached for the folder.

Benito looked at him and warned, "Don Cavalieri, it's not pretty."

He met Benito's look and nodded once before opening the folder.

There was a tense silence.

Papà flipped through several papers and photos, then said, "Homicide."

The room seemed to release a collective breath.

Matteo crossed to stand close to me, in a silent show of support. "Well, we already knew that. The question is what happens now?"

Benito cast a swift glance in my direction then shifted his gaze away. "An investigation, of course. Witnesses will have to be interviewed."

Cesare spoke. "Not Milana."

Benito rubbed his eyes. "Cesare, I can't control—"

Cesare wrapped his left palm over his right fist. "I'm telling you right now. Not Milana. She has already been through too much. It's still touch and go with the baby. I won't have her upset over that bitch."

The liquor in my empty stomach soured.

I resisted the urge to retch.

One more fallout from my choices.

One more stain on my soul.

One more casualty of that awful night.

Each time I witnessed my beloved brother's pain it was like a knife to my chest. I'd caused that. Me, and me alone. It didn't matter that Renata was the one who tried to kill Milana and damn near succeeded. Or that she was responsible for Milana's past trauma or the fear that still plagued her and my brother over the future of their unborn child.

If only I hadn't been stupid enough to accept that drugged cocktail that fateful night from Renata.

If only I hadn't slept with her.

If only I hadn't gotten her pregnant and compounded the mistake by insisting on doing the honorable thing by marrying her.

If I hadn't brought that viper into my family, none of this would have happened.

If.

If.

If.

I bore the weight of that guilt.

Papà leaned his palms on the metal rims of the barrel and

leveled a stern look at Benito. "Cesare is right, Benito. We all went to great lengths to cover up Renata's attempt on Milana's life, to avoid a family scandal. So there should be no reason to interview either of the girls in relation to Renata's disappearance and murder. They both have solid alibis, as does the entire family. We stick to the story. Milana accidentally got trapped in the wine cave and was rushed to the hospital. The entire family was standing vigil waiting on news during the time of Renata's disappearance."

He then gestured to the file. "And according to this report, she died within hours of her disappearance which means we were all still at the hospital."

Benito shuffled from foot to foot as he stared at the floor. "Not everyone."

Papà frowned. "What?"

Benito cocked his head toward me. "Not everyone was at the hospital at the time of her disappearance and murder."

All eyes in the room turned to me.

Benito continued. "Unfortunately, Don Cavalieri, it is well documented that Enzo stormed out of the hospital at some point and was not seen for quite some time afterward, until the alarm was raised over the cottage fire on the vineyard grounds."

No one spoke.

Cesare stepped forward. He placed a hand on Benito's shoulder. "Thank you for bringing this to us, Benito. There are some things we need to discuss as a family."

Benito nodded. Part of our family's *understanding* with the police department in the village was we didn't tell them what they didn't strictly need to know, and they didn't ask any questions.

Pulling his car keys from his jacket pocket, Benito gave us a final heads-up. "One more thing, the head office is bringing in an independent inspector to take over the case. I haven't been told anything about him, or even when he'll arrive. I'll keep you posted when I know more. Maybe we'll get lucky and he'll be *friendly*." He then turned and left.

Friendly, code for either bribable or vulnerable to blackmail.

No one said anything for several moments.

I stared at the file on the desk as if it would suddenly sprout teeth and claws and jump up and bite me.

Taking a deep breath, I broke the silence. "Was she pregnant?"

Papà frowned as he repeated my question. "Was she pregnant?"

I raised my chin toward the file. "Renata. Was she pregnant?"

Papà opened the file and scanned the coroner's report. Finally he looked up at me. I could tell by the look in his eyes, even before he spoke. "No, son. There is no evidence she was ever pregnant."

I threw my head back and laughed. The sound bitter and brittle.

All of this damage and destruction and she was never even pregnant. The sonograms and doctors' notes must have all been faked by Renata, just as I had begun to suspect.

Uncle Benedict exchanged a look with Papà. "Time for Plan B."

Cesare looked between them both. "Want to clue us in on Plan B?"

Uncle Benedict responded. "Matteo and I will leave for the north tonight and take Enzo with us. Worst case scenario, if charges are filed, Enzo will be able to slip over the border into Switzerland before they find him. There won't be a trail. We have loyal friends who will meet him on the other side."

Cesare cursed under his breath. He paced away and then pivoted back. "This is insane. He'd be a fugitive. He could never return to Italian soil. Papà, you can't be seriously considering this?"

"It might be our only option."

Cesare continued to object. "Bullshit. You weathered the scandal over Mom's death. And we all know you...."

He left the rest unspoken.

There was no need to say it out loud. We all knew my father was responsible for my mother's death.

"That was different. Your mother was sick and dying. Renata was...."

I spoke softly. "Beaten to death."

Everyone turned to stare at me.

Uncle Benedict drained his glass and set it down. "It's settled. We'll wait until the guests leave. Enzo, pack as little as possible. We don't want to raise any warning flags."

I inhaled deeply. "I'm not going."

My father faced me. "Son—"

I lifted my chin and met his gaze. "I'm not going, and that's final."

I had already caused my family enough pain with my choices and mistakes. I wasn't about to compound it by making another one. They would be under constant suspicion if I became a fugitive. I couldn't allow that. I would face the consequences of my actions.

I took a final sip and set my glass aside. Buttoning my suit jacket, I nodded to the men in the room. "Now, if you will excuse me, I have been neglecting my guests."

* * *

As I WALKED down the deserted hall, I couldn't help thinking, not one of them asked if I had killed her.

Over this entire long, excruciating week, from the moment they found my wife's body, through the frenzied cover-up and funeral preparations, to this moment, not one of them—not my father, not my brother, not my uncle or my cousin—not one of them had asked if I had actually killed Renata.

They all just assumed I had blood on my hands.

CHAPTER 5

ENZO

*A*fter the final mourner, and I used the term loosely, left, I climbed the stairs to my bedroom.

The burnished gold and hunter-green tapestries and heavy, dark mahogany furniture soothed me after hours of staring at Renata's appallingly tasteless decor. My bedroom and study were my two sanctuaries in the vast home I owned off the central piazza of Cavalieri village.

Since I never slept with Renata after that fateful night, there was no point in sharing a bedroom.

Ours was a marriage in name only.

I didn't want my child growing up a bastard.

It was the only reason why I'd married her. The only reason why I'd broken the heart of the woman I truly loved. It was to secure the safety and happiness of my future child.

The child that never existed.

I pulled off my tie and jacket and tossed them over the valet stand next to the wardrobe. Opening the watch case on top of my chest of drawers, I took out the key hidden in the folds of black velvet.

Palming it, I headed down the hallway to an arched doorway at the end.

Unlocking it, I threw open the double doors.

The air was stale with the scent of fresh paint and sawdust. I flicked on the light. The room came alive with vivid color. The walls were covered in lemon trees hand-painted on silk canvas with a subtle pale mint green background. Every few lemons featured hand-sewn embroidered sequins to give a shimmering, three-dimensional effect.

The ceiling was covered in a wide crown molding lattice to continue the lemon grove garden effect, complete with a chandelier made of yellow, green, and white crystals fashioned into a shower of flowers. The floor-to-ceiling arched windows were covered in wisps of white tulle to let in as much light as possible. All the handcrafted furniture was white.

Including the cradle which dominated the room.

I crossed to it and ran my hand over the smooth rail. I had made all the furniture myself. It had been a labor of love. I had designed the nursery after my own childhood memories of summers spent on the Amalfi Coast with my mother before she grew ill.

I had wanted to share a small part of my mother with my child, so that she would be with us at least in spirit.

"Your mother would have loved this room."

I pivoted to see Aunt Gabriella standing in the doorway. "I thought all the guests had left."

She held up two tulip-shaped glasses and a bottle of

chilled grappa. "I'm not guests, darling. I'm family. I told your father I would stay here tonight instead of the villa. I thought you could use the company."

"That is kind of you, but I'm fine."

She set the glasses down on the changing table and pulled the stopper off the bottle of grappa. "Posh." She poured a glass and pushed it toward me. "Now are you going to tell me about the girl?"

I took the glass and waited for her to pour her own.

She raised her glass. "*Alla salute!*"

I raised mine. "*Alla salute.*"

Instead of sipping, we both shot the liquor down.

She poured another round. "Don't play coy with me, Enzo. It doesn't suit you. The girl who slapped you in marvelous fashion in the middle of church today. The one you were later eye fucking from across the room all day. I believe her name is Bianca?"

I choked on my grappa. "Eye fucking? Really, Aunt Gabriella?"

"Oh, don't be such a prude, Enzo. You are so like your mother in that way."

"The last thing I am is a prude, Aunt Gabriella."

"What? Just because you might like to pull a girl's hair and spank her ass doesn't mean you're not still a prude, Mr. I Have to Marry a Chick Because I Knocked Her Up."

I finished my glass and poured another. "I'm not talking about my sex life with my elderly aunt."

She narrowed her gaze. "Watch it with the *elderly*."

She pulled out her cigarette case as we wandered over to the arched windows.

I opened two of them and we stepped over the low sills onto the narrow balcony. I took her lighter and lit her cigarette.

She took a sip of grappa and leaned her back and elbows against the wrought iron railing as she studied me.

I loved the view.

Italy.

Cavalieri village.

My home.

My legacy.

At this time of night, the usually crowded piazza was eerily still. It was the only time the smooth gray cobblestones, worn down from centuries of foot traffic, were visible. Usually they were covered by countless market stalls, coffee carts, and the small chess tables the old men of the village set up each morning to challenge one another to games.

The somnolent gurgling of the water fountain accentuated the peacefulness of the late October evening as its clear blue water eternally flowed from the stone jug of the toga-draped maiden in its center.

And looming over it all, in its forbidding gothic splendor, was Santa Maria Church.

The church where I was baptized.

The church where I was married.

And the church where I just buried my wife.

It was the church where I had hoped to baptize my son.

The child who never existed.

I drained my glass and poured another before topping off Aunt Gabriella's.

"You have your mother's eyes. Too bad that's not the only thing you inherited from her."

I paused in raising my glass to my lips. I cocked one eyebrow. "Thank you? I think?"

She exhaled several perfect rings of smoke. "I loved my sister, but the problem when someone dies when they are still young and beautiful is, the people who remain behind tend to beatify them. We turn them into sainted martyrs. We forget their flaws."

I leaned my forearms onto the railing and stared at the water in the fountain below as it swirled around the basin. "What are you trying to tell me, Aunt Gabriella?"

"Don't rush me, Enzo. It's been a torturous day with your horrible in-laws, I'm drunk, and I have something important to tell you."

I hid my smile and nodded. I snagged her cigarette from her, took a drag, and gave it back to her.

"As I was saying," she said pointedly. "Your mother has been turned into this martyr, when the truth of it is, she was not nearly as innocent and sweet as everyone remembers."

My shoulders stiffened.

She waved her hand at me. The glowing ember of her cigarette creating orange swirls in the darkness. "Calm down. You don't know the full truth. All families have secrets, Enzo."

I straightened and stared down at her. She seemed to be staring off into the distance, lost in the past.

She continued. "Your mother never loved your father. That's no secret. But what you don't know is that she did love someone else, desperately. I begged her to marry him instead. And before you start thinking this was some kind of rich girl,

43

poor boy fairy tale, it wasn't. He was rich. Not as rich as your father, few mortals are. Still, the boy had money. But your mother refused. Family. Duty. Loyalty. All that bullshit. She made her choice. She chose to bury herself alive in a life she didn't want in the name of family honor, rather than choose love, and happiness, and passion. In the end, it made her bitter and resentful. Sound familiar?"

I gripped the glass in my fist so hard, I was surprised it didn't shatter under the pressure.

My voice was hoarse and uneven when I spoke. "I may be my mother's son, repeating her mistakes, but it doesn't matter, not anymore. Renata is dead."

"There's something else you don't know about your mother. A secret I've never told anyone, not even your father. I'm only telling you it now because I know all too well how secrets, even well-intentioned ones, have a way of biting you in the ass."

She lit another cigarette and turned to face the piazza, hiding her face from me. "During the final months of your mother's illness, your father and I became extremely close. I will admit I may have developed a tiny, *fleeting* crush on him. I fell for that protective, strong-shoulder vibe he gives off so well."

Without turning, she said, "Don't give me that look. Your father is a very handsome, virile man. It was short-lived, and completely one-sided. I never acted upon it. Our relationship always has been and always will be platonic. Your mother accused me of having an affair with him, though. I denied it of course, and thought she believed me."

She paused, taking a long drag from her cigarette and a sip

of her grappa. She then cleared her throat. "So, feeling foolish for my little crush and thinking it was all resolved, I kept your mother's suspicions from your father. Your mother and I then discussed her... end of life plans. I will not get into the macabre details, but I will say it was a dramatically different plan than what actually happened. We both knew that any other plan would lay a lifetime of false suspicion on your father and ruin his life, because it's *always* the husband who gets blamed."

I flexed my tense shoulders, feeling the full weight of guilt and suspicion that had been resting on them since Renata's body was discovered.

She finally turned to face me. "Then, one evening, when I had been called away to Rome, she went behind my back and convinced your father that it was time. She deliberately tricked your father into killing her, knowing what the fallout would be for him. After the funeral, I was going through a small box of jewelry she had left me. Tucked inside was a note she had written to me the day she died."

Her eyes teared up as she took a deep breath. "It said, *now you'll both burn in hell.*"

I pivoted away and gripped the railing. "Christ."

There was a long, tense silence.

Finally, I looked over my shoulder. "You've never told Papà?"

"Never, and neither will you. Some secrets are better left rotting in the past."

"Why are you telling me this now?"

"Because the stench of that rotting secret is ruining your future."

"I don't know what you're talking about."

She stubbed out her cigarette. "Yes, you do. Of the two worst words in the entire world, one of them is regret. I regret keeping your mother's suspicions a secret from your father. Who knows what might have happened then? How things might have turned out differently. I felt guilty and foolish, so I kept silent. Thinking I was protecting them both, or perhaps I was just selfishly protecting myself from embarrassment."

We both stepped back inside. Gabriella replaced the stopper on her bottle of grappa. "Here is what your *elderly* aunt knows...."

I folded my arms and leaned against the window frame.

"I know you didn't kill Renata."

She lifted up her hand as I opened my mouth. "Don't try and object or ask me how I know... I just know. I know that you feel a sense of guilt for unleashing that dreadful woman on your family and for Milana's near death. You also feel foolish for believing Renata's lies about being pregnant. You think it is your penance to bear the burden of everyone's suspicion. A modern crucifixion."

I shifted my stance, uncomfortable with how close to the bone she was hitting.

She continued. "What you seem to have overlooked is, in your family's zeal to protect you against a murder charge and portray Renata as an innocent victim and not the homicidal bitch she was and thereby avoid a scandal, the *actual murderer*, possibly the third man who attacked poor Milana all those years ago, is walking free among us."

I lifted my shoulders away from the window frame.

Fuck.

She smirked. "You men. Honestly, if you'd just make sure we women are in the room more often when you are making these schemes, we could avoid sloppy oversights like this."

Fuck. She was right.

I was so busy beating myself up over my mistakes and convincing myself that I had to live with the consequences, regardless of if they were deserved, that I lost sight of the fact the real murderer was still out there… and still a threat to my family.

How could I have been so fucking stupid?

Whoever attacked Renata could still try to kill Milana.

Or go after the rest of Renata's family.

Bianca.

Whatever it took, I had to get her back on a plane to America where she would be safe, as soon as possible. Especially before she drew any more attention to herself than she did today with that slap in the church.

Aunt Gabriella patted my cheek. "I think my work here is done. I'm off to bed. I need my beauty sleep."

As she reached the threshold, I called out to her. "What is the other word?"

She turned with a frown. "What?"

"You said there are two terrible words, what is the other one?"

She gave me a sad smile. "*If*, darling. Perhaps the worst word of all… if. I will say one more thing. *If* Bianca is the one you want, don't make your mother's mistake and turn your chance for a life of love and happiness and passion into an *if only*…."

"It's not that easy, Aunt Gabriella. Even *if* I were able to convince her I didn't kill her sister, there are still countless obstacles, not to mention what people would say…."

After the warmth of her touch had faded, cold hard reason had returned.

A future with Bianca was not possible, at least not yet.

I had to face that fact. I couldn't cause her more pain by exposing her to another scandal, not to mention the unknown threat that was still stalking my family and hers.

She was better off far, far away from me.

Aunt Gabriella waved her hand dismissively. "Posh. It's always been my experience that the type of people who get talked about… are the ones having the most fun in life."

She winked and then left.

I turned to look out over the silent piazza.

I needed to get some sleep.

Tomorrow morning, I had to let my family know I wasn't a murderer.

Then I needed to enlist their help in kidnapping Bianca.

CHAPTER 6

BIANCA

I was awakened by the sound of crunching paper.

Crap.

I sat up and looked down at my cream silk nightgown. It was covered in dark gray smudges. I pulled back the covers and surveyed the damage.

Although I was in school to complete my Master of Fine Arts in Graphic Design, my first love was still sketching with charcoals.

My small box of charcoal sticks had tipped over while I slept.

Several of the delicate sticks had broken in half and been crushed into a fine dark powder that was now ground into the sheets. I tilted my head back and groaned. If my mother found out I was sketching in bed and ruined *yet another* set of sheets I would never hear the end of it.

I slipped out of bed and pushed my unruly hair back from my face.

Gathering up the broken pieces of charcoal, I replaced them in the slightly crushed box and stashed it in my nightstand. After surveying the full extent of the damage to the bedding, my only choice was to yank the blanket and pillows off the bed.

As I did so, several crumpled pieces of sketch paper floated to the floor.

I bent down to gather them up.

One was of the fountain from the center of the piazza.

Another was a close-up sketch of a withered old hand holding a rook, from the men I observed playing chess.

And the third was Enzo.

I had captured the first moment he wrapped his arm around my waist.

A moment burned into my memory.

The fierce yet protective look on his face. I traced the small exhaustion lines I had drawn around his eyes. He had looked so tired yesterday, but not from lack of sleep. No, it was deeper, more disturbing than that. It was that weary, bone-deep kind of exhaustion. The kind that came from too much disappointment and not enough hope, a resigned, stoic kind of exhaustion.

I didn't know what possessed me to draw him.

I had tossed and turned for hours before I finally turned the bedroom light on and grabbed my sketch pad and charcoals. Some people vented to friends, others scribbled in a journal... I drew. Trying to exorcise Enzo from my mind by putting his image to paper.

I didn't even want to think what would have happened if his father hadn't knocked on that study door.

Would I have allowed Enzo to take me?

Right there on his desk?

At my own sister's funeral?

I gripped the bedpost, leaned my forehead against it and closed my eyes as a wave of disappointment hit me so hard, it made me nauseous.

All those long days and terrible nights when I tried to forget him.

Hours spent listening to heart-wrenching songs while I drank cheap wine, sat on my balcony alone, and stared out at the busy New York skyline feeling sorry for myself.

All those stupid break-up rituals like burning sage, tearing up his pictures, and writing really bad poetry. Highlighting and placing tabs in books on female empowerment, which filled a bookshelf I had back in my apartment in America. Then there were the countless hours I'd spent burying myself in schoolwork and even taking on a few graphic design clients, so I could trick myself into believing I had moved on and had some semblance of a life without him.

And all for what?

So I could finally have one brief moment where I got a little of my own back?

I knew what I was doing when I marched into that church.

I had played it out in my head on the long flight over.

I didn't care that it might cause a scandal. I didn't care what people would say or think. I wanted everyone in that village to know that I was over Enzo. I didn't want anyone to pity me or to think I was still pining after him.

But I especially wanted *him* to know.

I wanted him to know he hadn't broken me.

That it was over between us.

That the chains which had bound my heart to his had been severed long before he had been accused of murdering my sister.

Murdering my sister.

Enzo had killed Renata.

Maybe.

I knew I told my mother that he did it, but I had my doubts.

I still hadn't processed it, and I didn't think it was just the shock.

As much as I hated them both for their betrayal, I never wished them dead. And yet...

I wasn't surprised to hear that Renata had been killed.

Or that Enzo was under suspicion for her murder.

What truly terrified me was the *inevitability* of what happened.

How fucked up was that?

It wasn't that Enzo was a violent man, although his temper was legendary, as was that of his father and brother. If anything, Enzo had always been violently protective of me.

No, it was more the dark cloud of fate that hung over their marriage.

It was an irrefutable law of nature. You couldn't put that much unwanted pressure on a powerful man like Enzo Cavalieri and not expect it to eventually explode back on you.

Renata hadn't been happy with just trapping Enzo. No, she'd kept pushing and pushing....

There was no excuse for murder and I wasn't victim blaming, but at the same time, Renata had always been one to cruelly fuck with people's lives with little care to the consequences. I should know. So it was only a matter of time before that kind of behavior caught up with her.

Still, I couldn't imagine Enzo, *my Enzo*, losing control enough to beat a woman, any woman, even one as horrible as Renata, to death.

No. Stop it.

He's not my Enzo.

He hadn't been *my Enzo* for a very long time.

I had to stop making excuses for him.

I slid down to sit on the floor, staring at the drawing on my lap.

I lightly touched his charcoal-drawn cheek. I imagined I could still feel the hot sting of the slap on my palm.

For one brief moment... I was whole again.

And then his touch shattered me into a million pieces.

I closed my eyes and leaned my head back against the bed.

My teeth sank into my still bruised lower lip, reigniting the feel of his punishing kiss. I flicked my tongue out between my lips as if I could still taste him, still taste his desperation.

It should have been my vindication.

It should have been a glorious moment of closure.

The ex-boyfriend who fucked me over still wanted me. Sweet revenge.

It was the type of moment countless women have wished for.

And yet... the ugly truth was... if Barone Cavalieri hadn't knocked on that door....

My hands slid under the drawing to rest on my upper thighs.

I pressed my fingertips into my soft flesh and opened my knees.

My breath caught, my imagination recreating the feel of Enzo stepping between them, the sound of his zipper lowering.

I grasped the fabric of my nightgown and inched it up over my knees.

What would he have done next?

Would he have torn open my dress to get to my breasts?

Or wrenched my hem up higher to tear at my panties?

My right hand slipped between my thighs.

Would he have teased me with just the tip of his cock?

Or grabbed my hips and thrust in forcefully, taking me brutally, right there on the top of his desk?

The tip of my finger slid over the wet cotton of my panties.

"Bianca?"

My eyes flew open.

"Bianca? Are you awake yet?"

I swallowed as I hastily pushed the hem of my nightgown down. "Yes, Mother. I mean, Claudia," I called out through my closed bedroom door, scrambling to shove the drawing of Enzo under my bed.

I rose and pressed my hands to my heated cheeks.

My mother yelled, "Stop lazing about. Your father and I are waiting in the breakfast room."

"Coming!"

I dropped my head and stared at the floor.

That man!

God damn that man!

He wasn't even here, and I was still responding to him.

Would I ever be free of him?

Yes. The answer was simple.

I would trade my freedom for his.

If I could prove to myself that Enzo was guilty of murdering my sister, then it would truly end all hope, even that tiny, obnoxious spark that refused to die deep inside of me.

If he is guilty, then I will have no regrets, excuses, or doubts about finally moving on.

We will be done... forever.

$$* \quad * \quad *$$

I STRIPPED the bed of the ruined sheet and shoved it in the laundry hamper before tossing a robe on. Casting a rueful glance at my flushed face, I hastened down the stairs.

Stopping to take a deep breath, I placed a hand over my stomach to calm the butterflies before entering the bright breakfast room.

Unfortunately, my mother shared my sister's love of garish decor.

The entire room was a vomit-inducing dusty pink with a glass and gold table and seventies-inspired rattan peacock fan chairs that creaked when you sat on them.

My mother's upper lip curled as she scanned me from head to toe. "Seven months in America and you come back a heathen. Since when do you come to the breakfast table half-dressed?"

I tightened the belt on my robe. "I'm hardly half-dressed," I responded under my breath, sitting down and cringing as the wicker chair shifted and creaked beneath my weight.

Her nose wrinkled. "What is that on your forehead? Dirt?"

I wiped my forehead and saw black on my fingertips. Snatching up my cloth napkin, I dipped the corner in my water and rubbed it over my face. "Nothing."

"You better not have been scribbling with those dirt sticks in bed ruining my sheets again."

My parents' view of my life's passion and chosen career in a nutshell—scribbling with dirt sticks.

My father set his paper aside. "Your mother—"

"Claudia," interrupted my mother.

My father sent her a disgruntled look. "Your *mother* is correct, Bianca. In the future, I expect you to display more decorum. You will come to the breakfast table precisely at seven o'clock dressed appropriately for the day."

I smiled my thanks to the female servant who placed a cappuccino in front of me. I didn't know her name yet. My parents had a history of running staff off every few months, so it was no surprise I didn't recognize anyone in the household. I reached for a brioche and the crystal jar of preserves. "Since I plan to return to America and school by the end of the week, I don't see that being a problem, Father."

My father cleared his throat and picked up his newspaper. Snapping it open, he covered his face as he said, "You aren't returning to school."

The spoon I was holding clattered to my plate. "What?"

He cleared his throat again. "You heard me."

I looked between him and my mother. "Why? What is going on?"

My mother picked up her knife and scraped the nonexistent burnt edge off her toast. "Now that your poor, beautiful sister is gone, you have a duty to your family to marry."

I shook my head. "What does Renata's death have to do with me marrying?"

My mother let out a long-suffering sigh. "Honestly, Bianca, I am disgusted you could be so selfish at a time like this. I thought I raised you better than that."

I blinked several times. The fact that I wasn't *more* self-centered was actually the miracle, and given my mother's complete lack of maternal instincts, I was pretty sure I would have been better off being raised by a pack of wolves than in this family.

My father slammed his fist down on the table, tipping my cappuccino over. The hot liquid pooled over the tablecloth and dribbled onto the floor. The servant rushed forward with a towel only to be screamed at by my father. I gave her a sympathetic look and whispered to her to return to the safety of the kitchen, then knelt down with my napkin in hand to mop up the mess.

"Get off the fucking floor," my father blustered at me, shoving his chair backward. "You're not some common laborer."

I rose and lowered my gaze to avoid reacting to my father's finger wagging in my face. "Your sister's death cost this family a great deal of money."

And there it was.

"We need a Cavalieri connection."

My mouth dropped open in shock. "You are not suggesting I marry Enzo Cavalieri!"

My mother scoffed, giving me a scathing once-over. "Don't be ridiculous. That would be unseemly. Besides, he already rejected you once. No one would believe he wanted you now."

I bit the inside of my cheek to keep from saying anything.

My father continued. "There is an unmarried cousin, Matteo. You will marry him."

"The hell I will!"

My father's arm struck out so quickly I didn't have time to duck.

He backhanded me across the face, sending me flying into the adjacent wall. My vision blurred and there was a sharp ringing in my ears as he shouted his final command.

"You will do as you are told, young lady. There is no money for New York. We have already closed your bank account and cancelled your tuition payment for next semester. We have also cancelled the lease on your apartment. You will do your duty and charm the Cavalieri cousin into a marriage proposal or so help me God, you will wish it was you instead of your sister in that grave."

With that he stormed out.

I held a shaking hand to my burning cheek and stared at my mother through blurry, tear-filled eyes.

She held up a knife and checked her lipstick in the reflection. "I don't understand why you are fussing, Bianca. You will be rich and a Cavalieri."

"I don't care about the money and the last thing in the world I want is to be a Cavalieri."

"Only people with money say they don't care about money."

"I won't marry him."

She shrugged. "Then you will be cut off."

She rose and smoothed her skirt over her thighs. "New York is a very expensive city, daughter. You're not a good enough artist to make it there on your own merit."

She didn't know that I already had a few clients. Good ones. Companies based in Italy who appreciated a designer who spoke Italian. The problem was, I didn't have long-term contracts with any of them. If the money dried up, I could be left destitute.

My mother circled around the breakfast table and stepped up to me. She lifted up my chin. "I think your father did you a favor. You were looking too pale. Now your cheeks are nice and bright."

My eyes widened.

She walked toward the door but turned to face me before leaving. "Be a good daughter and do as you're told, Bianca. I warned you. There are things at play here that are beyond your comprehension. Trust me. This is the best solution. If you can't get Matteo Cavalieri to propose, and quickly, you won't like our other option."

With that threat, she left.

Something seriously fucked up was going on here.

My parents' obstinate refusal to talk about Renata's murder.

Their strange insistence that it was an accident.

Now, their hints at money issues and threats about forcing me to marry Matteo Cavalieri.

What weren't they telling me?

What secret were they keeping?

There was only one way to find out.

The way anyone learned anything when living in a mountain village in Italy.

I looked at the clock on the wall. If I hurried, I would be just in time for the stalls to open on market day in the piazza.

If the villagers were going to gossip about my family, I might as well know what they were saying. If I headed to the market, maybe I'd get lucky and someone would gossip within earshot of me.

CHAPTER 7

ENZO

"You want us to kidnap Bianca Moretti?" asked Cesare.

He shifted in his chair, tossing an elbow over the back. "I'm not objecting. I just want to be clear on our new family project."

Papà finished making his espresso and turned to lean against the kitchen counter. "Call me old-fashioned, but don't you think kidnapping the sister of the woman you are about to be accused of murdering a bit risky?"

He raised an eyebrow before taking a sip.

I rubbed my index finger over my lower lip. "About that...."

I took one of the kitchen chairs and spun it around to straddle it, leaning my forearms on the back.

Cesare's expression fell. He pushed his breakfast plate aside and leaned forward.

I couldn't look either of them in the eye.

I stared at the table. Focusing on the random constellation of pastry crumbs scattered across the cream linen and lace tablecloth. "The day we were at the hospital. When we weren't sure Milana was going to make it. When we learned—"

My throat closed around the words. I couldn't say her name. My entire being rebelled against saying *my wife* as well. *My wife* was worse. *My wife* was taking ownership over the entire mess. *My wife* was taking full responsibility for inviting this destructive chaos into my family's life.

Saying *my wife* was admitting my guilt.

I swallowed past the dry, bitter taste in my mouth and continued. "When we learned my wife was—"

My father stepped forward. "Cesare, leave us."

Cesare rubbed the back of his neck, clearly upset. "No, Papà. I'm staying. What Enzo did—"

Papà roared, "Enough! Not another word."

He slammed his palms down on the table and shifted his narrowed gaze between us. "*Someone* ordered that coroner's report *after* we went to great lengths to prevent one. *Someone* with enough influence and inside knowledge to get it done under the radar, and before we hastened her body into the ground. We know it wasn't her parents because they have their own reasons for toeing the line and claiming it was an accident. *Someone* wanted this investigation."

He straightened up and crossed his arms over his chest. "Which means Cesare will be as much of a suspect as Enzo. You had just as much motive."

"I was at the hospital keeping vigil over Milana."

"We can't assume that alibi will hold. Either way, if we

can't stop this investigation, the less you know about what actually happened the better."

Cesare stood and faced Papà. "I'm not going to slink off and stay ignorant in the shadows like some fucking coward while my brother sacrifices his entire future. Not after what he did *for me* to protect the woman I love!"

Papà squared off with him. "You can and you will. You have a family of your own now to worry about. Focus on Milana and the baby. I will worry about your brother."

Cesare fought back. "Fuck that! We face this as a family, same as we always do!"

I vaulted out of the chair, knocking it over. "I didn't do it."

Both heads turned.

Papà lowered his head. "This isn't helping, son. I told you that night I'd be the last person to judge you, but—"

I paced away a few steps and turned. "I didn't do it."

Papà frowned, "Then why did you say—"

I rubbed the back of my neck. "I never said I did. Everyone just assumed. No one actually asked me."

Cesare and Papà both sat down and stared at me.

I righted the chair and gripped the back. "I'm no saint. After learning it was... her... who attacked Milana, I left the hospital in a rage. After shaking off Vito and not finding her at our house or her parents', I headed to the cottage. The truth is, I'm not sure what I would have done if I *had* actually found her. I was so fucking pissed. I can't remember ever being that angry at another human being in my entire life."

I slumped down in the chair and buried my head in my hands, like hiding from the morning sunshine would somehow prevent it from revealing the darkness of my words. "I wanted the bitch dead. I wanted her out of my life, out of my family's life. By that time I was pretty certain she wasn't even pregnant. I wasn't sure if there had been a baby and she got rid of it or if it had all been a lie. The coroner's report confirmed it for me."

My father laid a comforting hand on my shoulder. "Son...."

I shrugged him off. "Don't. I don't deserve it. You both tried to warn me about her, and I wouldn't listen."

Cesare frowned. "Enzo, this isn't your fault."

I looked up at him.

My younger brother.

My closest friend.

The idea that my choices nearly cost him the love of his life *and his child* tore at my insides like acid.

"Yeah, it is. I may not have been the one to kill her, but this whole disgusting mess is definitely my fucking fault. It was my 'doomed from the start' wedding."

My father pinched the bridge of his nose as he closed his eyes. Without opening them he asked, "Is that why you let us believe you were responsible?"

I threw my head back and stared at the ceiling, letting out a bitter laugh. "One more stupid choice. I thought it was what I deserved for all the pain I'd caused to Milana, to Bianca, and to my family because of my actions and choices. To have everyone think I was capable of beating a woman to death with my bare fists. I was wallowing in my own self-pity when Aunt Gabriella pointed out the flaws in my plan in her usual blunt way."

Papà clasped his hands together. "So if you didn't kill her... who did?"

I leaned back in my chair. "That's the thing. I assumed it was some lover she pissed off. I never touched her after that first night."

Cesare nodded. "Sounds plausible. We know for a fact she was playing with fire with the Agnellos as well. She probably just pissed off the wrong person. Fuck knows she was good at pissing people off."

Papà shook his head. "We're missing something."

"The third man." Aunt Gabriella sauntered into the room wearing an emerald-green and gold silk caftan.

Cesare checked his watch. "It's barely nine a.m., what are you doing up?"

She pointed at him. "Don't be cheeky! Your brother knows why." Papà rose to make her an espresso.

"Aunt Gabriella pointed out—"

"Helpfully," interjected Aunt Gabriella.

I corrected myself. "Aunt Gabriella *helpfully* pointed out that by focusing on all the reasons why someone would want to kill Renata—"

"Of which there were many," quipped Cesare.

"—we lost focus on why she tried to kill Milana."

It was as if someone sucked the air out of the room.

We all sat in silence for a moment.

Cesare broke it by muttering, "Fuck."

Aunt Gabriella nodded sagely. "The third man."

Papà turned in his seat and looked at her before repeating, "The third man."

Cesare leaned back in his chair. "Of course. It makes sense. We were getting close. Renata must have been involved that day at school. She must have been the female."

Papà looked at Cesare. "Does Milana remember anything from the day Renata attacked her? Anything at all?"

He shook his head. "No. And I don't want to ask her. You know her. She's stubborn as fuck. It bothers the hell out of her that she can't remember. She suspects that Renata must have said something to her before locking her inside and it is driving her crazy that her mind is blocking it out."

Papà let out a frustrated sigh. "We're not going to mention this to her or Amara. I don't want either of them upset. I want them focused on Milana's health and the baby."

We all nodded.

He continued. "In the meantime, I think it is safe to assume it was the third man. Judging by the information we have collected so far, we know he is an enforcer for the Agnellos, and he is someone local. That means he has influence and insider knowledge."

I looked at my father. "The coroner's report."

"Exactly. He's covering his tracks. He wants you charged for Renata's murder. He knows you're vulnerable to an accusation. He must assume that we would be so busy defending you, we'd stop looking for him."

"In the meantime, he'll continue covering his tracks, which may include the rest of Renata's family. I need to get Bianca out of the country. Now. Today."

Aunt Gabriella patted the top of my hand with her long, elegant fingers heavily weighed down with thick gold rings. "You don't think she'll go willingly? I mean, I know you were probably hoping she'd stay, but she's started to build a life for herself in New York."

I averted my gaze. "What I want is immaterial. I think

Bianca would leave, it's her parents I'm worried about. The guards who mingled among the crowd picked up some disturbing talk. It seems they may try and keep Bianca here."

"Why?"

I shrugged. "They didn't learn why."

My father grimaced. "You can be sure whatever the reason, money is involved."

My eyes narrowed. "And possibly the Agnellos."

Cesare rubbed his hands together. "So kidnapping it is! What's the plan?"

Footsteps from the direction of the doorway broke into our conversation.

Vito held up his palms. "Sorry to interrupt, Don Cavalieri."

He nodded toward me. "Enzo, one of the guards from last night just came to the villa gate. He thought you'd want to know Bianca Moretti is in town. She's asking a lot of... as he put it... *awkward questions.*"

I shot out of my chair and stormed toward the door. "Goddammit!"

My father called out to me, "Do you need some help?"

I shouted over my shoulder, "No, I can handle Bianca on my own."

Moments later I was on my motorcycle roaring toward the piazza.

CHAPTER 8

BIANCA

I watched the old woman with the bright kerchief knotted tightly under her chin pick up a sharp knife and place it on top of the wheel of Pecorino Romano cheese.

She looked up at me expectantly.

I pinched my fingers. *"Un po' di più."*

She moved the knife.

I clapped my hands. *"Perfetta."*

She cut a thick wedge and gingerly wrapped the cheese in wax paper.

I shifted the fresh tonnarelli pasta I just purchased one stall over to make room for my cheese purchase in my basket. I knew better than to bring a purse to market day.

Tourist season may be over, but that didn't mean there still weren't pickpockets and thieves working the crowd.

All I had with me was a simple woven basket and a handful of euro for my food supply shopping.

One surprising thing about living alone in New York was I had learned to cook over these last few months. Growing up in a house filled with servants and a mother who thought talking down to the help was a sign of good breeding, I had rarely been allowed inside the kitchen.

So it had been a pleasure to learn I didn't just enjoy cooking, I was actually quite good at it. In many respects, a well-crafted meal was an expression of art.

I looked forward to gathering up some fresh, local ingredients and making my favorite autumn dish, *Cacio de Pepe*. I could practically taste the rich, creamy sauce with its salty earthiness from the black pepper clinging to each delicate *al dente* noodle.

After the last few days, I could use a few comfort carbs. Plus it was the perfect excuse to move about the market, quietly asking questions.

So far, I had learned that I had missed nothing by skipping out on Enzo and Renata's wedding.

Apparently, it had been a rather morbid affair. There was even talk of a fight between Enzo and Renata over her flirting with the male guests. Some overheard them yelling and Enzo was seen later with bruised knuckles.

I was also pleased to learn, although I hated to admit it, there was gossip they slept in separate rooms. A woman who sold old clothes and rag linens said her granddaughter worked as a maid in the household and she usually had to clean two bedrooms, not one.

There was also almost universal consensus that Enzo was the one who killed Renata.

The villagers seemed to calmly brush off his heinous actions as acceptable.

Not surprising, since the Cavalieris practically walked on water in this area of Italy, especially the eldest son, the heir to the throne.

But also, it had to be admitted, because neither my sister nor my parents had many friends in the village. People tended not to mourn the deaths of those who thought they were above common kindness and decency. *God's will* and all that.

I pulled my hat down a little lower. I was wearing a tight black pencil skirt with a fitted black sweater. I had concealed my hair with a red, black, and white silk scarf, knotted in the back and topped with a large-brimmed, black straw hat. I had completed the look with a pair of large, dark glasses that obscured the top half of my face.

If anyone recognized me as Bianca Moretti in the midst of the bustling market crowd, no one said so.

Adjusting the soft wicker handles of my market basket on my forearm, I headed to the market stall selling *porchetta* sandwiches.

I had always loved the simplicity of the pork, slow roasted with savory fennel seeds, sage, and rosemary and served on a small roll. With its crispy edges and salty, anise flavor, it was a taste of home and the ultimate street food.

The popular New York hot dog, which spent who knew how long bobbing about in a foul-smelling soup of tepid water before being placed on a bland white flour roll and covered with sugary tomato paste and raw onions, didn't even come close in my opinion.

Seeming to wait patiently for my turn, I watched skewers

of *arrosticini* sizzling over an open flame while I stood slightly behind the other customers to listen in on their conversations, hoping to glean some information or gossip.

Dios mio!

I was shoved so violently from behind I lurched forward.

With the market basket blocking my arms, I was unable to raise them in time to prevent my falling face-first onto the hot grill surface.

Time seemed to slow as the hot, glowing coals inched closer to my face, their radiating heat scorching my neck and cheeks.

My sunglasses fell off onto the grill. I could smell melting plastic and smoke as the brim of my hat caught fire.

At the last possible second, a strong arm swept across my shoulders and pulled me back.

I was spun around, and powerful hands gripped my upper arms. A man swept the burning hat off my head.

"Are you okay?"

I couldn't hear what he was saying. I swayed as I dropped my market basket. The contents spilling out onto the smooth cobblestones to be trampled under the onlookers' feet. The terror of the near miss caused the blood to pound a harsh cadence of a drumbeat in my ears.

I stared up at him, trying to focus. The bright sunshine was at his back, throwing his tall frame into shadow.

He placed his hands on my face. "Answer me, beautiful. Is English better? Do you not speak Italian?"

I blinked several times. How odd, he thought I was a tourist. Slowly, rational thought was fighting through my startled near-death fog. I nodded.

He lifted his head. "Stand back, give the lady some room to breathe," he commanded in an authoritative voice.

He released his grip on my face and I swayed slightly.

"Easy, beautiful." He steadied me with an arm around my waist.

A woman standing nearby offered us a glass of water. "Thank you." He accepted it and held it up to my lips. "Here. Sip this."

Like a child, I dutifully sipped from the glass he held.

I looked up at him. In addition to being tall, he was extremely handsome in that classic Italian way. He also seemed oddly familiar.

I took the glass from his grasp and stepped back, breaking his hold.

He turned to a smaller man, clearly a tourist, who had been jockeying among the crowd to get a photo of the vendor.

He grabbed him by the collar. "You idiot! You could have hurt the lady!" He thrust the man toward me. "Apologize. Now."

The man stared at me wide-eyed with fright. His mouth opened and closed several times but nothing except a high-pitched squeak came out.

The taller man wrenched him off the ground by the back of his shirt. "I said, apologize!"

"I'm very sorry, miss! I didn't mean it! I'm so sorry!"

Bothered by the display and the attention we were drawing, I hastily said, "It's fine. Really."

The tall man dropped the tourist to the ground. The man scrambled to his feet and scurried away.

My rescuer then turned to me. "Are you sure you are okay? Do you need to sit down?"

Casting a nervous glance around at the crowd, I shook my head. "I'm fine. Thank you for saving me."

He smiled. "It is always a pleasure to save a gorgeous woman." He reached up and stroked my cheek. "It would have been a crime against nature to mar beauty such as this."

Uncomfortable with his intense regard but not wanting to seem ungracious, I lowered my head to break his contact. "Thank you again."

"I'm sorry I mistook you for a tourist. Clearly a beauty such as yourself could only be a daughter of Italy."

I smiled, used to such flagrant flattery from Italian men. "That's very kind of you. I shouldn't keep you any longer."

His gaze narrowed. "You look familiar. Your name wouldn't be Bianca, would it?"

I stilled. There was no reason why I should be on edge. I grew up in this village. Many people knew me. The man was obviously near my age. There was a very good chance we had crossed paths at some point.

And yet... there was something about him....

His smile widened but it didn't seem to reach his eyes. "Bianca Moretti. It is you."

Casting a glance over at the grill where my sunglasses were now a melted mess adhered to the metal grates, then at my crushed basket on the ground, I turned my head up sharply at hearing my name. "Yes. Do we know one another?"

His gaze wandered over my face and body appreciatively. "Let's just say I know you, but I don't think you know me."

I bristled.

My grip tightened on the glass of water I was holding.

Shielding my eyes from the glare of the sun to get a better look at him, I asked, "And what is that supposed to mean?"

He laughed as he placed a palm over his heart. "Forgive me. I meant no offense. We went to school together. You were a very pretty girl, and I was just a poor boy in the shadows."

I relaxed. My sister's murder and my parents' threats had me seeing demons and evil plots around every corner. "Sorry."

"I had quite the crush on you back in school."

I blushed. There was something both flattering and strangely off-putting learning someone I didn't know had been thinking about me in that way. It was hard to articulate. It gave me an odd sense of a lack of control. Not knowing how to respond, I averted my face as I set the empty water glass on a nearby stall. "Really?"

"Yes. I even left you one of those silly Valentine cards in your desk one day. It said *Bee Mine*, with a silly little bee on it."

I actually remembered getting that card.

It was tucked into my desk next to my art supplies.

It hadn't been signed, but on it was a note asking me to meet my secret admirer in the music room after school. Since I was secretly harboring a huge crush on Enzo even way back then, I had ignored it.

"I remember. I'm sorry, what is your name again?"

He looked over my shoulder at the roar of an approaching motorcycle.

He gave me a wink. "Some other time, beautiful."

With that he disappeared into the crowd.

How strange.

A hand grabbed me from behind and spun me around.

Enzo glared down at me. "What the hell do you think you're doing?"

I matched his glare as I placed my fisted hands on my hips. "I beg your pardon?"

He stepped close, towering over me. "Who was that man touching you?"

He was so near, I could smell his cologne mixed with the scent of gasoline and leather from his motorcycle.

Unlike yesterday, today he was simply dressed in a pair of jeans with a thick leather belt and a loosely tucked-in, thin white T-shirt that seemed to hint at every sculpted muscle on his chest.

I had to tilt my head back to maintain eye contact. "None of your fucking business."

His gaze zeroed in on my lips. "Watch your mouth," he ground out.

I had forgotten he never liked it when I cursed.

Knowing I was playing a dangerous game but unable to stop myself, I leaned in. I flicked the tip of my tongue out to lick my lips before saying, "I will *fucking* say whatever I *fucking* want because my *fucking* mouth, and the things it can do, are none of your *fucking* concern."

A growl vibrated from deep inside his chest.

He reached for me.

I stepped back, evading his grasp. "Careful, *dear brother-in-law*, you wouldn't want to make a scene with your sister-in-law in front of all of these people in the middle of the piazza, now would you?"

He followed me, standing even closer. "You foolish little

girl, these people think I'm capable of murder and yet they showed up at my home yesterday, ate my food...drank my wine...and looked me in the eye as they shook my hand and offered me their *sincerest* condolences."

He raised one eyebrow. "And you think they will be the ones to protect you from me?"

All bravado left me. How could I have forgotten he was a Cavalieri? No one in this village defied a Cavalieri. No one.

I tried to pivot away, but his arm whipped out.

He grasped my forearm, holding me in place. "Go ahead, call out for help," he challenged.

I tried to pull free, but his hold tightened. "Let me go or I'll—"

"Or you'll what? Scream? Do it. I dare you. Scream and see what happens."

I opened my mouth, but nothing came out.

His mouth twisted in a smirk. "That's what I thought."

He dragged me over to his motorcycle. "We're leaving. It's time you and I came to an understanding. Get on the bike."

"Where are you taking me?"

"Get on the bike, Bianca."

"I can't get on that thing. My skirt is too tight. Just let me leave, Enzo."

My black pencil skirt was wrapped tightly around my hips to just below my knees.

His gaze raked over me. "No."

He reached into his saddle bag and pulled out a switch-blade that he flicked open. The sharp blade gleamed in the sun.

My eyes widened. I held up my palms and tried to pull out of his grasp. "Wait! What are you—"

He wrenched my body against his. His breath brushed my mouth as he spoke. "Hold still."

The air in my lungs seized.

There was an insistent pressure between my thighs.

Oh God.

Then the sound of fabric tearing.

He had sliced the blade down between my thighs, cutting the front of my skirt from my panties to the hem.

I bent over and grasped at the edges, trying to pull them back into place. "Are you insane?"

"Quite possibly."

He wrapped his hands around my waist and lifted me onto his motorcycle. The warm metal pressed against my inner thighs.

I frantically reached for the handlebars as the metal beast pitched awkwardly to the side and righted itself as he climbed on behind me.

His mouth brushed my ear. "Put your feet on the crash bars."

I placed my feet on the metal bars on either side of the front wheel.

The motorcycle roared to life and pitched forward.

The crowd of onlookers separated as we raced out of town.

CHAPTER 9

BIANCA

The motorcycle picked up speed as soon as we passed Santa Maria Church and hit the country lane which led to the smaller farm cottages on the outskirts of the village.

My sweating palms slipped on the smooth metal handlebars, making it a challenge to pull my body forward as I held my back rigid in an attempt to not touch him.

Enzo pressed his left hand flat against my stomach, pulling me back until my ass slid into the junction of his thighs. "Lean back against me," he commanded over the sound of the engine.

His arm brushed the side of my breast as he reached for and gripped the left handlebar.

Nestled securely between his strong legs, my arms weren't long enough for me to hold onto the handlebars. My only option was to grasp the sides of his legs for purchase.

Enzo brushed his jaw against my cheek; my head was practically resting against his shoulder.

It was as intimate as an embrace.

The vibration of the motorcycle and his nearness played havoc with my senses.

I was very aware that my skirt was split up the center, exposing my naked thighs straddling his bike. If I looked down, I could see glimpses of the pale pink silk of my panties.

I squeezed my eyes shut and just absorbed the entire experience.

The swift speed of the bike.

The wind rushing past us.

My racing heart.

The feel of his thighs pressing against my hips.

The scruff of his beard rubbing against my cheek.

The rumbling hum of the engine between my thighs.

My mouth opened on a gasp as my fingertips dug into his legs.

Enzo tilted his head. His lips grazed my ear.

I moaned.

A fierce blush bloomed on my cheeks. I prayed he hadn't heard it.

His deep chuckle told me he had.

His teeth nipped at my earlobe.

My right hand moved to caress my clit before I caught myself. What the hell was I doing?

Was I seriously close to coming just from riding on this man's motorcycle?

He pulled into the gravel drive of a small farmhouse that was set away from the surrounding houses. There was evidence of recent construction. A few sawhorses on the lawn. Stacks of marble tiles. Recently planted cypress trees and wisteria bushes. And a freshly painted, arched double door.

The moment Enzo turned off the motorcycle and swung his leg over, I awkwardly climbed off without his help. Holding the scraps of my skirt closed, I demanded, "Where are we?"

He grasped my forearm. "Inside."

He opened the door and thrust me over the threshold. He then closed and locked the doors before crossing his arms and leaning back against the dark wood.

I looked around.

Inside, the walls were freshly painted a welcoming, off-white cream. There was what looked like a newly installed, Roman-inspired, bright mosaic-tiled entrance depicting dancing animals carrying trays laden with fruit.

The entire cottage was furnished in a rustic, elegant manner, filled with gently distressed, sturdy wood furniture topped with handcrafted canary-yellow and cobalt-blue ceramic pieces and the occasional vintage-looking bronze figurine. Through a large, arched doorway, I could just glimpse a classic, Tuscan-style kitchen with open shelves and a farmhouse white porcelain sink.

"Whose cottage is this?"

"Amara Beneventi's. I'm refurbishing it as a wedding present to her and my father."

I nodded. I remembered my mother complaining about Amara being a gold digger going after Don Cavalieri.

That was the last time I spoke to her before Renata's death.

I couldn't abide the bitter vitriol she was spitting out.

I hadn't been close friends with Amara in school, but we had been friends and I liked her. She didn't deserve my mother's scathing remarks, especially since my own sister was guilty of the same thing... and worse, where Enzo was concerned.

I walked further into the room. I ran my fingers over the back of the sofa. "They're getting married?"

I could feel Enzo's gaze on me as he followed me.

The tension in the room was a looming presence, like creeping smoke. As if the swirls of dust in the beams of sunlight would suddenly coalesce into a dark, twisting storm that would rise up and close around our bodies... choking us.

"Not yet. She refuses to allow my father to propose."

"Good for her." I faced him and crossed my arms over my chest, inhaling a shaking breath. "You wanted to talk. Talk. Say what you have to say and then let me leave."

His bright green eyes stared at me, studying my face. His eyes were his most striking feature. So different from the usual dark brown of most Italian men and women. They gave his already intense gaze an unsettling quality.

I shifted under his scrutiny.

"Who was that man you were talking to? In the piazza just now."

"That's what you want to talk about?"

"Who was he, Bianca? I know he's not your boyfriend because you don't have one, so who the hell is he and why did he think it was acceptable to *touch you*?"

I sighed. "He's not anyone— Wait. How do you know he's

not my boyfriend? Maybe he is. Maybe he came with me from New York to offer support."

Enzo stalked toward me. "You really think it's smart to play that game with me, babygirl?"

I backed up, circling around the sofa.

My suspicion rose faster than my sense of caution. "How do you know I don't have a boyfriend, Enzo?"

His eyes narrowed as his lips thinned.

Realization dawned.

I covered my mouth with my hand as I slowly shook my head.

I lowered my hand and hugged my arms around my middle. "No. No. You couldn't... you wouldn't...no one is that... *cruel.*"

Enzo stood there staring at me, saying nothing.

The truth set in.

The class projects where my male partner would suddenly be switched out for a female.

The cute guy who would ask for my number, but then never call.

The way a black sedan always seemed to be parked either outside my apartment or my school.

I bit the inside of my cheek, hoping the pain would cut through the dizzying darkness that had me swaying on my feet.

"The clients? The Italian businesses which contacted me claiming to have seen my work from the school classwork exhibits?"

Enzo remained stoic.

How could I have been so stupid? How could I have fallen

for such a scheme and believed that not one, but several Italian companies had somehow viewed the work of a lowly graphic design student and sought me out?

I almost moved back to New York with no money, foolishly believing I could make it on my own because of those clients.

Clients that didn't exist. It was a lie. All a lie.

I tightened my arms around my middle as if by doing so I could somehow hold the pieces of my life together while everything seemed to be falling apart.

My lower lip trembled. "Why? Why would you do all that to me?"

His hands curled into fists at his sides as his brow lowered. "Dammit, because *you're mine.*"

I stared at him for several seconds, certain I hadn't heard him correctly. I couldn't possibly have heard him correctly because what he said would be the words of an absolute sociopath. "But I'm *not* yours."

He spoke through clenched teeth. "Don't say that."

I blinked. "Don't say what? The truth?"

He rubbed the back of his neck. "I know it was wrong. I tried a thousand times to call off the surveillance. To sever the link to you. To let you just move on with your life."

He stormed up to me, wrapping his hands around my jaw.

He looked down at me, desperation etched into the lines around his eyes. "But each time I saw one of your designs, it was like I was touching a small piece of you. My day didn't start until I saw a photo of you and knew you were safe and protected."

I wrapped my hands around his wrists, unwittingly being

drawn into the green depths of his eyes as he gazed down at me.

I could physically feel his pain and longing. My soul cried out to him. The part of me that still deeply loved him sparked to life at his words.

He leaned in.

His mouth brushed mine.

My lips opened under the gentle caress.

I breathed his air.

Time stood still.

I knew he was waiting...

Waiting for me...

All I needed to do was rise up on my toes, just the barest of inches.

His thumbs rubbed circles on the edge of my jaw.

Just the slightest of touches.

The smallest brush of my mouth against his, and he would take over... claim, possess, dominate.

I would be tossed on the turbulent storm of his embrace.

Sucked under.

Drowned.

But it would be worth it.

I would be with him again. The man I loved. The man I longed for. The man I cried out for in the night. The man I ached for.

Who cared about the rest?

Why should I if I was once again in his arms? Why should anything else matter?

I inched up onto the balls of my feet, desperately, with

every fiber of my being, wanting all of that to be true. I truly wanted nothing else to matter.

But it did.

I fell back to earth.

Everything about this was wrong.

If I gave in to him now, I would be forever lost.

Where would be my self-respect? My self-worth? My sense of self, if I sent him the message that this was even the slightest bit okay?

I stepped back, breaking his hold. "No. You don't get to twist this into something romantic, Enzo. You made your choice. You don't get to toss me aside, break my heart, and then stop me from finding love with someone else by using your money and power to fucking spy on me!"

He reached for me again, but I avoided his grasp.

He turned away in anger then pivoted back to face me.

He gestured wildly with his arm. "You don't think I wanted to be a better man? To be the kind of man who could let you find happiness in someone else's arms? I wanted that for you, Bianca. God, how I fucking wanted that for you. I couldn't do it."

He thumped his fist against his chest. "You're mine. You were always meant to be mine and you always will be mine. Nothing that has happened will change that."

Bile burned the back of my throat.

It was no secret my sister had trapped Enzo into marriage by tricking him into bed and then claiming to be pregnant. A pregnancy that had been a lie. My mother had confessed it to me in a drunken moment the night she called to tell me Renata was dead. She had let that secret and *much worse* slip.

I had assumed Enzo finding out about the fake pregnancy had caused the tragic fight which led to her death. It was an obvious conclusion.

Now a more sinister motive was becoming disgustingly clear.

I backed further away. Casting a glance over my shoulder, I eased toward the front door. "Did you kill Renata to be with me?" I asked, the words barely above a whisper, as if saying them too loudly would make them even more true.

"That was what I was trying to tell you yesterday. *I didn't kill Renata.*"

"I don't believe you."

"I swear to God, I didn't kill your sister."

"Don't bring God into this. God has no place in this conversation, Enzo. Did you kill my sister so that we could be together?"

"No. I'm not going to stand here and say that it hadn't occurred to me." He let out a frustrated sigh and looked away for a moment. "Your sister… she did something pretty fucked up right before she died, and it pissed off— You have to trust me, baby. There are things about your sister's death that involve some very dangerous people, and to tell you anything else would put you at risk. All I can say is that it wasn't me," he finished in a rush.

I must be a fool because I believed him.

I couldn't decide if I believed him because I *truly* believed him, or because I desperately *wanted* to believe him.

I knew Enzo was no saint.

I also wasn't stupid.

I knew he had done violent things.

There were rumors about his family.

Yet, even with his betrayal of my privacy, I couldn't make myself believe he was truly capable of beating Renata to death like that. And what he said did track with how suspicious my parents had been acting.

Either way, it didn't matter. We were still done. Everything about us was tainted, toxic to the core. No relationship could survive after so many secrets and betrayals.

My anger at his deception flared up again.

He stepped closer. "Say you believe me."

I inched toward the door. My voice was flat, devoid of emotion. "I believe you."

He moved forward.

I raised my hand to stop him. "It changes nothing between us. I meant what I said yesterday. I want nothing more than to forget I ever knew you. Ever loved you."

His eyes narrowed. "I won't apologize for wanting to protect you as best I could. Or for refusing to share you, Bianca. I may be going to hell for it, but no man was going to touch what was mine."

All sense of self-preservation was burned to cinders in the flames of my fury.

How dare he act like the fucking protective, caring boyfriend?

He had no fucking right.

I silenced the small voice in my head that was screaming for me to just keep my mouth shut and leave.

Finally.

Finally.

Here was my moment to cause him a fraction of the pain and heartbreak he had caused me.

I tilted my head to one side as I raised an eyebrow. "Apparently your surveillance wasn't as good as you thought, Enzo."

His upper lip curled on a snarl. "What?"

I leaned forward. "One man slipped through your net. I'm not as innocent as you believe me to be."

Enzo stalked toward me. "What did you just say?" he growled.

I stumbled backward, reaching behind me for the doorknob. I twisted it. It was only in that moment I remembered... he had locked it.

It was too late.

I was in too deep.

I met his gaze defiantly. "I'm no longer yours. I'm *his*."

CHAPTER 10

ENZO

*N*ow I know why those I loved thought it was plausible I would be capable of murderous violence.

My tentative hold, at best, on all rational thought...snapped.

I slammed my body against hers, pinning her to the door.

Stretching her arms over her head, I captured her fragile wrists in one hand and secured her jaw in my other. I breathed heavily through clenched teeth as I stared down into her frightened face.

I knew she was terrified.

She should be.

I was no longer in control.

I pressed my lips against hers as I snarled, "You let another man touch you?"

It wasn't fair.

It wasn't even close to right.

I was a complete bastard for being angry.

And I didn't give a fuck.

"Enzo, wait—"

I pressed my fingertips into her soft cheeks, forcing her lower jaw down and her mouth open.

I then fell on her.

Pushing my tongue inside.

Tasting her. Claiming her. Sucking the air from her body.

Her torso bucked as she pulled on her wrists.

I wouldn't relent.

No one would call this a kiss. I was smothering her.

Stealing her breath. It was as if I were trying to swallow her essence whole.

When I finally relented, she gulped in great gasps of air.

Her mouth was bruised and the delicate flesh around her lips red from the brush of my beard.

I released her wrists.

She immediately turned and yanked on the doorknob, reaching for the key. It fell from the keyhole and rattled to the tile floor.

I reached for the hem of her sweater and yanked it violently over her head.

She screeched in protest.

I tossed it aside as I pulled at the clasp of her bra, bending the thin metal hooks until they snapped. The straps fell loose over her shoulders.

She cast a glance over her shoulder, wrapping her arms over her breasts to cover them. "Enzo, don't do this!"

The silk scarf which had been covering her hair hung loose, exposing her silky, mink-brown curls. Her head snapped back as I wrenched the scarf off and stuffed it into my back pocket. I then reached around her body to yank off her bra.

She resisted.

I won.

Bare from the waist up, Bianca raised her arms and banged on the door. "Help! Someone!"

Pulling her body back flush against mine, I palmed her breasts. "No one can hear your cries."

I fell on her neck, dragging my teeth up its length as I pinched her nipples.

I moved my right hand over her stomach, down to her torn skirt. Fisting the fabric, I tore it the rest of the way until it fell in a useless pile at her feet.

She was now standing in only her pretty pink panties and high heels.

Looking like an innocent wanton.

Except she wasn't innocent. Not anymore.

Some other man had taken her innocence.

Some other man had touched her. Kissed her.

Had his cock inside of her.

The very idea caused a red haze of rage to fall over my vision.

Until all I could think about was erasing all memory of that man from her body. I wanted to brand her physically and mentally, until there was nothing left but my mark. And even that wouldn't be enough. Not even close. Not until I hunted the man down and wiped his existence from the face of the earth for touching what was mine.

I shoved my hand down her panties, palming her pussy.

Bianca moved up on her toes in a helpless effort to escape my touch. "Don't," she moaned.

I sank my teeth into her earlobe. "Did you moan for him, *tesoro mio?*" I rasped in her ear.

I pushed my two middle fingers between her pussy lips.

Her hips jerked forward.

I shifted my left hand to grasp her right breast, as I moved my fingers rapidly back and forth.

Her arm swept up to clasp around my neck.

I sucked harder on her neck, wanting her to bear my mark.

I applied more pressure with my fingers as I increased the pace, teasing her clit.

"Oh God," she moaned again.

"That's it, baby. Come for me."

I vibrated my hand, moving it faster and faster, until she came undone in my arms.

The moment her body went limp, I turned her around and pushed my shoulder into her stomach, hefting her high.

I carried her into the bedroom.

Shoving aside the canopy curtains on the Sicilian wrought iron marriage bed, I tossed her into the center. Before she could escape, I placed her on her knees and whipped out her silk scarf, securing her wrists to the headboard, ignoring the intricately carved images of doves and hearts.

"What are you doing?"

"What I should have done the first moment I met you."

I had never shown her this dark side of myself when we dated. Not even close. I had treated her like a delicate piece of precious glass. I hadn't even let her suck my cock.

There was just something so sheltered, so innocent and sweet about her.

I had wanted to preserve it, treasure it.

She was *tesoro mio.*

My treasure.

I didn't want to dirty what we had with my dark, perverted needs.

Maybe that had been the problem.

Maybe keeping that side of myself secret from her was what allowed events to unfold as they did. I was so afraid I would scare her off with my rough touch and brutal needs, I had insisted on taking things slowly. I didn't want to push her.

My plan had been to make her my wife so we had a lifetime ahead of us.

That *had* been the plan.

Now some other man had stolen my treasure.

Stolen what was mine.

Stolen her first moment of pleasure.

Stolen her innocence.

And I was determined to claw back every moan, every tremble, every touch.

When I was finished with her, we would be like Adam and Eve after the fall. No other human being would exist on this earth. It would just be the two of us.

And my unforgivable sin.

Standing over her, I tore off my T-shirt and reached for my belt. As I pulled the thick leather from the jean belt loops, I folded it in half in my hands, testing its weight.

Bianca stared up at me with wide eyes, saying nothing.

I reached over and tore her panties off her, exposing the generous curves of her ass.

She leaned to the side and tried to kick at me.

I grasped each of her ankles and ripped her high heels off and threw them across the room.

I palmed my leather belt again. "How many times, Bianca?"

Her chest rose and fell as she breathed heavily. "What?"

I repeated through clenched teeth, "How many times did you *fuck* him?"

Her eyes narrowed. She jutted out her chin. "None of your business!"

I whipped the flat of my belt over her ass.

She cried out.

I spanked her with my belt again. "How many times? How many times was his cock inside of you?"

She was right. I had no goddamn business asking, but I didn't care. I was a man possessed.

"Fuck you!"

I tossed the belt aside and climbed onto the bed. Grasping her hips, I kneeled behind her and stared down at her ass, the flesh pink from my belt. I spread her cheeks. Her tiny, puckered asshole clenched. "Did he fuck you in the ass, too?"

I pressed my fingertip against her hole.

Bianca's back arched as she tried to clench her cheeks closed.

"Tell me, babygirl. Are you still a virgin here?"

She stayed quiet.

I sucked my thumb and pressed the wet digit against her resisting hole.

"Ow! Don't! I am! I am!"

I forced my thumb inside her tiny hole, taking a sick pleasure in how tightly it squeezed around my digit. I pumped my thumb in and out several times. Watching as the pale pink skin smoothed and whitened with the pressure.

Bianca groaned as her hips bucked.

I ground my crotch against her thigh. Fuck. As angry as I was, I knew I was too big to fuck her virgin asshole raw. I lowered the zipper to my jeans. Pulling my hard cock free, I wrapped my fist around the thick shaft and ran my hand up and down its length several times.

I flipped her onto her back.

I wrenched her knees open and wedged my hips between them. Placing my forearm near her head, I leaned over her. "Do you love him?"

She pulled on her restrained wrists. "Let me go, Enzo!"

My body shook with emotion. I blinked past the mist in my eyes. I notched the head of my cock at her wet entrance. "Answer me," I growled, "do you love him?"

I didn't want to know.

I needed to know.

Even though the answer might shred my very soul.

A tear escaped from the corner of her eye. "I love you," she screamed. "Are you happy now? As stupid as it sounds, I still love you."

The blood boiled in my veins with a possessive heat so intense I wasn't sure I would survive.

With an absolute feral mating roar, I thrust deep inside of her.

Crashing through her maidenhead.

Shocked to my core, I pulled partially out and stared at my cock.

It was faintly streaked with virgin blood. "Jesus fucking Christ, Bianca!"

I stared down at her flushed, tearstained face. She sniffed. Fixing me with a defiant glare, she whispered, "You're not the only one who can lie, Enzo."

I pushed her hair back from her cheeks, cupping her face. My brow furrowed. "Why, baby? Why would you say something like that?"

She swallowed before licking her kiss-bruised lips. "Because I wanted to hurt you, like you hurt me."

I pressed my forehead to hers and closed my eyes, "Goddammit, Bianca," I groaned.

She jerked on her wrists, tears beginning to fall. "Untie me. I want to leave. Now!"

I pushed slowly back inside of her. "I'm sorry, *tesoro mio*. I can't let you go."

I shifted my hand to cup the back of her head as I pressed my mouth to hers. My tongue teased a response from her; my left hand shifted to gently caress her breast.

It took all the willpower I possessed not to thrust.

My cock was deep inside of her, but I kept my hips still as I kissed the corner of her mouth, the edge of her jaw, her neck. I placed open-mouthed kisses along the slim column of her neck, arching my back and bending to suck her nipple between my lips.

I flicked the hard nub with the tip of my tongue as I continued to cup and massage her other breast.

Waiting.

I slid my hand over her silky skin to her waist, then caressed her hip as I returned to kiss her neck.

I shifted to lean over her to run the tip of my tongue over her lower lip. "Give in to me, *tesoro mio*," I whispered softly against her mouth.

She whimpered.

Then I felt it. Her body clenched around my cock as her hips shifted upward.

A tremor raced down my spine.

Bracing my forearms on either side of her head, I kept my gaze on her as I pulled out halfway and then carefully pushed back in. I did it again, and again, slowly increasing my pace.

Her lips opened as her breath quickened.

I thrust faster.

Her eyes started to close.

"Eyes on me, babygirl."

Her beautiful eyes flashed open.

"That's it, baby. Stay with me." I thrust faster.

Her body clenched around my cock.

"Good girl."

I thrust deeper.

She moaned as her head tilted back.

I reached up and released the knot on the silk scarf binding her wrists. "Touch me, baby. I need to feel your hands on my skin."

She placed her hands on my chest. Her fingers weaved into my chest hair.

I quirked an eyebrow. "Pull it."

She looked at me with wide, uncertain eyes.

My breath was harsh against her lips. "Pull it hard. Do it, baby."

I wrapped my hand around her knee and lifted her left leg up higher over my hip as I thrust harder and faster.

Bianca twisted her fingers into my chest hair and pulled.

"Harder," I commanded.

She pulled harder. The sting of pain spurred me on.

I reached between us and teased her clit. "Come for me again. I want to hear you moan."

Her fingernails dug into my chest. "Enzo, I'm… I'm…."

I knew she was about to find her release.

I couldn't hold back my own any longer.

I flipped our bodies until I was on my back, and she was straddling me. Grabbing onto her long hair with one hand and her hip with my other, I thrust violently upward, bouncing her on my cock.

I then used my grip on her hair to force her head down to my chest. "Bite me!" I growled. "Mark me, babygirl. Draw my blood like I drew yours."

I felt the hesitant press of her teeth just over my heart.

I pounded into her. "Bite me, Bianca!" I commanded.

She sank her teeth into my flesh but without breaking the skin.

In that moment, I came.

I pressed her head against my heart as I released my hot come deep inside of her. My body jerking with each violent spasm. Relishing the sharp sting of pain from her teeth. Hoping it scarred.

She collapsed on top of me.

I wrapped my arms around her, clasping her to me.

Neither of us spoke.

The only sound in the room was our harsh, mingled breaths.

After several minutes, I gently slid her beside me on the bed and left the room.

I crossed the hall into the bathroom I had finished refurbishing.

In its center was a massive, slightly chipped, antique porcelain claw-footed tub. I turned the polished brass spigots and tested the water until it was the perfect temperature. I then placed the stopper in the drain to fill it so she could take a bath.

Before leaving the bathroom, I paused and stared into the mirror.

Over my heart were two tiny red crescent-shaped bite marks.

When I returned to the bedroom, she was wrapped in a blanket leaning against the headboard, her knees drawn up to her chest.

Her eyes were wide. Her expression drawn.

She flicked her eyes down my chest to my open jeans and back up to the bite mark on my chest.

I pulled my jeans up over my hips and raised the zipper. I then stepped toward the bed.

She stiffened.

I stilled.

She clutched the blanket more firmly around her shoulders. "What we just did...what just happened...it can never happen again." She swiped at a fresh tear on her cheek. "This whole situation. *Us.* It's toxic. It's fucked up. It's not healthy."

Her gaze swept over the rumpled and stained sheets. "It nearly broke me getting over you. I can't go through that pain again."

I stood there and watched her.

There was nothing I could say.

I wasn't going to apologize because it would be a lie.

I was sorry for how it happened, but I wasn't the least bit sorry it *had* happened. If that made me a monster, then so be it. I was already headed to hell for so many other things, I would gladly skip down that path for this one.

I fisted my hand. But at what cost? I would rather cut off an arm than cause her more pain, and yet every fiber of my being raged at the idea of letting her go.

She stared at me for several heartbeats.

When I remained silent, she lowered her head. She then got off the bed and, keeping the blanket tightly wrapped around her shoulders, swept past me into the hall. She crossed to the bathroom, where the water for the hot bath I had drawn for her was still running.

She turned to face me. Her dark eyes were filled with tears. "Loving you is a weakness, Enzo, not a strength."

With that she closed the door.

She couldn't have wounded me more deeply than if she had actually plunged that letter opener straight into my aching heart the other day.

* * *

I OPENED the cottage door to the soft knock.

Aunt Gabriella stood there with a Louis Vuitton weekender bag resting on her forearm. "With all the clothes I lend you, your brother, *and* your father's lovers, I'm lucky I have any wardrobe left."

Her smile faded the moment she saw my expression. She frowned. "What's happened?"

I gave her a kiss on the cheek. "She's in the tub. Just... take care of her for me. See that she gets home safely. You brought the two guards I asked for in the separate car?"

"Yes. They are waiting at the end of the street, like you asked."

I nodded. "Good. They'll follow you at a distance. After you drop her off, the second guard will ride back with you to the villa while the first remains behind, out of sight. I don't want her to know she's being watched."

I left the cottage and walked toward my motorcycle.

"Of course, darling. And what about the plans we talked about earlier? Have they changed?" she called out.

I didn't turn around. "Just take her home."

CHAPTER 11

BIANCA

I sank lower into the water at the sound of the knock. "I don't want to talk, Enzo."

"It's not Enzo, dear."

I frowned at the unexpected feminine voice. Sitting up in the tub, I stretched my arm over the edge to try and reach for a towel. Before my fingertips could touch it, the door swung open.

Soapy water sloshed over the edge as I slunk down, covering my nakedness. "I'm not decent."

The woman giggled. "Well then, you are in good company, darling," she teased with a wink.

My mouth opened.

It was Gabriella De Luca, Barone Cavalieri's sister-in-law.

Although I had never met her in person, everyone knew her by reputation.

It was hard not to be cowed.

In the quaint, shabby chic, cottage bathroom she was like fireworks going off in a closet. All bright, sparkling light.

Dressed in head-to-toe Gucci, she practically shimmered from all the gold, cobalt blue and ruby red. Her glossy black hair, expertly swept up into a loose chignon, didn't show a single gray strand, and her cat-eye makeup was perfect. She practically vibrated with glamorous energy.

Gabriella effortlessly achieved what my mother could only hope to cheaply copy, no matter how much money she spent.

Next to her, I felt like a common little dormouse drowning in a bucket of water.

I tried to reach for the towel again. "I should get out of the tub."

She waved her hand. "Don't be silly. You just got in there, and you look like you could use a nice, relaxing soak... with some wine of course."

I awkwardly sat back in the tub, making sure the suds covered my naked breasts.

Wineglasses clinked as she set them on the sink countertop. She held up a bottle of red wine. "This is all I could find in the cupboard. It's not Cavalieri. Seems to be a simple table red wine but needs must and all that, right sweetie?"

I was too confused and awestruck to respond.

She twisted a corkscrew into the top and pulled. Half the cork popped off. Gabriella frowned. "Dry cork. Should have expected as much from a cheap wine. No worries. I learned this from a rather randy machine laborer when I was probably too young and he was probably too old, which is the best kind of romance."

She hiked up her skirt and wedged the wine bottle between her thighs. She inserted the corkscrew into the bottle again and gave the top a good smack. It drove the second half of the cork into the bottle. She raised it triumphantly. "There we are!" She poured two glasses. "We don't mind a bit of cork in our wine, now do we?"

She handed me a glass and sat on the closed toilet as if it were a chair at the Plaza. Crossing her legs, she took an elegant sip of her wine and then asked, "So what's the problem, is my nephew bad in bed?"

I choked on the swallow of wine I had taken. "I'm sorry? What?"

Gabriella shrugged one shoulder. "Just because he is a Cavalieri does not automatically mean he is good in bed. I mean, look at me and my sister. Technically we were both De Lucas. She was a prude. And yet, by all accounts, I am unforgettably fabulous between the sheets."

My cheeks flamed. I wondered if you could drown yourself in only a few feet of water?

"I...I...I don't think I can answer that."

She raised an eyebrow. "It's like that is it?"

I blinked. "Like what?"

She tilted her head and slid her gaze to the side as she smiled slyly. "It's always the quiet ones."

My stomach twisted. I had a nasty feeling this conversation was rapidly getting away from me. "What is always the quiet ones?"

"Who hide their freak flag of course." She patted the top of my hand. "Don't worry. Your secret is safe with me."

I rose up in the tub, exposing my breasts. I quickly sank back below the water, to my chin. The violent movement caused a wave of water to crest and splash against my face as I tried to talk. "No," I choked on bathwater. "I didn't say that!"

Good God! How did she know?

Thoughts of Enzo roughly commanding me to pull his chest hair and bite him after he had spanked me with his belt came crashing into my mind like out-of-control boulders tumbling down a mountain.

This conversation was *definitely* getting away from me.

Gabriella tried to soothe my agitated state. "It's all right, darling. Truth be told, *I'm relieved.*"

That caught my attention. "Relieved?"

She leaned forward, resting her forearms on her thighs. She twirled the stem of her wineglass. "Enzo has always been a bit uptight, prudish. He gets it from his mother. It's good to know behind closed doors he loosens up and gets a little kinky."

Enzo a prude? She couldn't possibly be serious. And oh my God, did his aunt just say *kinky?*

Gabriella continued. "Everything was about preserving the family's reputation and keeping within society's rules. Even at the cost of his own happiness."

She regarded me thoughtfully over the rim of her wine-glass as she took a sip.

I couldn't hold her scrutinizing gaze.

Leaning against the tub back, I focused instead on the remaining clouds of soap bubbles I was pushing around on the water's surface with the bottom of my wineglass. As a casualty of that side of his personality, she wouldn't get an argument from me on that point, at least.

Gabriella cleared her throat. "Forgive me for saying so, you don't seem that upset over your sister's death."

I bit the inside of my cheek before answering.

Finally, taking a deep breath, I said, "I'm not." It felt terrible to say it out loud like that in such a matter-of-fact way, but it was the truth. "We weren't close. Even before… what happened with Enzo. Do you think I'm a horrible person?"

Gabriella let out a relieved breath. "We'll have to get drunk together for me to know your true measure, but so far, I think you're delightful. Now your sister, on the other hand…." She made the sign of the cross and looked up at the ceiling. "Forgive me, Madonna, for speaking ill of the dead. She was a nasty piece of work, that one. It's nice to know I won't have to pretend to be sorry she's gone to spare your feelings."

Damn. Well, okay then. Gabriella certainly didn't hold back.

I gave her a rueful smile. "I see my sister endeared herself to your family after the wedding."

Gabriella opened her mouth as if to speak then closed it.

Then said, "I've been sworn to secrecy on a certain matter, but all I'm going to say is, if you knew the full truth, you wouldn't be feeling quite as guilty for not being sad right now."

How odd.

As strange as her statement was, I didn't want to dwell on it.

I was already feeling all kinds of weird about what I'd just done with Enzo. I folded my hands on the edge of the tub and rested my chin on them. "Can I ask you a question?"

"As long as it's personal."

I gave her a half-hearted smile before asking her, "Do you think it's wrong... I mean, do you think I'm a bad person...that is—"

"Should you have fucked your sister's widower the day after her funeral?"

"Oh my God!" I groaned.

It was even worse when she put it that bluntly... and it was already pretty fucking bad.

I dunked my head below the water.

Gabriella pulled me to the surface by my hair.

I gasped for air as I swiped the water from my eyes and face.

"Don't be so dramatic. You and Enzo are so alike. You both think the world should be viewed in stark black-and-white terms. Well, it's not like that. It's not even gray. It's a messed up, mottled Jackson Pollock painting of splats, smears, and drips of all three colors."

"What is that even supposed to mean?" I sputtered.

She threw her hand up in the air. "*Who cares?* is what it's supposed to mean. Who the fuck cares who you are fucking?"

I snatched at the towel and wiped my face. "People care!"

She shrugged. "People? What people?"

"I don't know. People! My parents. People in the village. Enzo's father and brother. People! People will talk."

"For starters, Enzo's father is the last man on earth to pass judgment on anyone's bed partner. I doubt his brother would give a damn. Your parents shouldn't be commenting on your sex life, and as for the rest, why would you care?"

"What do you mean why?"

"Exactly that. Why would you care? What is the point in caring what others say? Talk is just talk. It doesn't harm you, so who the fuck cares what they say. Let them talk."

I drained my wineglass. "That's all well and good to say, but that's not how the real world works."

"You're what, twenty-one, twenty-two? You're a baby, what do you know of the real world?"

"I know I have no intention of getting my heart stomped on again," I sighed. "And I know that loving someone and them being the right person for you, the right choice, are not the same things."

Gabriella was quiet for several moments. Her voice was uncharacteristically soft and low when she finally spoke. "It seems I was wrong. Seems you do know a lot about how the real world works."

She stood. Taking the wineglass from my hand, she gathered up the half empty bottle and corkscrew. "I'll let you finish your bath. I've laid out a cute Valentino A-line dress in burnt umber and gold from last season for you."

"Thank you."

"I'll take you home when you're ready." She closed the door behind her.

Home.

I didn't have a home.

My childhood home was a viper's nest now. My New York home was gone. I couldn't return to school. I didn't have enough of my own money to afford the fees. Fuck. My life was a complete freaking mess, and that was before I factored in the insanity of my attraction to Enzo.

Holy hell. Enzo.

The sex had been unbelievably *intense*.

In the past when I imagined my first time, there was always candlelight, romance, love, and gentleness. What we just did had none of that. It was raw, primal lust. I might be inexperienced, but I was pretty sure that was what they called hate fucking.

And the worst part?

It had been amazing. Every fucked-up, brutally rough moment of it.

My world was a bubble of affectation my parents created, a warped illusion. Everything was thinly gilded in cheap gold to keep up the appearance of wealth and affluence. My whole life was about knowing the *right* people, vacationing in the *right* places, wearing the *right* clothes, saying and doing the *right* thing.

Be a good girl, Bianca. Stay silent and step aside so your sister can marry Enzo Cavalieri for the good of the family. Don't fault your sister. It is not her fault you were not beautiful or charming enough to snare him for yourself.

In that fake world, sex would have been all roses, gentle kisses, and candlelight.

In the real world, sex with Enzo had been frenzied, wild, and untamed.

For the first time in my life, I had done something wrong, something twisted, something seriously fucked up.

And it felt good.

It felt good to be bad...in the moment.

But cold reality was creeping back in.

I looked down at the now tepid bathwater, the fizzled remnants of what once were big, fluffy clouds of shimmering bubbles now floating listlessly on top.

With a resigned sigh, I pulled out the drain stopper and got out of the tub.

CHAPTER 12

MILANA

"*M*ilana? Milana Carbone? Is that you?"

I turned to see Bianca Moretti waving to me from across the small cafe as she approached.

She was wearing a gorgeous, flared-sleeve cream blouse with fabulous brass button details and a brown suede skirt, a beautiful Ralph Lauren Leonarda Wrap camel coat tossed casually over her shoulders.

I inwardly sighed. Compared to the garish vulgarity of Renata, Bianca had such an understated, classic style. She was so elegant and chic.

Even when she stormed down the church aisle to embarrassingly slap Enzo at the funeral.

As much as I felt for my future brother-in-law—I couldn't argue with the girl's style and panache.

Damn! The dress. The heels. That fabulous Saint Fort black pearl wheel hat and gauze veil.

If her intent was to return to town and send a message

that she was *over* her ex-boyfriend and the humiliation of him marrying her sister, then that was definitely the way to do it.

Why couldn't Enzo have married her instead?

She would have made a fun sister-in-law.

I looked her over as she weaved her way through the chairs and tables.

Especially since we looked to be about the same clothing size.

Alfonso rose and stepped forward, intending to run interference.

"It's fine."

He looked down at me. "Cesare won't like it."

"Since when has that ever stopped me?"

I was still on ordered rest and not allowed back in the office yet.

Although I was sneaking some work in when Cesare wasn't around, between being cooped up in the villa and the round-the-clock nursing staff he insisted on hiring to watch over me, the excursion to the cafe had been a welcomed relief.

Alfonso was acting as a guard for my safety while we waited for Cesare to join us.

An expert physician was traveling in from Rome to Dr. Pontano's offices to examine me.

We were finally going to learn if my pregnancy was still viable.

Cesare wanted the best doctor in the country to run his tests and write up his reports. And that was fine. That was what he needed to get past the trauma and guilt over what happened.

I placed a hand over my stomach.

I knew my baby was alive.

There was no rationale. No science. No medical tests. *I just knew.*

I had struggled and fought for too long to finally find happiness for it to be taken away. Besides, there was no way a baby of mine didn't inherit at least some of my stubbornness.

Alfonso shook his head. He nodded toward a seat one table over. "I'll be right over there if you need me."

I stood to greet Bianca.

We clasped hands as we gave each other a kiss on each cheek. I then gestured toward the nearest chair. "Please, sit. Did you want a caffe?"

She set her Saint Laurent Sac De Jour Nano crocodile purse to the side. "Yes, that would be wonderful," she agreed as she took off her brown suede gloves.

I gestured for the waiter, and she ordered.

Bianca looked at me. "You look beautiful, Milana. Is that Valentino? It's made for you. How have you been?"

I clasped the charm around my neck. This wasn't awkward at all. Totally normal to be sitting at a cafe enjoying a drink on a chilly autumn morning with the sister of the person who tried to murder you.

Nope. Not awkward. At. All.

Especially since I was fairly certain poor Bianca was absolutely clueless as to her sister's crime.

Although Barone and Cesare had said they would leave the final decision up to me, the family wanted everything kept quiet to avoid any suspicion or scandal. In the end, I agreed.

It wasn't like my own family name was spotless. I didn't want malicious gossip any more than they did.

It was driving me crazy that I couldn't remember anything from the afternoon Renata locked me in the wine cave.

It was pretty obvious now, though, that she must have been the female from that horrible day back in school. It would have been nice to have closure, but in the end, it didn't really matter. She was dead. Did I really need to hear from her the twisted, jealous reasons for why she targeted me?

I knew why. She wanted Cesare.

Well, she lost. I got him.

She'd then turned her sights on poor Enzo, fucking over her sister in the process.

And again, she wasn't satisfied with that. Nothing was good enough for her.

Greed did that to a person.

She always wanted more than her fair share.

She sowed malice and discord all around her, all for the sake of money.

And what was all that money she valued above all else buying her now?

The threat was over. It was best to bury the entire sordid business with her.

Besides, we might not have been friends, but I'd been passing acquaintances with Bianca in school and had always liked her. Truth be told, I had felt sorry for her. I wasn't the only one Renata was cruel to. She often openly bullied and talked down to Bianca in front of others.

I forced a smile. "I'm well. I was sorry to hear about your sister." I picked up my spoon and added an extra spoonful of sugar to my latte macchiato. I would need it to wash away the bile that stuck in the back of my throat.

Bianca's own expression seemed to freeze in place. She reached for her caffe. "Yes. Thank you," she responded stiffly. "I thought I saw you at the funeral, but I wasn't sure."

"I was there, briefly, to pay my respects."

And to witness the slap heard around Italy, but best not to mention that.

Why make this more awkward than it already is?

"That was kind of you. I know Renata wasn't particularly nice to you at school."

I set my spoon aside. "No, she wasn't, but that is all in the past now."

Bianca looked to each side of us as if checking to see if we were being observed.

I cast a quick glance in Alfonso's direction. He was quietly reading a newspaper, looking for all the world completely uninterested in the conversation of two women. I knew differently. I knew full well he was listening to every word, waiting for any sign of danger.

"Speaking of school, are you still close friends with Amara Beneventi?"

Alfonso ruffled his newspaper and cleared his throat.

I could understand Alfonso's unspoken concern.

Were we wrong about Bianca? Had she somehow been involved in Renata's schemes?

I looked over my shoulder and adjusted my seat. "Yes, why?"

She shook her head. "I'm so sorry. That must be so difficult for you. I think I know a little bit about what you're going through, so if you want a friend to talk to about it, I'm here for you."

Wait, what?

I wanted to keep her talking to see what I could learn, just in case there was something suspicious going on, but at the same time, I had no clue what the fuck she was talking about. "I'm not sure—"

"Your hatred for the Cavalieris?"

My eyes widened. "My *hatred* for the Cavalieris?"

"Everyone knows how much you hate Cesare Cavalieri. I'm sure it can't be easy having your best friend date his father."

Santo inferno! Do her parents not tell her anything?

Bianca looked around again and then leaned forward before continuing. "Actually, I was really glad to spot you today. I could use a friend, and it's impossible to find anyone within a thousand kilometers who doesn't worship the Cavalieris like some kind of living gods."

Alfonso snort-laughed and covered it with a cough.

Feeling like a fraud, I shook my head. "Bianca, I'm not sure I'm the—"

"Please, Milana. I'm desperate for some advice."

Cazzo! What the hell am I supposed to do now?

Before I could respond, she rushed on in a heightened whisper, "I slept with Enzo."

Decision made.

I leaned forward and whispered back, "Holy shit! When? Where? How did it happen?"

She propped her elbow on the table and covered her eyes. "Yesterday. I know what you're thinking. I'm a horrible person."

I frowned. "Why would I be thinking that?"

"Because he's my ex. Because we broke up. Because he's my brother-in-law. Because my sister just died. Because he's a Cavalieri"—once again, she glanced around her— "and there are *rumors*."

I lowered my voice. "Rumors?"

"About how my sister died."

I played with the handle of my spoon. "I wouldn't put much stock in those rumors. You know how the people in this village like to gossip."

"So you've heard them too?"

Oops.

I shrugged. "I've heard some nonsense, but I didn't believe it. Enzo isn't capable of murder."

Bianca's shoulders sagged with relief. "You have no idea how glad I am to hear you say that."

"Really?"

"I was worried I was letting my past feelings for him cloud my judgment. I don't think he did it either." She gestured toward me. "But if someone who hates the Cavalieris as much as you do would give Enzo the benefit of the doubt, then that makes me feel better."

I let out a short laugh. "Yes! Yes, *totally* because I *really hate* them."

I was *so* going to hell for this conversation.

She played with the handle of her caffe cup. "Although it won't make a difference in the end, at least I didn't sleep with a murderer."

"You mean, you're not going to try things again with Enzo?"

Bianca looked up at me. "Can you imagine allowing your-self to fall in love with a man who betrayed you?"

And just like that, this gets even more awkward.

I cleared my throat. "Actually... yes. I can. As lame as it may sound, the heart wants what it wants. And you know, like you said, sometimes emotion can cloud our judgment. That works both ways. Would it be so terrible to give him a second chance? I mean you're obviously still attracted to him."

"Enzo and I together isn't a relationship, it's a plot from a soap opera."

"I'll admit dating your sister's widower sounds a bit melo-dramatic, but let's be honest, I was a catering server at your sister's wedding, and even I could see it wasn't a real marriage. Talk about hearing rumors!"

She leaned back in her seat and rested her forearms on the armrests. "I thought you'd be the one person in this town to knock some sense into me by raining fire and brimstone-level hatred for the Cavalieris down on my head. Why are you defending Enzo? It's almost like you want me to get together with him?"

"It's not that. It's just I think you're being too hard on both of you. You guys had barely started dating when he... fucked up."

"Knocked up my sister and then married her, you mean?"

"Yeah, that. Although, speaking of rumors, I had heard a rumor that Renata put something in his drink that night."

She played with the edge of the tablecloth. "That rumor is true. Don't tell anyone. I wouldn't want people thinking I'm going around trashing Renata's memory or anything, but yes, she put something in his drink."

"So it's not really his fault? And no offense, but the man was married to your sister. I think he's been punished enough."

She sighed. "It's worse than that."

My stomach muscles tightened. "What do you mean?"

"Can you keep a secret?"

Fuck, no. Not if it concerns your psychotic bitch of a sister.

"Absolutely."

"Enzo probably never slept with Renata."

My mouth dropped open. "What? But the whole pregnancy thing?"

"I only just found out a few days ago. My mother was trashed when she called to tell me about Renata. She let it slip that Renata was never pregnant."

"Not to be crude, but that doesn't mean, you know…."

"She gave him too much of whatever the drug was. It knocked him out cold. When he woke up, she let him think they had slept together."

"No offense, but your sister was a real piece of work. Are you going to tell Enzo?"

"Fuck no."

"Why not?"

"Are you crazy? My parents are already freaking out about losing the *great Cavalieri* connection. They are worried as it is about all the millions they will miss out on by not being in their inner circle. They are even trying to pawn me off on some cousin named Matteo. If I tell Enzo, he'll be furious. Who knows what kind of revenge his family would be capable of? You know what the Cavalieris are secretly like. You don't get all that power and money by playing nice in the sandbox. Besides, would you want to know the reason you were forced to marry someone was a complete lie?"

I decided to play along. "It's been months. I'm sure he figured out by now she wasn't pregnant."

"Yeah, but he might not know the other part."

"Don't you think he deserves to know he didn't betray you?"

She bit her lip. "It's my only protection."

I frowned. "What do you mean?"

"I wish I could be like you. I really want to hate him, like you hate Cesare. I know I have plenty of reasons, but I'm not strong enough to resist him. I know he's all wrong for me. Toxic. I just can't stop thinking about him, especially since being back in Italy. I missed him so much. I tried everything to get over him and I really thought I had...but then you know what happened. So him thinking that we can't get beyond the past, that I can't forgive him for his betrayal, is the only thing protecting me from making a terrible mistake."

I raised an eyebrow. "Didn't you kind of already make that mistake?"

"Yes, but it was a one-time thing. It's not going to happen again."

I said under my breath, "Sounds familiar."

"What?"

I waved my hand. "Nothing. Just a word of caution, the Cavalieri men have a funny way of *overlooking* your objections."

She picked up her caffe cup and brought it to her lips. "You almost sound like you are speaking from experience."

In that moment, Cesare walked up. He leaned down and

gave me a kiss on the cheek. "Sorry that paperwork took so long, *carissima*." He placed a protective hand on my shoulder as he stared down at Bianca. "Why is Alfonso not sitting with you?"

Translation, why the fuck is Bianca Moretti sitting with you?

Bianca's cup clattered to the saucer. Her gaze shifted between me and Cesare and back.

She reached into her purse as she rose. Tossing a few euro onto the table, she glared at me. "It seems you *were* speaking from experience."

I stood. "I can explain."

Her eyes narrowed. "Don't bother."

She turned and stormed away.

Cesare rubbed his forehead. "I can't leave you alone for one moment without you getting into trouble."

"This is hardly my fault. Alfonso is my witness. She walked up to my table and sat down!"

Alfonso raised up both of his palms. "Leave me out of this. I'm heading back to the villa."

With that, he folded up his newspaper and walked off.

I slung my Alexandra De Curtis Loren navy tote over my forearm and pulled on the matching soft leather gloves, then turned so Cesare could slip my Falconeri Sabled Cashmere cream coat over my shoulders.

He hugged me briefly from behind before giving me a quick kiss on the neck. With his arm wrapped around my waist, he led me to his car parked around the building on the other side of the piazza.

"It was dangerous talking to her, Milana. The third man is still out there. We suspect Renata's parents were involved in the Agnello property scheme and we can't rule out that Bianca wasn't as well."

I rolled my eyes. "Trust me. She's not involved. "

He opened the car door for me. "How do you know that?"

I turned to face him before getting in. "That poor girl is clueless, about a *lot* of things."

He pulled up the collar of my coat, inching me closer to him. I inhaled the familiar scent of his cologne, always a turn-on for me.

Leaning down, he kissed the edge of my mouth. "So did you at least learn anything interesting?"

CHAPTER 13

AMARA

"Oh my God!"

Barone had just yanked the heavy wicker picnic basket out of the back seat of the Fiat Spider Lusso.

He dropped it back onto the seat and approached me. Cupping his hand around mine, he tilted the phone in my grasp so he could see the screen. "What has happened? Have they heard?"

We had come to the point in our relationship where we now *shared* my phone for work and family. Since Barone's disdain for mobiles was well known, staff and family had slowly started calling me to get ahold of him since we were almost always together. Now it was just an accepted thing.

"No. They are headed to Dr. Pontano's now. Milana had a run-in with Bianca Moretti, Renata's sister, at the cafe while she was waiting for Cesare."

Barone frowned as he returned to unpacking the car.

We were at my mother's cottage.

Enzo had thoughtfully repaired the damage wrought by my stepfather and stepbrother.

He had even made some amazing improvements to the interior as well as the exterior landscaping. He really was a very talented architect. It was almost a shame so much of his time was spent running the family winery.

The cottage would be ready by spring for me to start renting it out to tourists as an authentic Italian countryside experience. I was offering it as part of a package linked to the Cavalieri winery tours. It was a fun little side business and a way to ensure I still kept making a little of my own money.

It didn't compare to Barone's billions, but it was important to me.

Today we were hanging lace curtains in the kitchen, similar to the ones my mother and I had made when I was a child. Rosa and I had sewn them together from a wedding gown we had found in the market, just like the originals.

We were about to start bottling at the winery and things were ramping up with the new promotions, which meant I had been working nonstop on finalizing an artist for the new labels and campaign.

So between that and the scare with Milana, things had been hectic.

Barone and I decided to sneak off for an afternoon, just the two of us.

I had packed a special picnic lunch for the occasion.

Barone unlocked the door and entered first. He scanned the cottage before allowing me to enter. It was a force of habit since it remained unoccupied most of the week.

He closed the door behind us and carried the basket into the kitchen. I followed.

"So Milana says—"

Barone snatched me around the waist and lifted me onto the countertop, stepping between my knees.

"What are you doing? Don't you want to know what she found out?"

He grabbed the phone from my hand and tossed it across the kitchen to land on the parlor sofa. "Later."

Wrapping his hand around my neck, he pulled me in to claim my mouth, his warm hand finding my thigh under my skirt. His thumb caressed my inner thigh as he inched higher.

I moaned against his mouth and wrapped my legs around his hips, locking the ankles of my knee-high leather boots behind his back.

He curled a hand around my throat, breathing against my mouth, "Twice now I've tried to fuck you in this kitchen and twice we've been interrupted. Not today."

I flicked my tongue over his lower lip. "So is this now a goal of yours?"

He raised an eyebrow. "To fuck you in every room of every house we own? Absolutely."

He slipped his fingers inside my panties.

I gasped and arched my back as I gripped his shoulder. "I've been a bad girl, *daddy*."

Initiating one of our favorite bedroom games.

With a guttural growl, Barone grabbed me around the hips and swept me off the counter to lay me on the kitchen table. Bending my legs to plant my feet on the surface with my knees up high, he flipped my skirt up over my thighs, exposing my panties. I lifted my hips and feet so he could pull them down and off.

He placed four fingers over my pussy, rubbing them back and forth. "Tell me where you want my cock."

I licked my bottom lip as I stared at his imposing form towering over me. "Inside of me."

He whipped his black thermal shirt over his head, exposing his tanned, muscled chest. He reached for his thick, leather belt.

I tried to close my knees to capture a delicious tremor rippling between my legs.

He placed his large hands on my legs, prying them open. "*Tsk. Tsk. Tsk.* If you block my view of this pretty pussy, I might have to punish you."

He flipped the lid off the picnic basket and reached inside to pull out one of the tiny cobalt-blue glass goblets of rhubarb and cardamom *dolci al cucchiaio* spoon desserts I had made for us. He dipped two fingers in the still-chilled whipped cream topping and held them up to my mouth. "Open."

I obeyed.

He pushed his whipped cream-coated fingers past my lips. "Now suck."

I sucked the sweet creamy mixture from his fingers. Pulling his hand from my mouth, he dipped his fingers into the goblet again, this time getting some of the sweet-tart rhubarb.

Like a little baby bird, I opened my mouth.

He pushed three fingers inside and I swirled my tongue around the thick digits. He pushed them in deep, almost gagging me, my lips stretched around the width.

With his eyes still on me, he reached around inside the basket and pulled out a jar of honey.

Bringing the jar to his mouth, he pulled the cork stopper out with his teeth. "Let's see if I can make this sweet pussy even sweeter. Open your legs wider."

I shifted my hips up as I widened my knees.

The sunlight from a nearby window glinted off the thick, amber syrup as he tilted the jar and we both watched it slowly drip down onto my lower stomach and shaved pussy.

Barone braced his fists on either side of my hips and leaned over the table. His dark eyes captured mine as he opened his mouth and swept the tip of his tongue along my stomach, tracing the swirling, drizzled line of honey.

I moaned.

He reached into the basket again and pulled out a peach half. Picking up the honey jar, he drizzled the golden nectar over the luscious fruit.

Setting the jar aside, he held the fruit a few inches over my mouth and gave it a slight squeeze. Sweet peach juice droplets mixed with honey fell onto my waiting tongue.

Barone swooped down and kissed me, sweeping his tongue inside.

When he pulled back, he held the peach up to my mouth. "I want you to lick this, like I'm about to lick you."

I took the peach from his grasp as he kissed his way down my stomach to back between my legs. He swept his tongue over my pussy lips. He then raised an eyebrow, his intent gaze trained on me.

I pushed my tongue out and swept it up the center of the peach, licking the sweet honey.

"Brava ragazza."

He swirled his tongue around my clit.

I matched the movement by swirling my tongue around the scooped-out center of the peach.

My body rocked back and forth on the table, held in place by his hands wrapped around my thighs.

There was an illicit eroticism from matching the movement of his tongue with my own.

It was as if I were getting myself off.

My chin and lips were covered in peach juice from the fruit I had crushed in one hand while I gripped Barone's hair and pushed his head against my core with my other.

"So sweet," he growled against my pussy, sending vibrations over my sensitive skin.

My shoulders came off the hard table surface as my breath seized in my lungs. My thighs clenched around his head, my orgasm coming fast and hard, bursting in a shower of sparks behind my eyelids.

I screamed his name before falling back onto the kitchen table surface.

He reared up. "You're not done yet, babygirl."

Barone lowered the zipper to his jeans and pulled his engorged cock free. He positioned himself at my entrance with one hand while he dipped the tips of his two center fingers in the honey jar.

"Grab my wrist. Guide my fingers to your mouth."

I wrapped my hands around his thick wrist and brought his hand close, the tips of his honey-coated fingers caressing my bottom lip.

"Choke yourself on my fingers while I fuck you," he commanded darkly.

"Yes, daddy."

Knowing he liked it when I kept my eyes trained on him, my gaze didn't waver. I opened my mouth and slipped his two center fingers inside as he pushed his cock into me.

The deeper he pushed his cock, the deeper I pushed forward on his fingers, showing him what a good, obedient girl I was. I dipped the tip of my tongue between the digits, licking the honey off them.

Barone's upper lip curled on a snarl, his eyes flaring.

His free hand gripped my hip as he pulled out and thrust back in. Hard.

I followed his motion, but this time I accepted a third finger into my mouth.

Wrapping both my hands around his thick wrist, I tilted my head back, my lips stretched around the fingers dominating my mouth and throat. Thrusting in and out, matching the movements of his cock.

"Fuck, babygirl."

He pulled his hand free and flipped me onto my stomach.

In one movement, he wrapped his hands around my hips and pulled me to the edge of the table, pinning me there like a butterfly.

Wrenching my legs open, he pounded into me hard, deep, and fast.

The kitchen table creaked and swayed beneath us so violently I feared it was going to collapse.

I reached under my hips and teased my clit as I slapped my open palm onto the table, feeling another release building.

"That's it, baby. Come for me. Come for daddy."

Breathing heavily from the force of his thrusts, I teased, "Are you going to give me something to suck on if I come like a good girl?"

I gloried in his deep, chuckling response.

He dipped his finger in the *dolci al cucchiaio* and swept up the remaining whipped cream. "Suck the cream off my finger while I fill you with more cream," he teased back.

I took his finger into my mouth, scraping my teeth along the bottom edge.

He groaned before thrusting deep. I could feel his cock swell inside of me before he released his seed.

* * *

AFTER CLEANING off in the shower, Barone carried me naked into the main bedroom.

We both stared down at the stripped bed.

I tightened my arms around his neck as I frowned down at the bare mattress. "I could have sworn there were sheets and blankets on this bed."

Barone shrugged. "No matter."

He carried me to the smaller back room, my original bedroom.

Gone was the tiny, windowless shed of a room. It had been transformed into an ethereal space. The back wall had been knocked out and extended into a classic wrought iron-framed mini conservatory, so it felt almost like sleeping outside.

Barone set me down in the center of the bed and left.

I was curled up in the quilt when he returned with a bottle

of *Masciarelli Villa Gemma Cerasuaolo d'Abruzzo* and a warmed-up bowl of *polpette di ricotta*. He snuggled in next to me.

We rested our backs against the headboard and stared out at the newly landscaped, walled-in garden through the hand-blown glass conservatory walls.

I lifted the wine to my lips and drank straight from the bottle, enjoying the light cherry and blackberry bouquet.

Barone chuckled as he spooned a ricotta dumpling dipped in fresh tomato sauce into his mouth. "This right here is the peak of living."

He wrapped his left arm around my shoulders while he held the spoon up to my mouth with his right hand.

I opened my lips, and he slipped a spoonful of savory ricotta dumpling inside. I licked a drop of tomato sauce from the corner of my mouth, chewing before saying, "You can't be serious. You're a cazillionaire. You've stayed in... I don't know... probably golden palaces with golden toilets all around the world."

"Pretty sure I have, what's your point?"

I laid my head on his shoulder. "Swigging wine from a bottle while we lay in a bed in what used to be a meat drying shed? *That's* your idea of the *peak of living?*"

He kissed the top of my head. "It's not the location. It's the company."

I squirmed. "This *company* is still sticky in some unmentionable places."

He nuzzled my neck. "I'll lick them later."

I wrapped my hand around his middle. We fell silent for a few moments as he stroked my back.

He broke the silence. "Are *you* happy?"

I tilted my head back to look up at him. "Yes, very. I'm the happiest I've ever been."

He cupped my cheek as his thumb caressed my lower lip. "You know, *dolcezza*, this room is sort of where our relationship started… so it would be romantic if…."

I pulled out of his arms. "Nice try."

"What?"

I snatched up the blanket to cover my naked breasts. "You're not proposing right now."

"Amara—"

My ringing mobile interrupted him.

I sprang from the bed and raced out of the room to get it, avoiding Barone's arm as he tried to snatch me back.

"Dammit woman. Get back here!"

I returned a few moments later and jumped on the bed, straddling him. I wrapped my arms around his neck. "The baby is fine!"

"Milana and Cesare?"

I nodded.

We both laughed and hugged.

He pulled me close and kissed me. I could feel his cock stirring back to life.

"Oh no, you don't. We have to head back to the villa. Everyone is meeting there to celebrate."

I tossed Barone his jeans as he grumbled about how much he hated fucking mobiles.

CHAPTER 14

ENZO

"You are aware there is a party going on inside?"

I looked over my shoulder to see Cesare cross the private terrace toward me. I turned back to rest my forearms on the wrought iron railing, the darkened mountain valley stretched out in front of me.

I hated this time of year.

After the harvest.

When the vines were naked branches, stripped of their fruit, their once glossy green foliage shriveled to dried brown husks.

Soon, cold winds would sweep down from the mountains to usher in winter and drive most activity indoors.

Traditionally, this was a time for hearth and home. When farming families would gather around the fire and wait out the harsh weather together until spring.

This had been the time my child would have been born.

A time for family.

Heritage.

A continuation of the Cavalieri legacy.

Cesare joined me at the railing. He reached into his inside jacket pocket and pulled out two cigars. He gave me a wink. "Swiped these from Papà's study when he wasn't looking."

I took a cigar from him and placed it under my nose, inhaling the robust earthy yet sweet aroma of the tobacco.

Cesare set an unlabeled bottle of wine on the lower narrow marble ledge and pulled two glasses from his jacket pockets. "And this is compliments of Vito. He wants our opinion. It's the *Riserva*. It's been two years. He thinks it's ready. If we agree, they'll start bottling next week."

He pulled the cork out with his teeth and poured two glasses.

The liquid shimmered like deep, dark garnets in the moonlight.

I rested two fingers on either side of the stem at the base of the glass and swirled the goblet gently, letting the wine breathe. I lifted the glass to my nose and inhaled.

After the palette cleanser of the tobacco, the bouquet of black cherry, plum, leather, and pepper was that much more pronounced. Taking a sip, I savored the more complex, full-bodied flavor profile of the *Riserva* produced from its longer aging process in oak barrels, holding it on my tongue before letting it slide down my throat.

Cesare did the same. He nodded. "Going to be another good vintage."

He set the glass aside and pulled out a pack of wooden matches.

My lips quirked up in a smile. "Do you have a cheese platter in there somewhere too?"

"I tried, but Rosa gave me the stink eye. You know how she guards her antique pewter platters."

He lit a match and handed me the packet. I did the same, hovering the open flame just under the cigar so the heat would warm the tobacco enough to light it, but not burn it and ruin the flavor.

After inhaling a strangely calming puff of acrid smoke, I exhaled and watched it drift off in the wind. Picking up my glass, I swirled the contents further before saying, "You know I couldn't be happier about the baby."

Cesare rubbed the back of his neck as he smiled. "Fuck, I'll admit it to you, brother. I was scared as hell to get those results, but I should have known better. Milana is too stubborn to lose our baby."

My chest tightened. "I want you to know—"

Cesare clapped me on the shoulder. "Don't even think about finishing that sentence." He took a generous puff from his cigar. "You thought you were doing the right thing by marrying that woman. None of what followed was your fault. It's in the past. Bury it with her."

"The investigation isn't in the past. Neither is finding the third man."

Cesare turned and leaned his back against the railing. He gestured with his wineglass. "He can't hide forever. We'll find the bastard. And as far as the investigation is concerned, unlike other times, we are actually *not guilty* this time. A rather refreshing change of pace, don't you think?"

The tightness in my chest eased at the dark humor of the

situation. I lifted the cigar to my mouth. "Well, you do have a point."

"We'll deal with the bullshit of the investigation like we always do."

I smiled. "With guns, money, and a disgusting amount of arrogance?"

"The unofficial family motto."

We clinked glasses.

Cesare raised his again for another toast after taking a sip. "The baby is healthy. Milana said yes. And according to Papà, Amara turned down *yet another* would-be marriage proposal. For tonight at least, all is right with the world."

"At this point, I think she's doing it just to fuck with him."

"Oh she's totally fucking with him, and God love her for it."

We clinked glasses a second time and drank.

I wished I shared his optimism.

I just couldn't shake this sense of impending doom. It wasn't just the investigation. It was Bianca. My life. Everything.

I was a man who valued control and right now, nothing felt within my control, and that made for a very dangerous situation.

What happened between Bianca and me yesterday was only a taste of what I was capable of. I had spent a lifetime reining in the darker side of my personality, but it only worked when my life was in order.

When it was not...

We stood in silence for a few minutes.

I refilled my glass and studied Cesare. "I have to ask, how did you pull it off? With Milana?"

He frowned. "What do you mean?"

"That woman hated the very sight of you. From what I understand, even the mere mention of your name would send her into an existential crisis of rage. She refused to be in the same room with you. Alfonso showed me what she did to the car you bought her. Matteo told me about the time in the office—"

Cesare rolled his cigar between his fingers. "Yeah, I know. I was there. She hated me. Do you have a point to this *super fun* trip down memory lane?"

"How did you do it? How did you move past her hatred of you?"

He raised an eyebrow. "Wait, is my big brother asking *me* for dating advice?"

I threw my hand up. "*Vaffanculo!*"

"I'm sorry. I'll be serious. Is this about Bianca?"

I stiffened. "Why? What have you heard?"

"Has some *other* female slapped you in a spectacular fashion in front of the entire village in the last week?"

I relaxed. "No."

"Out with it."

"What?"

"You know what."

I stared at the glowing tip of my cigar. "I fucked up."

He remained silent.

I continued. "I crossed a line, *in more ways than one*. Now she hates me more than ever."

"Are you sure it's hate?"

141

My eyes narrowed. "If you spew some romantic bullshit about the thin line between love and hate, I'll throw you off this terrace."

He turned back to face the valley. "I'll consider myself warned. It must be hard having her back. I know you missed her."

Missed her? No.

Ached for her? Yes.

Spent every waking minute feeling as though there was a sucking hole in my chest from the very moment I made the decision to do the supposed right thing and marry her sister instead of her? Absolutely.

Felt the agonizing weight of an endless stretch of days, months, years ahead of me without her by my side? Yes, again.

Realized the paralyzing truth that my life would be a torturous purgatory of constantly wondering if she was safe, if she was happy, if she was loved, or worse yet, if she was in love? For my sins…yes.

Lied awake on countless evenings staring at old photos and videos on my phone so the memory of her laugh, of her smile, of the cute charcoal smudges that were always on her hands and cheeks from her drawings never faded from the front of my mind? Fuck yeah.

I tapped my cigar on the edge of the iron railing, watching as the ash crumbled into dust to be carried away on the chilly late October evening wind. "Yeah, I missed her."

"You asked how I did it with Milana. I wasted years staying away from her because I thought she hated me. It's one of the biggest regrets of my life, because I was fucking wrong."

I put my cigar aside and leaned forward, my entire focus on Cesare.

He shook his head. "It wasn't hate. It was hurt. I had hurt her. Betrayed her."

My own betrayal of Bianca sat like a stone in my stomach.

He continued. "The thing is, brother, you can't hurt someone who is indifferent to you."

He turned to face me, leaning one elbow on the railing. "The moment you realize you're not battling their hate, you're battling their pain, a pain you caused, fuck... that's the moment you fight like hell to make it right, to heal the hurt."

I swallowed past the lump in my throat. "What if making it right means letting them go?"

"Fuck that. You don't mean that."

I pushed back from the railing and paced away deeper into the darkness before turning back. "You were too young when our mother first died. You didn't have to bear the brunt of the scandal and all the horrible rumors. Everybody trashing the Cavalieri name. I've spent my entire life trying to recapture that honor and do what's right."

"Honor? Our ancestral tree is riddled with thieves, bastards, and murderers. How do you think we got our billions? From crushed fucking grapes? Honor is for fairy tales, not the real world. You don't keep power and influence by always worrying about being honorable. A true Cavalieri takes what he wants and holds on to it."

"That's not true. I wish I could be more like you and Papà. I wish I could take what I want, and the rest of the world be damned, but someone has to care about the Cavalieri name. Someone has to care about our legacy."

"And how's that working out for you?"

"*Vai all'inferno.*"

"I'm not trying to be a dick."

"Try harder."

"You're the only member of the family who seems concerned about the family's reputation. No one asked you to martyr your life for the sake of the fucking family crest. The Cavalieri name has survived for hundreds of years and will keep surviving regardless of who you fuck and marry or don't marry."

Dammit. Aunt Gabriella practically told me the same thing the other night.

"It's really annoying when you're right."

Cesare drained his glass and poured another. "I have to take advantage of it with you. I rarely win an argument against Milana...Well, unless I play dirty."

"Even if I did say fuck it, and selfishly didn't care about the family's reputation or what people would say or what the right or wrong thing to do would be... it still doesn't mean it's the right thing for her."

"Have you asked Bianca?"

I let out a frustrated sigh. "Yes."

"I'm assuming it didn't go well?"

I frowned. "Depends on who you ask."

"Just for fun, let's say I asked her."

I rubbed my hand over my eyes. "Then no."

"So would this be a good or bad time to tell you Milana met up with her today at the cafe?"

"We've been standing here chatting about our *feelings* like two old women for ten minutes and *now* you tell me that?

What happened?"

"It wasn't planned. Bianca spotted her and sat down... and said some things."

Fuck.

Now my future sister-in-law probably thinks I'm a fucking monster, and she'd be right.

I had completely lost control.

I couldn't seem to keep my emotions in check where Bianca was concerned... not anymore.

"What Bianca said is true. I was so fucking jealous. Next thing I knew I had her pinned against the door—"

"Whoa! Keep that shit to yourself."

"Bianca didn't tell Milana about...."

"Whatever kinky shit you and she did? Fuck no. But it's bad. Real bad."

"Tell me."

"You're not going to like it."

"Tell me anyway."

"Before I do, Bianca made it clear she only learned of this a few days ago and only because that shit excuse of a mother of hers was drunk or high or both."

My jaw clenched as the fingers of my right hand curled into a fist. "Tell. Me."

"The night Renata drugged you. The night you supposedly got her pregnant?"

"Yeah?"

"The reason why you can't remember any of it was not just the drug. It never happened. Renata gave you too much and you passed out. You never fucked her. She just made you believe you had to trap you into marriage. She then faked the whole pregnancy thing."

Until the coroner's report, I'd had no way of knowing if Renata had lied about being pregnant from the beginning or had lost the baby early on and just continued to pretend, but I never thought to question whether I had actually fucked her that night. Learning she had never been pregnant had been an enormous blow, but it hadn't taken away my initial betrayal of Bianca's trust.

"I never fucked Renata? It was all a setup from the start?"

"Yep."

"And Bianca knows it?"

"Apparently."

So Bianca was holding me at arm's length by hiding behind a gold-digging scheme her own family perpetrated against me?

The heavy stone of guilt I had been carrying around in my stomach since the morning I woke up lying naked next to Renata was suddenly pulverized into dust.

I blew a cloud of fragrant cigar smoke into the frigid air.

This changed... *everything.*

I turned and placed my hand on Cesare's shoulder. "Thank you, brother. Suddenly, I'm in the mood to join the party."

"Not going to lie. I saw you taking that news differently. What am I missing?"

I crushed my cigar out, twisting the stump until the hot flame weakened and gave out.

"Let's just say I've decided I'm a true Cavalieri after all."

CHAPTER 15

BIANCA

I climbed the worn stone steps of Santa Maria Church.

Balancing the heavy tray of *caggionetti* on one hip, I gripped the wrought iron handle and pulled on the massive oak door.

The somber interior of the church was even cooler than the autumn weather outside.

The moment I entered, the cloying scents of floral, clove, and frankincense made my stomach turn.

My gaze turned to the altar. It was already covered in large arrangements of yellow chrysanthemums and white candles in preparation for tomorrow's *Tutti i Santi* celebrations.

With my sister's recent passing, my mother was in full drama mode for this year's All Saints' Day, which was fitting since she only seemed to grieve when there was an audience.

One of the village widows, dressed in all black with the traditional black lace head covering, approached me. After eyeing my bare head with displeasure, she gestured to the platter in my hands. "Is this for tomorrow?"

Playing the dutiful daughter, I recited the speech my mother gave me. "Yes, my mother was up early this morning making it special from the chestnuts in our garden, in memory of my sister."

Bitter bile roiled my stomach.

I hated that I still tried to please a woman who'd clearly never felt even the tiniest drop of motherly affection for me.

Hated that I allowed myself to be a puppet in the stupid pantomime she put on for those around her.

What did I think was going to happen?

That if I kept my mouth shut and did as I was told, suddenly she would wake up one morning and hug and kiss me and tell me she loved me?

That all the passive-aggressive digs about my art, my looks, my personality, would just be forgotten memories?

The widow bowed her head as she took the platter from me. "How kind."

It was a lie of course.

The only time my mother entered the kitchen was to scream at our cook. She wouldn't be caught dead baking, let alone making an involved traditional All Saints' Day dish like chestnut, chocolate, and almond-stuffed sweet ravioli.

As the widow shuffled off, I approached the votive candle-stand stationed in a small side alcove. I stared up at the serene gaze of the Madonna statue, which I had always adored as a child.

The black iron tier at her feet glowed from all the lit candles nestled inside ruby-colored glass votive candleholders. Placing a few euro in the metal donation box nearby, I selected a long, thin taper from the jar and held the tip to an existing candle flame until it ignited.

I then held the taper to an unlit wick. I wasn't sure who I was lighting the candle for. I knew it wasn't my sister. I refused to feel guilty for not mourning her death. There had never been any sisterly affection between us since long before her betrayal with Enzo.

Enzo.

My Enzo.

Letting go of him had been nearly impossible before. I didn't know how I was going to manage it now. Before, what we had was like an ideal version of dating, almost a fantasy. I had often even wondered if it had been real.

But now? Now I knew what I felt for him was real.

And raw. And intense. And painful.

Only real love hurts like this.

Before, I had held him up in my mind as this ideal boyfriend, an almost girlish blend of bittersweet memories and myth.

Now he was a flesh and blood man.

Now I knew what it felt like to have him press his weight down on me, to feel him move between my thighs... *to be inside of me.*

I closed my eyes.

Even now I could almost imagine the scent of his cologne.

A warm hand closed over mine.

My eyes sprang open.

Before I could react, a strong arm wrapped around my waist as a body stepped close.

Enzo whispered darkly in my ear. "Miss me, my treasure?"

My lips opened, but no sound came out.

He raised our clasped hands to his lips and blew out the taper. We were surrounded by a soft swirl of smoke and the lingering scent of sulfur, the signs of a demon's entrance.

I finally found my voice. "What are you doing here?"

His fingers pressed into my side. "I've come to hear your confession," he ground out.

My brow furrowed. Then realization dawned.

My conversation with Milana. It must have gotten back to Enzo.

Madonna santa!

My gaze flashed up to the sightless eyes of the Madonna statue.

Even she could not help me now.

I spun around to face him, knowing outrage would be my only defense.

I jutted my chin out as I tilted my head back. "What a pity to learn that even Milana Carbone, who once hated your family as much as I do now, has fallen prey to the Cavalieri curse. It didn't take long for your family to turn her into a deceitful bitch willing to do your bidding."

His jaw clenched as he bared his front teeth. "You have no fucking idea what you're talking about, little girl. So I suggest you tread very carefully."

I backed away from him.

Unfortunately, his imposing form was blocking the main exit to the church, so I had no choice but to move further into the dark interior.

A quick glance over my shoulder showed that we were

alone in the gothic, cavernous space. The widows having completed their task of decorating the altar.

"Or you'll what, Enzo? We're in a church. There's nothing you can do to me here."

His lips lifted at the corners in a macabre semblance of a smile that didn't reach his cold jade eyes. "Babygirl, you are seriously mistaken if you think God is going to save you from my wrath."

I continued to back up, running my hand over the heavily varnished edges of the pews as a guide, keeping my frightened gaze on Enzo's determined approach. "How dare Milana betray my confidence. She had no right to tell you what I said. The damage was already done. It changes nothing between us."

His brow lowered. "She had *every* right."

My back struck a wide marble column. "Why? Because she's a Cavalieri now? So she can do whatever she wants just like the rest of you?"

It wasn't fair to be attacking Milana like this. I knew that. My reason for being angry was threadbare at best, but I was clinging to that meager strand with everything I had.

The walls I had placed between Enzo and me had already crumbled.

I was weak and vulnerable against his slightest attack to my heart. I had to use every weapon at my disposal, or I'd be lost.

Before I could move around the column, Enzo caged me in. "No, because your sister tried to kill her."

I blinked, not sure I'd heard him correctly. "That can't be true."

He leaned in close. "A few days before your sister's murder, the woman you were so quick to call a *deceitful bitch* was locked in a wine cave and ruthlessly starved of oxygen by *your sister*. My brother barely found her in time. She came extremely close to dying. Despite that, she greeted you with grace and warmth yesterday. She deserves none of your vitriol."

I was too stunned to speak. More secrets.

Was this why my parents refused to discuss her death?

Wait... a few days before my sister's murder?

I licked my dry lips. "You said *before*, was that why—"

He ran the backs of his knuckles down my cheek, then covered my lips with his fingertips. "Don't even say it."

To any passersby the gesture would look like a gentle, romantic caress.

I knew better.

I kept my mouth closed.

He breathed heavily as he glared down at me. "My answer hasn't changed. I didn't kill your sister. Neither did my brother. I've told you before, your family got involved with some dangerous people, and it got your sister killed."

His gaze traveled from my mouth to my eyes and back.

He then gripped my upper arm and moved us away from the column. "That's what happens when you manipulate people's lives," he said suggestively.

He marched me toward a dark recess of the church, toward a wall of heavily varnished walnut cabinet chambers.

The confessionals.

"I didn't know. I swear. I only found out a few days ago."

Enzo reached past me and swung open a narrow door

before pushing me inside the dimly lit priest's confessional.

It was a narrow space barely big enough for two people.

The varying dark chocolate and honeyed tones of the walnut-grain cabinet had an ethereal glow from the recessed lighting above the doorway. At the back of the cabinet-like space was a deep bench topped with a purple velvet cushion where the priest usually sat during confession.

Enzo released his grip and placed his palms on either side of the wall. He loomed over me. "Kneel on the bench."

I swallowed. "Enzo—"

"Kneel."

Knowing it was foolhardy to argue with him, I slipped out of my heels and gathered up my skirt, only as high as was absolutely necessary to kneel on the purple velvet cushion. Because of his superior height and the low seat of the bench, my head barely reached his mid-abdomen.

He cupped my chin and raised my head. "I'm ready to hear your confession."

The blood pounded in my ears as I curled my fingers into the fabric of my skirt. "My confession?"

He stroked my lower lip with his thumb. "Yes. I want to hear straight from this pretty mouth how you weren't planning on telling me that I didn't *fuck* your sister that night. That I didn't betray you."

I flinched at his harsh language, made all the harsher given our setting.

He stepped closer as he widened his stance. "Tell me, Bianca. Tell me how your family conspired to drug me and trap me into marriage and how you knew all about it."

My lower lip trembled. "Please, Enzo."

In the confined space, his anger was like a hand reaching inside my chest and squeezing the air from my lungs.

"Were you part of the plan?"

He tore off his gray cable-knit sweater, exposing his tanned, muscled chest. The raw, red bite mark from my teeth was still visible over his heart. "Answer me, Bianca."

I didn't know how to answer him.

There were so many secrets.

So many terrible deeds.

So many ruined lives.

So much pain.

All caused by my family.

And yet I was the one who had been accusing him of the most heinous crime of all.

He moved his hands to cup my cheeks. "Were you the *bait*? Was your sweet innocence part of the plan to lure me in? Did you lose your nerve in the end? Is that why your sister stepped in and drugged me? Your family would get their hands on the Cavalieri fortune one way or another, right?" he hissed through clenched teeth.

Tears blurred my vision. "No," I whispered. "Please believe me. I had no idea what my sister was planning."

His thumbs caressed my cheekbones as he leaned threateningly over me. "You were my perfect little treasure. So shy and untried. Unspoiled. I was afraid to touch you. To even kiss you. Despite your age, there was just something so innocent and almost unreal about you."

He moved his hand to press his thumb against my lower lip, applying pressure until my mouth opened.

He forced his thumb inside. "So many nights, I lay awake,

fantasizing about your beautiful mouth."

He reached for the zipper of his jeans.

My eyes widened.

He slowly lowered the zipper.

"I imagined what it would feel like to see those full lips stretched around my cock. What it would feel like to have your tiny throat clench around my shaft."

He pushed his thumb in deeper, forcing me to suck it. "But I never acted on it. Because I was stupid enough to buy into your sweet, innocent ploy. I was dumb enough to want to preserve and protect that virginal innocence."

I wrenched my head back, breaking free. "It wasn't a ploy. You know that better than anyone," I accused, reminding him of our heated encounter a few days ago.

He chuckled. The sound held no mirth. "If I recall, you goaded me into that as well, with yet another lie. Was that Plan B? Your family's second attempt at the brass ring?"

How dare he think I would try to trap him into marriage like my sister!

Without thinking, I whipped my arm up to slap him.

He snatched my wrist and slammed it against the back of the confessional, before capturing the other one. "I'm afraid one slap in church is all I'm willing to allow, babygirl."

Because I was kneeling, his grip on my wrists caused my back to arch slightly, my chin tilting upward to counterbalance my body's off-kilter position.

He reached inside of his jeans, pulled out his hard cock, and wrapped his fist around the girth.

He stroked it several times.

"Time for your penance."

CHAPTER 16

ENZO

I watched as the tears gathered in her dark eyes, making them shine bright in the dim light.

My soul was truly damned because it did not deter me from my purpose.

I shifted my hips to press the tip of my cock against her lips. "Open your mouth."

She turned her head away. "I'm not sucking your cock because you're mad at my family, Enzo. That's insane."

I grabbed her under the jaw and forced her head back. "No. You're sucking my cock because I'm done treating you like some precious little doll."

I pressed my fingertips into her cheeks, forcing her mouth open. "You're sucking my cock because I'm done hiding my true nature from you."

I pushed the head past her lips.

Her tongue swept over my shaft.

I stifled a groan as I used every ounce of restraint I

possessed not to shove all the way to the back of her throat, choking her.

I placed my hand at the base of her skull and pushed in slowly.

She whimpered as my cock filled her mouth.

Her hands pressed against the tops of my thighs, but I was relentless.

I pulled back slightly and pushed back in, her tongue helplessly moving around my shaft.

I pushed in deeper.

Her shoulders curled as her throat clenched.

I pulled out.

She gasped for air.

"Have you ever sucked a cock before?"

She sucked in another desperate breath.

"Answer me."

She opened her mouth.

Before she could respond, I warned her, "Don't you dare lie to me."

She lowered her eyes. "I tried. Once. I didn't like it."

I grasped my cock and used the tip to caress her lower lip. "Why?"

It was a special kind of torture hearing about another man touching her.

It was like I was punishing myself for punishing her.

"I don't want to talk to you about this."

"I don't care. Tell me why."

She avoided eye contact with me. Her cheeks warmed into a pretty, dark-pink blush. "It was... awkward. He was... timid about it. It made it weird. I don't want to talk about this!"

Time stopped.

My heartbeat stopped.

Everything in that tiny space became unnaturally still.

As if in slow motion, Bianca turned her beautiful face up to meet my gaze.

If some tiny, sane corner of my mind wasn't worried about giving away our illicit location, I would have let out a feral howl of pleasure.

My sweet, innocent little treasure had a secret dark side.

One that perhaps she wasn't even fully aware of.

One that I and I alone would experience and possess.

I snatched both her wrists and stretched them high over her head, pressing them against the confessional wall. "Open your mouth and this time I'm not going to stop until you're choking on my come," I growled.

She yanked on her wrists, but I held firm.

"I could scream for help," she challenged, her dark eyes bright with fire.

"Do it. I dare you. And I'll drag you out of this confessional by your hair and fuck you on the altar right in front of the priest. What's it going to be, babygirl? Your choice."

I stared down at her for the span of several breaths.

Truly not caring which she chose.

I was prepared to see my threat through.

There was no salvation for me, so hell held no sway.

Keeping her still defiant gaze trained on me, Bianca slowly opened her lips.

Her show of submission wasn't enough, not nearly enough.

"Wider."

159

Her eyes narrowed slightly as her wrists twisted in my grip, but then she obeyed, opening her lips wider.

I pushed inside, relishing the soft warm feel of her mouth. I pulled back slightly. "Move your tongue over the tip."

Her tongue swept over the sensitive head, sending a shockwave of pleasure right up my spine. I threw my head back, restraining myself from thrusting in too deep, too fast. "Good girl."

I thrust in a little further. Back and forth, each time pushing in deeper.

I released her wrists and planted my palms on the confessional walls over her head, widening my stance and bracing my feet. "Relax your throat, baby."

I pushed inside her wet mouth until I felt the resistance at the back of her throat.

She gagged and gripped the tops of my thighs.

I thrust in deeper, feeling the tight ring of muscle at the top of her throat clench around the head of my cock.

With my right hand, I brushed back her hair and stared deeply into her tear-filled eyes. Fisting her thick hair at the base of her skull, I pulled, wrenching her head all the way back as I leaned in and up. "This time you're going to take me all the way in."

Her beautiful eyes pleaded with me as she tried to wrench free.

I tightened my grasp.

She squeezed her eyes shut as her shoulders jerked. Her nails dug into my flesh through the denim of my jeans.

I twisted the hair in my grip. "Eyes on me."

Her eyes sprang open.

I wanted to see the look in them the very moment she was forced to swallow my cock balls deep.

Pulling back until the head rested on the base of her tongue, I let her suck in a quick breath through her nose before ruthlessly thrusting in deep. I didn't stop until the top of her pretty little nose brushed against my stomach.

Bianca struggled, her whimpers muffled by my hard flesh.

After a few more seconds, I pulled back. Before she could fully recover, I thrust in again. Then again. Fucking her sweet mouth.

It was better than in my fantasies.

With each thrust there was a twinge of delicious pain as her bottom teeth dragged along the sensitive underside of my shaft.

My balls tightened.

As much as I wanted to prolong my sinful entrance into heaven, I wouldn't be able to hold out much longer. The feel of her tight mouth was too much. The sight of her full lips stretched around my shaft as her cheeks hollowed out with each suck was enough to drive me to madness. I hoped the fires of hell burned the image forever in my mind.

Since I was certainly going to hell for taking advantage and defiling her shy innocence in such a sacred place.

I thrust several more times, before the pressure built too great to contain.

Not truly wanting her to choke, I pulled back until the head of my cock was just past her lips. I then gripped the shaft and threw my head back as stream after stream of hot come spurted directly onto her waiting tongue.

Breathing heavily, I stared down at her. Her cheeks were

flushed, her lips swollen and bruised a dark cherry red. Pulling free, I ordered gruffly, "Open your mouth. Show me your tongue."

My come pooled in the center of her perfect pink tongue.

I cupped her cheeks. "Swallow."

She closed her mouth and swallowed. I watched the delicate play of her throat muscles contract as she ingested my seed deep inside of her.

My thumb swiped at the tears which fell over her cheeks.

She inhaled a shaking breath. "Did you get what you wanted, Enzo? Have I been punished and humiliated enough?"

"Not quite."

Her eyes widened.

I reached for her shoulders and lifted her off the bench. Spinning her around until she faced the wall of the confessional, I flipped her skirt up over her ass. My fingers pressed against her lower back as I gripped the edge of her panties. It was simple work, tearing the soft silk off her. I couldn't help the smirk that crossed my lips at her little squeak of surprise.

Before she could recover and move away, I shoved the torn remnants of her panties in my jeans pocket and slid my left foot to the inside of her foot, forcing her legs wide with my right.

Reaching from behind, I cupped her pussy.

Bianca gasped.

I slipped a single finger between her folds as I whispered against her ear, "You're wet for me."

Keeping two fingers together, I caressed her pussy, teasing

her clit before pushing them inside of her. Bianca rose up on her toes.

I continued to taunt her. "Such a bad girl to have such a wet pussy in church. Did you like being forced onto your knees? Did you like having that cute mouth of yours filled with my cock?"

She jerked her body sideways, trying to break my grasp. I easily secured her wrists over her head.

Her ass needed a spank and I obliged.

The sound seemed to reverberate beyond the close quarters of the confessional.

She stilled.

I swept my hand over the skin I'd just spanked, feeling the heat rise to the surface. "I want to hear you say it. Tell me what a bad girl you've been."

"*Vaffanculo!*"

I spanked her again. This time even harder. "Watch that mouth or I'll be forced to teach it another lesson. Now tell me that you've been a bad girl."

When she still refused to answer, I palmed her ass cheek and squeezed.

She rose up on her toes again. "Please, I don't know what you want me to say."

"I want you to say you were a bad girl for lying to me."

Her breath came in short, rapid gasps. "I was a bad girl for lying to you."

I slipped my hand between her legs again. Using my same two fingers, I teased her clit. "Now tell me why sucking my cock got you all wet."

"Please don't make me."

I pushed those two fingers inside of her. "Tell me, Bianca. Tell me why being forced to open those lips and take my cock down your throat until you choked made your pretty pussy wet."

She sniffed. "I don't know why."

I moved my fingers in and out of her snug hole as the pad of my thumb pressed against her tight bottom hole.

Bianca hissed through her teeth and clenched her ass cheeks.

I slid my hand free and spanked her again. "Don't clench or I'll put you over my knee and give you a real spanking."

She sniffed again before relaxing her body.

I returned and pushed a third finger inside her. "It's the same reason why you liked it when I fuck you hard and fast like an animal. You, my dear sweet innocent treasure, like it *rough and dirty*."

"That's not true!"

"You like being forced to submit. You like when I dominate you."

"Stop it right now. This has gone too far, Enzo." She pulled on her wrists. "I mean it. I really will scream this time."

I placed the head of my cock at her entrance and thrust, impaling her.

The moment she cried out, I covered her mouth with my hand.

Releasing her wrists to wrap my other arm around her waist, I spun her to the side of the booth so I could flatten her flush against the wall, away from the bench. In profile, her smooth complexion grew flushed as I pressed the side of her head to the wall, simultaneously pulling her hips out slightly so I could pound into her soft flesh more deeply. Her body was left braced and open to me, yielding under my grasp as I thrust.

The walnut confessional's ancient walls creaked from the force of our bodies thumping together.

I knew it was only a matter of time before we were discovered.

As much as I wanted revenge against Bianca for the part she may have played in her family's schemes, I did not want to destroy her reputation in the village, especially since my plans for our future had not changed.

With that in mind, I reached around her front to tease her clit, matching the movement of my fingers with the timing of my thrusts.

I held back until her pussy clenched around my cock and I heard her sharp intake of breath as she came.

For the second time, I then came. This time inside her pussy. It was all the sweeter, knowing I may have gotten her pregnant. I was no longer a man constrained by morals or a sense of honor. I would chain her to me by fair means or foul.

I had played by society's rules once, and it had almost cost me not only the love of my life, but my family's happiness as well.

Fuck those rules. I was going to play by my own set of rules from now on.

I was now following the true Cavalieri family legacy.

Feeling almost light-headed with a sense of euphoria, I slammed my body against the other wall as I released her.

Bianca quickly faced me as she pulled her skirt down.

My gaze drifted over her as I tucked my cock back inside my jeans.

Her gaze narrowed. "Are you satisfied now?"

I wrapped my hand around her neck and kissed her hard on the lips. "I'm satisfied knowing as you walk out of this church you will still taste my come on your lips and feel it dripping out of your pussy onto your inner thighs."

"You're disgusting."

I looked down at her from my superior height. "That's two holes. I wonder when I'll sample the last one."

Her mouth opened in shock.

My lips quirked as I caressed her lower lip. "You can close your mouth. I'm done with it. For now."

I was being deliberately cruel.

She didn't deserve it.

In many ways, she was just as much a victim of her family's machinations as me. Part of me had stupidly hoped that when she learned the truth, she would have come to me. Instead, she stayed silent. The truth that we were no longer close, that I wasn't the man she would choose to run to for help and protection, made me angry and bitter.

It made me want to lash out and punish her.

As if I were using her submission as a poor substitute for her acceptance.

In the end, that's what I wanted, what I needed... and what I would get.

She could fight me all she wanted, but eventually she would accept that we were meant to be together. No matter the past, the obstacles, or what her family or society might say. She was mine.

She reached down and put her high heels back on before straightening her shoulders. "You can act smug all you want, Enzo Cavalieri. What we had was nothing but an illusion. It was fake, and not because of any secret plan of my parents and sister. Because of you. You admitted as much yourself. The person I fell in love with doesn't exist. Never did. You've shown me your true nature now. What you're truly capable of. So thank you for that."

She swung open the confessional door.

After pausing a moment to make sure the church was still empty, she exited and turned. "It makes leaving you for good that much easier. Goodbye."

She slammed the door shut.

The hard clack of her heels resonated against the marble tile as she stormed away.

I sat on the bench.

The scent of her perfume lingered in the small, enclosed space.

I leaned my head against the wall and closed my eyes.

If I hadn't decided to finally embrace my family's true legacy, those final words from the woman I loved might have been the end of it all.

Instead, all I heard was a challenge.

CHAPTER 17

BIANCA

S anto inferno!

It was a fitting exclamation since I was fairly certain people who had dirty, hot sex in church received a first-class ticket straight to hell.

After racing directly home and changing out of my wrinkled clothes, I'd spent the last two hours cloistered in our family's rarely used library with my sketch pad.

Every time I heard the scuff of a heel outside the closed doors, my stomach clenched, and I braced myself for the possibility of my scandalized mother crashing into the room, telling me I was excommunicated because I had been seen on my knees sucking Enzo Cavalieri's cock like a Jezebel.

My mind still reeled from the revelations he'd forced on me.

Renata had tried to kill Milana. What the fuck?

Judging by how my mother spewed venom when Amara appeared in Barone's life, I couldn't imagine either she or my sister took Milana's appearance any better, but to try and kill her? Why?

It didn't make any sense.

And what could my parents possibly be involved in that would have gotten Renata killed?

I knew they needed money. Not in the way normal people needed money. We weren't hurting to pay our bills or put food on the table. No, my parents were upset that their obscene amount of money had dwindled to merely a ridiculous amount, especially now with the lost Cavalieri connection. I knew my father and sister had exploited that connection for at least one land purchase.

I had overheard them talking about it before I left for New York.

Something about a warehouse and a man named Agnello.

Thinking about this wasn't getting me any answers and it was only providing a thin distraction from thinking about what was really bothering me. Enzo.

I meant what I said.

At least I *wanted* to mean what I said.

We were over. Done. Finished.

We had now been in each other's presence three times since the death of my sister and all three times we'd had a fight that then led to an explosion of unholy passion. As if our anger was driving our desires. That might make for exciting drama in romance novels or in movies but in the real world, that was a dangerous and toxic foundation to build a relationship on. Never mind the fact that ours was already teetering on shaky moral ground.

Secrets. Lies. Betrayals. Murder. And now sex in a church.

If that wasn't a recipe for a relationship doomed to burn in the fires of hell, I didn't know what was.

My only recourse was to stay as far away as possible from the man.

I would play nice with my parents and save up what money I could until I had enough to return to New York. It was a crap plan but for now it was all I had.

I stared down at the charcoal sketch I had been making. It was a heart wrapped in chains with a dagger pierced through it. A little sentimentally macabre but apt for how I was feeling right now. I wonder how big a fit my mother would have if I got this as a tattoo on my arm?

A loud *bang* startled me out of my thoughts when the door to the library swung open and hit the wall so violently, the landscape painting in the heavy gilt frame to the right of it lurched sideways on its hook.

"You deceitful, wretched, spoiled brat!"

I closed the flap cover on my sketch pad and set it aside. "Hello Claudia, what can I do for you?"

"You were seen in the church."

The room tilted. My cheeks burned with embarrassment at being caught. "I can explain."

No, I couldn't. How could I possibly explain?

You see, Mother, Enzo appeared like a handsome devil and seduced me.

Even though I could claim I was an unwilling participant… that would be a lie.

True, he bullied me into that confessional and threatened me, but I didn't really believe he would have followed through. If I had *truly* tried to escape or cry out or object, he would have stopped. I knew that deep down. He would have stopped. He didn't because I didn't want him to stop... and he knew it.

He saw straight into my deepest, darkest fantasy.

One I didn't even acknowledge I had.

To be overpowered and dominated by him.

It was terrifying and exhilarating. Just like when he took my virginity.

There was something electrifying about a strong man gripping your wrists, holding you down and having his way with you. No, that was too prosaic of a phrase.

Fucking you senseless was more like it.

The way he stared intently into my eyes as he pushed his cock deeper and deeper into my throat, inch by inch, stealing my breath, practically holding my life in his hands.

It was an out-of-body experience.

I felt nothing like myself.

To be on my knees, sucking his cock like a wanton whore, in church?

And yet, I'd never felt so connected to my body as I did in that moment.

Every nerve, every inch of skin, every sense had been on fire.

It was odd to be completely and utterly humiliated and regret something while at the same time knowing that the moment would be relived over and over in your dreams for years to come.

My mother lit a cigarette, deliberately blowing the smoke in my face. "Really? You can explain why you were seen walking into the church moments before Enzo Cavalieri?

Did you arrange to meet him there? What did you say to him?"

Was this a trap?

I stood and faced her, feeling more well-matched meeting her at eye-level. "Why? What have you heard?"

She gestured with her cigarette hand, her bracelets rattling. "Ah ha! So you don't deny it!"

I placed my hands on my hips. "Are you forgetting you asked me to drop off the *caggionetti* for the church *Tutti i Santi* celebration tomorrow?"

One of her false eyelashes had come partially unglued at the corner, making her eye twitch in an unsettling manner. "You probably used that as a cover. Pretending to play the dutiful daughter. I should have known." She grabbed my upper arm, her nails digging into my skin. "What did you say to him?"

"He knows."

"Knows about what?"

"He knows Renata was never pregnant. He knows it was all a marriage trap."

She leaned in close. "You stupid bitch! You betrayed your family?"

The scent of her perfume mixed with the cigarette smoke and her stale breath made me want to vomit. "I didn't tell him anything. He already knew. That's why he followed me into the church. To confront me."

She released my arm and paced away, puffing on her cigarette. "What else did he say?"

"Nothing."

"You're lying."

I sighed. "He made some crazy accusation about Renata trying to hurt Milana before she died."

I watched her closely.

Her arm froze halfway to her lips.

The cigarette ash lengthened as she just stood there and stared at me. "Milana Carbone? We heard what happened at the villa was just an accident." The cigarette ash fell onto the tip of her designer shoe. She didn't even notice. "They know it was Renata?"

I stepped back, tripping over a small table and falling against the bookcase. I rubbed my elbow where it caught the edge of one of the shelves as I stared at my mother. "You mean it's true?"

She stubbed out her cigarette. "I've told you before. Renata was willing to do whatever it took to help this family. She was loyal. Unlike you."

"Are you insane? What could Milana have possibly done to deserve Renata wanting her dead?"

"That is none of your concern. Obviously, we need to do damage control." She paced back and forth across the library carpet. "The Cavalieris won't let you marry into the family now, not even the cousin, even if we could get close enough to drug him."

"Why? Why did you drug Enzo like that, trap him into thinking Renata was pregnant? He was my boyfriend! I loved him!"

She lit another cigarette. "Love? Oh, don't be so middle-class. You were never going to get a man like Enzo Cavalieri to the altar. Renata tried to lure him away, but he wouldn't take the bait, so we had to use… other measures. It was for the good of the family."

There had never been a chance I was going to marry Matteo but at least now that my mother knew it, she would stop pushing me. Maybe they would change their minds and let me return to my studies in New York?

"I'll have to talk to your father. It seems we'll need to move forward with our other plans."

"Well, keep me out of them."

She grabbed my chin and squeezed my cheeks. "That will be hard to do since you're the bride."

I pulled away just as she blew another cloud of smoke in my face. "You just said the Cavalieris won't allow another marriage between our families."

"That doesn't mean there won't be a wedding. And we still need the Cavalieri connection. In fact, we'll be attending a party at the villa tomorrow night. They may not want us there, but they need to keep up appearances as much as we do."

"I'm not going."

"Oh yes, you are. And you'll have a date."

I frowned. "Who?"

She smirked as she leaned over to crush out her cigarette. "Your future groom, of course."

I gripped the back of a chair, afraid I would pass out. "Why can't you just let me return to New York? I want nothing to do with any of your plans. What you and father and Renata did to Enzo was despicable!"

"You will do as you're told."

"I'm twenty-two years old. I don't need your permission."

She pulled something from her pocket. "I thought you might say that."

She held my passport and my birth certificate in her hand.

"Where did you get my passport? Did you go through my things?"

She flicked open her gold-plated lighter and held the flame just below the open booklet. "Of course, I did."

I stretched out my arm. "Mother, no!"

It was too late.

She set my passport and original *Atto di Nascita* on fire.

She tossed the now useless documents into the cold grate of the fireplace where I watched in horror as they burned to ash. Brushing her palms together, she turned to face me. "I'll pick out the gown I want you to wear. We want to make sure you make a good first impression on your future husband."

CHAPTER 18

BIANCA

I yanked on the bodice of my dress.

It figured my mother would choose the Tom Ford Gucci dominatrix dress. The champagne silk corset dress with its black bodice piping hid very little from the imagination.

The woman had no shame.

Neither of my parents did.

It turned out this wasn't just any party at the villa.

It was Milana and Cesare's engagement party.

The outright gall it took for them to insist on attending after what their daughter did was staggering. I hated that I was playing any part in it, but I had no choice.

Until I could figure a way out of this twisted web I found myself in, I had to play along.

My so-called date was chatting animatedly with my parents as I came down the front staircase. He sounded vaguely familiar.

As I crossed the threshold, he turned.

It was the man who had rescued me that day at the market.

Dressed in a Brunello tuxedo, his black hair slicked back with perhaps a bit too much gel making it look still wet, he smoothly stepped forward and took my hand.

My father made the introductions. "Nevio Zettici, this is my daughter, Bianca."

He raised my hand to his lips while his gaze remained steady on mine. "I am charmed by your beauty." He then kissed the back of my hand.

I pulled my hand free and pressed it against my lower back. "Thank you again for helping me that day in the market."

My mother frowned. Her laugh was high-pitched and shrill. "You already know one another? You must tell me all the details, at once. Right now. Immediately."

Nevio straightened and stood next to me. The acrid smell of his aftershave burned the inside of my nose.

"Your daughter and I met at the market a few days ago. I had the pleasure of playing the knight in shining armor by rescuing her from a fiery death."

My mother gasped, causing her to choke rather unattractively.

My father pounded her on the back which sent her tipping forward.

The false hair she had added to give her hairstyle extra volume flipped up. When she straightened, it fell back onto her head at an awkward angle.

I had no intention of telling her.

I looked up at Nevio and caught him staring at my breasts

which were indecently on display because of the corset design of the dress.

I stepped to the side, breaking his line of vision. "It was hardly that dramatic. Someone in the crowd shoved me from behind near the *arrosticini* skewer grill. I briefly lost my footing."

My mother clapped. "What a wonderful first meeting story to be able to tell your children!"

I lowered my head and glanced at Nevio through my lashes to see his reaction. Just because my parents were planning a wedding between the two of us didn't mean this man was on board. After all, we had only just met. There was no reason to believe he would be interested. This could all be wishful thinking on my parents' part.

Despite him saying that he knew me from school and had even had a crush on me, something about leaving me a valentine in my desk one year, I didn't recall him or his family name. I could only presume he came from crazy-stupid money or else why would my parents be trying to play matchmaker?

Nevio placed an arm around my middle and pulled me close to his side as he beamed at my mother. "I couldn't agree more."

My father handed Nevio a rocks glass with a shot of Amaro over ice. "Here you go, son. We'll share a quick one while the women finish getting dressed."

Son?

I sidestepped again, breaking Nevio's hold. One more step and I'd be sitting in the potted plant.

My mother snatched me around the upper arm and

ushered me out of the room and into the powder room across the hall where she had left her purse.

She leaned over the counter and straightened her wig before she reapplied her thick, bright red lipstick. "I'm warning you. You had better put a smile on your face and behave tonight."

"What exactly have you told that man?"

She tossed her lipstick in her purse. "What do you mean?"

"Is Nevio aware of your plan to marry us off?"

Something is not right.

No man in his twenties reacted that calmly to the idea of being married off to a woman he'd just met. How did my parents know Nevio and why was my father already calling him *son*? And what was with that whole bit about him being a knight in shining armor and me almost dying? Was it possible that had been a setup? It had seemed odd that I had been shoved so violently when there hadn't been that big of a crowd and everyone had been standing calmly in line up until that point.

It felt like I was in one of those escape rooms in a movie and the walls were slowly closing in on me, but I didn't have enough clues to solve the puzzle to save myself.

She ran her finger over her front teeth. "We have to go. They're waiting."

"Let me just run upstairs. I want to get a wrap for the party and my coat."

Thankfully, I had a black gauze wrap I planned to wear during the event which would preserve at least some of my modesty.

"You're not covering up."

"Mother—"

"Claudia."

"Claudia, it's freezing outside for one and secondly my tits are hanging out of this dress."

"Don't say tits. Only trollops say tits."

"You seem to know an awful lot about what trollops say and do, Mother."

She slapped me across the cheek.

I held my hand to my burning face.

She pointed at me. "That is your last warning. Behave. Your father and I are trying to get this done the *nice way*, Bianca. Don't make us get *nasty*. Now fix your face before joining us."

She stormed out of the bathroom.

I turned to face the mirror. There was a faint scratch from where her diamond ring caught my cheekbone. With shaking hands, I opened the drawer where my mother kept extra makeup and picked up one of her compacts. I pressed some powder to my cheek, hiding the red handprint and scratch behind a layer of makeup.

Blinking away the unshed tears from my eyes, I took a deep breath and joined them in the entrance hall.

Nevio offered his arm. "You look even more beautiful."

I caught my father's glare. My mother must have told him about my outburst.

I forced a smile before placing my hand in the crook of his arm. "Thank you."

I allowed him to usher me out into the frigid November evening. I stood on the marble staircase entrance to our home as we waited for the car to be brought around. The cold seeped through the thin leather soles of my high heels. I tensed my arms and legs as my body shook.

Both my father and Nevio had black wool overcoats on.

My mother had her mink fur coat.

I was the only one without a coat and yet no one seemed to notice or care.

When the car arrived, Nevio crossed around to the driver's side and hopped into the back, leaving me to open my own door. My fingers were so frozen, they slipped on the handle twice before I finally opened it.

The moment I sat down, the tight corset pushed my breasts up even higher. I pulled my long hair over my shoulders to cover them as best I could.

As my father slipped behind the wheel and the car drove off into the night toward the Cavalieri villa, Nevio leaned over, his gaze on my breasts. "I cannot wait to show you off as my date to all the guests tonight."

Oh God.

I was headed to the Cavalieri villa, Enzo's family home… with a date.

I bit the inside of my cheek as sheer panic set in.

It was a Cavalieri engagement party.

There would probably be hundreds of people in attendance.

Maybe I would get lucky, and he wouldn't even see me there.

CHAPTER 19

ENZO

I was wrong to think the hypocrisy of the funeral could not be matched.

This was worse.

At least at the funeral there was a shallow veneer of social grace.

Those in attendance followed the custom of pretending the deceased was a decent person who would be missed. They offered the usual platitudes, all the while skillfully ignoring the nasty, inconvenient questions over how my wife had died.

There were no such niceties now.

Armed with the hard metal of righteous judgment forged in the fires of religious devotion, the guests in attendance showed their displeasure by just as skillfully aiming poison-tipped barbs at me.

It was nothing overt. My family was too powerful for an outright assault.

It was subtle.

Death by a thousand cuts.

A sly word here. A dropped comment there. The side looks. Hushed whispers. Turned backs. Conversation that hushed at my approach.

It was clear. I had been accused, tried, and sentenced in society's eyes.

Murderer.

I raised my glass to my lips and sipped slowly as I surveyed the guests, taking their measure.

They would still do business with my family. Business was business and money was money, after all. They just wanted it clear they objected to the idea of being forced to socialize with someone such as me.

Murderer.

There was no point in proclaiming my innocence. I wouldn't give them the satisfaction of thinking, even for a moment, that their opinion of me mattered.

But I was taking stock, and I would remember who stood by me... and who didn't.

And those who didn't would regret it.

"You get used to it."

I cast a glance at my approaching father before returning my gaze to the assembled guests. "I never realized how difficult it must have been for you."

He leaned his shoulder against the wall next to me. "To be fair, I deserved it. You don't."

"I admire your restraint."

He raised an eyebrow. "How so?"

I narrowed my gaze. "I'm calculating the relatively infinitesimal cost it would take to put these self-righteous bastards out of business. I could ruin half these people before the end of the night and the other half casually over breakfast."

My father chuckled. "I won't say it didn't cross my mind on occasion. We could put a stop to this."

I shook my head. "No. Tonight is about Cesare and Milana, not me. Besides, the more they suspect me, the more the third man thinks his plan is working. It's our only advantage, because right now, we have nothing leading us to him."

He placed a hand on my shoulder. "It will be over soon. Then things will be back to normal."

Normal.

What was normal?

I didn't want my life to go back to normal.

I wanted Bianca.

The problem was, that possibility was becoming more complicated with each fucked-up revelation. It was like we were both caught in a sticky spider web and the more we struggled the more entangled we became. I could hardly blame her for fighting me, for wanting to escape, to move on and just forget.

If I wasn't such a monster, I'd be the bigger man and let her go.

I'd let her find love with another man.

A clean slate. Someone not tainted with the blood of all these secrets and betrayals.

Yet the thought of another man even touching her, let alone loving her, sent me into a rage.

I couldn't do it.

I couldn't let her go.

Ever.

I did that once and it nearly killed me. I'd never make that mistake again.

One of our security guards approached and whispered something to my father. His lips thinned as he turned to me.

I frowned. "What?"

"The Morettis have arrived."

I nodded. I'd received a text from the man watching the house the moment they left. "I know. We all knew they wouldn't miss an opportunity to press their connection to us."

He cleared his throat. "There appears to be a man with Bianca."

Everything faded into the background.

The people around me were just flashes of color and garbled noises.

My hand clenched into a fist, snapping the delicate crystal stem of the wineglass I was holding. The goblet portion toppled to the polished marble tile and smashed at my feet.

All conversation around us stopped and countless pairs of eyes turned and stared.

My jaw was clenched so tight I could barely form the words. "Where is she?"

Papà gestured for a server to clean up the glass. He stood facing the guests, a false smile on his face as he spoke to me. "Do I need to remind you, this is your brother's engagement party?"

I stared straight ahead, unseeing. "Where. Is. She?"

He let out a frustrated sigh. "Somewhere among the guests. I want your word. No scenes."

Before I could answer, Amara hurried up to us both,

blocking my path. "Enzo! There you are! You look so handsome in your tuxedo!" she exclaimed before throwing her arms around my neck.

As the guests observed what looked like a friendly, sisterly hug, she whispered into my ear, "I heard about Bianca's date. You know I love you, but if you ruin Milana's party, I'll make you wish you were dead."

She then broke free and brushed some nonexistent lint off my shoulder. "Do we understand one another?"

I caught my father's questioning look before responding. "Perfectly."

Papà looked between us. "Is there something I should know?"

Amara gazed at me, a sweet smile that wouldn't melt butter pasted on her seemingly innocent face.

I pulled on the suddenly tight collar of my tuxedo shirt. "Only that the two of you are well matched."

I stepped over the shards of shattered glass and went in search of Bianca.

I SPOTTED her across the room.

Releasing the button on my jacket I shrugged it off as I shouldered my way through the throng of guests to reach her.

The moment I did, I threw my jacket over her shoulders. "Cover yourself."

That her beautiful breasts were on obscene display for every ogling man in the room made me want to rip out the throat of anyone who dared look at her.

What could she have been thinking to wear such a dress in public?

And for another man.

Bianca clasped the lapels and pulled them over her chest.

Before she could respond, a hand reached out and pulled the jacket off her shoulders, tossing it back to me. "Thank you for the offer, friend, but it would be a crime to hide such beauty."

I looked over to see the man from that day in the piazza. Although tall, he was nothing compared to my height. I raised my chin and looked down my nose at him. "I'm not your friend."

I moved to place the jacket back on Bianca.

She stepped to the side as she deliberately avoided my gaze. Her voice was strained and strangely emotionless. "Thank you, Signor Cavalieri, but I'm fine."

My brow furrowed as I surveyed her more closely. She was wearing significantly more makeup than usual. The pressed powder made her look pale and ashy. Her hand shook as she drained her wineglass and reached for another from a passing servant.

I took the glass from her hand. Our fingers touched. Her startled gaze clashed with mine.

Fear.

There was fear in their depths.

My shoulders tensed. Something was wrong. Very wrong. "I think you've had enough."

The man she was with wrapped an arm around her lower back as he pressed his glass of wine into her hand and guided it to her mouth. "Bianca is my date, and I will determine when she has had enough."

My gaze narrowed as I raised my right arm and adjusted my cuff with my left hand. I spoke softly and calmly. "If you don't get your hands off her. This instant. I'm going to break that wineglass in half and slice your jugular with it."

Bianca stepped away, breaking the man's hold for him. She visibly trembled as she lowered her head and rasped, "Enzo, please, I don't want to draw any attention. It's fine."

Keeping my eyes trained on the man, I once again placed my tuxedo coat over her shoulders, covering her breasts from his view. "I don't think I caught your name."

He slid his hands in his pockets as he smirked. "That's because unlike the Cavalieris... I don't throw it around."

The corner of my mouth lifted. "I'm going to enjoy killing you."

The man tilted his head. "Are you sure? It might prove to be a challenge. From what I hear, you and your family only kill defenseless women."

There were several gasps from nearby guests, proving our conversation was not going unnoticed. Fuck.

Still, engagement party or not, an insult like that could not go unpunished.

I clenched my fist and stepped forward, pushing Bianca behind me with my other arm.

As I pulled my arm back to throw a punch... a shower of foamy prosecco arched over my head to hit the man square in the face.

The man sputtered, "What the fuck?"

A second arc of prosecco doused me and Bianca.

189

We turned to see Milana and Aunt Gabriella laughing and cheering as they held up the empty bottles.

"Oops! Sorry! Did we get you?"

"Sorry! These corks just popped!"

As the crowd cheered along with them, Milana sidled up to me. "Kill him later, when there are fewer witnesses." She then winked and turned back to the crowd as she raised up her arm and yelled, "I'm getting married!"

Cesare broke free from the crowd, snatched her around the waist, lifted her high and spun her around as the guests chanted, "Kiss! Kiss! Kiss! Kiss!"

I pivoted back, but the man was gone.

I turned my gaze on Bianca.

With wide eyes, she turned on her heels, intent on disappearing into the crowd.

I wrapped my arm around her from behind and yanked her flush against my body before whispering harshly into her ear, "Not so fast, *tesoro mio.*"

She clawed at my restraining arm. "You don't understand."

"It's you who doesn't understand, babygirl, but I'm going to change that, right now."

CHAPTER 20

ENZO

orcing a laugh, I said louder than necessary for the benefit of the onlookers, "Let me show you where you can get cleaned up, *sister*."

I squeezed her side and gave Bianca a warning look. She swallowed. "Thank you, *brother*."

I ushered her out of the room. The moment we reached the empty entrance hall, she broke free and bolted for the door. My jacket slipped from her shoulders as she ran.

I easily caught up with her. Snatching her wrist, I pulled her into a concealed alcove, pinning her to the wall with my body. My forearms rested above her head, caging her in.

Her chest rose and fell with her heavy breath. The curled, prosecco-drenched tips of her hair clung to her partially exposed breasts. Thinking how she appeared before all those leering eyes, half-dressed like this, made me furious all over again. "Who the fuck is he, Bianca? I want an answer this time."

She turned her head to the side. "None of your—"

I pounded the wall over her head with my fist. "I swear to fucking God, if you say none of my business, I will rip this fucking dress off your body and whip your ass with my belt right here, right now."

She remained stubbornly silent.

"Have it your way, babygirl."

I wrapped my hand around her small wrist and dragged her out of the alcove into the hallway toward the stairs.

"Where are you taking me?"

I glared down at her. "None of your business."

I marched her up the servants' hidden side staircase and down the upstairs hall toward the bedroom I still kept in the villa for when I worked long nights at the winery.

I kicked open the doors and shoved her inside before closing and locking them behind me. I pulled the key from the door and crossed to the mahogany wardrobe, setting it on top, out of her reach.

She stood facing me.

Neither of us said a word for several moments.

You could hear the muffled din of music and laughter from the party below. It gave the dim bedroom a strange, ethereal quality, as if both of us were existing on another plane than the rest of the world.

I pulled at the bow tie at my throat. I then unbuttoned my collar. I twisted off one cuff link, then the second as I crossed to the fireplace. I put the cuff links on the mantel and lifted the lid on the nearby black and gold enameled box.

Selecting one long match, I went down on my haunches, struck the match against the brick, and held the flame to the sticks artfully arranged around the central log until they caught fire.

Tossing the match into the fire, I rose and turned to face Bianca.

The entire time she had just stood there in the center of the room, watching me like a rabbit staring at a wolf.

I crossed my arms over my chest and leaned against the mantle. I took a deep breath, choosing my words carefully. "You have until the count of three to tell me who the fuck that man was and why you are dressed like a whore before I tear that dress off you."

She crossed her arms over her breasts. "First off, this is Gucci. And second, I don't owe you any explanations, Enzo."

I lifted my shoulders away from the mantel. "One."

"We aren't together. I'm free to date whoever I want."

I uncrossed my arms and took two steps toward her. "Two."

"I don't belong to you! You can't threaten me like this."

"Three."

Despite knowing it was locked, she bolted for the bedroom door and pulled on the knob.

I crossed to her in two strides, pressing her back to the door... and that's when I saw it. "What the fuck?"

The prosecco had splashed her face, washing away a thin streak of the caked-on makeup. I cupped her cheek and gently swiped my thumb over her cheekbone, exposing a faint bruise below her eye and an angry red scratch.

She hissed in pain at the contact.

Through clenched teeth I seethed, "I'll kill him."

I stormed toward the wardrobe to retrieve the key.

Bianca followed, pulling on my arm. "It's not what you think."

"He's a dead man."

"It was my mother!"

I pivoted to look down at her, staring intently to see if she was lying to me.

She lowered her head. "It was my mother," she whispered.

I ran my hand through my hair. "Why?"

"I confronted her about what you told me… about Renata and Milana."

Damn it. I never should have told her. I'd let my anger get the best of me.

I placed my hands gently on her shoulders. "So she hit you?"

"Not exactly."

When she refused to raise her gaze, I put a finger under her chin and tilted her head back. "I've got all night. And I'm not going anywhere until you tell me the truth."

"Whatever my parents are involved in, it has them freaked out about money. They are refusing to let me return to New York and are pushing me to marry."

"The man you were with tonight?"

She nodded. "His name is Nevio Zettici."

I made a mental note to have my men learn everything that was possible about the man, especially any connections he might have. It would be useful information to know before I killed him.

And I would kill him.

He dared lay claim to what was mine. For that he would die.

And as for her parents? I would ruin them.

They only thought they had money problems. By the time I was through, they wouldn't have a pot to piss in. I was over their bullshit.

Fuck the investigation. Fuck playing nice for appearances.

I was going to burn their world to the ground for daring to put my girl in this position, for daring to strike her. Enough was enough. It would be preferable if I could have arranged a more permanent answer to the problem they presented as well, but that would look too suspicious.

I nodded slowly. "We'll stay here for tonight. Tomorrow I'll send my men to pack up your things. I'll use my connections at town hall to waive the notification of intent and waiting period for a license. I have a friend at the Vatican who will waive the Marriage Banns and marry us without the Pre-Cana sessions by the weekend."

She blinked. "Marry us? This weekend?"

"Possibly sooner if I can arrange it."

She backed out of my embrace. "I'm not marrying you, Enzo."

"The hell you're not."

It was the best way to protect her and to put a stop to her parents' machinations. Cut the head off the snake. The fact that it was what I wanted as well was just a bonus.

She placed a hand over her stomach. "What do you think is happening here?"

I rubbed my jaw as I stared at her with narrowed eyes. "I'm protecting you."

Her shoulders shook as she laughed. The sound was bitter and brittle, like cracking ice. It chilled me straight to the bone and made me want to reach for her, comfort her, anything to stop that terrifyingly hopeless laugh.

The moment I raised my arms and stepped toward her, she backed away toward the windows.

She ran the tips of her fingers under her eyes as she sniffed. "Do you think you're the hero of this *fairy tale*? That I'm some damsel in distress and you're going to ride up on your noble steed and save me from my *evil parents*? You're not the hero, Enzo. You're one of the villains."

The truth of her words sliced through me. For all my talk about family and legacy and falling on my sword by marrying her sister, I had dishonored and betrayed Bianca.

"So what about these last few days? What has that been?"

Her head tilted to the side as her beautiful eyes again filled with tears. "Closure."

My gaze shifted away as I took in that one damning word.

She sighed. "You're just the ex-boyfriend who broke my heart. I needed closure to move on. I'll deal with my parents. I'll scrape together some money, get a new passport, and find my way back to New York. I was building a life there. A life without you."

I took a deep breath. Going back to having her not in my life was not an option. If the only part of her story she would allow me to play was the villain, then so be it.

I stalked toward her, deliberately blocking the door. "You're not going anywhere."

She crossed her arms as she shifted her weight onto one hip. "You act like you have a say in the matter."

I reached for my belt buckle. "No… you act like I'm giving you a choice."

CHAPTER 21

BIANCA

He pulled his belt off, folded it in half, and snapped it.

I jumped at the sound.

He jutted his chin upward. "Take that fucking dress off."

The dress I had scorned as an immodest scrap of silk earlier this evening now took on the sanctity of a nun's habit.

"I will not."

He twisted the leather belt between his fists, clenching it so hard, his knuckles were white. "I don't think you fully understand what's happening right now, babygirl."

I blinked several times, hating the heavy, caked feel of my lashes as the tear-soaked mascara weighed them down. "I know exactly what's happening here. You're trying to bully me just like my parents. Well, I won't stand for it."

"No. Your parents want to use you. I'm trying to protect you. There's a difference."

"I fail to see it."

He raised an eyebrow. "Take off that dress and I'll show you."

"This is absurd. Being married to you didn't protect Renata." It was cruel, but I was desperate for him to see reason.

His jaw tightened. "That was different, and you know it. Renata got herself killed because of the people she crossed. Your parents are trying to drag you into that same trap, but I'll be damned if I let that happen."

"I already told you in the church. We're finished. Done. It's over. I'm not your responsibility!"

With a frustrated sigh, he tossed the belt aside. "Fine. Have it your way." He then turned his back on me and walked out of the room, into the en suite bathroom.

My chest tightened. I should be taking advantage of his absence to grab the key and escape, but all I could do was stand there, dumbfounded.

I swallowed past the lump in my throat as fresh tears formed. I bit the inside of my cheek until I tasted blood, but the shock of pain did nothing to dull the torrent of conflicting emotions spinning around in my stomach so violently I wanted to vomit.

I reached out blindly for something to hold on to. My fingers grasped the heavy maroon and gold brocade drapes which framed the massive arched windows.

The realization that I had been fighting him all this time as some form of test... a test he just failed...hit me with sickening clarity. Part of me wanted to make him hurt and suffer for the pain he had caused me. Another part wanted to make him prove that it was me he had always wanted, not my sister.

I had wanted him to fight for me... to choose me this time.

And now it really was over. For real this time. I couldn't complain. I had told him emphatically over and over and over again that he no longer meant anything to me, that I didn't want him, that I had moved on.

I couldn't expect the man to read my mind when I didn't even know it myself.

One moment I loved him more than life itself, and the next I hated him.

I covered my mouth to stifle a sob.

I really thought....

I guess I was stupid for thinking....

Oh God.

It was over. No mental tricks. No what ifs. No maybes.

That was the double-edged sword with closure. You thought you wanted it. You thought you needed it, but you didn't realize that it took away that tiny kernel of hope, that silly fantasy that kept you going, that maybe...one day....

I just... I really believed he was going to fight for me, for us... this time.

Which was insane, since I wasn't even sure I wanted there to be an us.

Except that I did... maybe.

Dammit. Everything was so confused and jumbled.

I squeezed my eyes shut as I lowered my head.

I didn't hear him approach.

He swept me into his arms before I had a chance to object.

"What are you doing?"

Forced to wrap my arms around his neck for purchase, I realized he was naked except for a towel wrapped low around his hips.

He refused to respond as he carried me into the bathroom. The moment we crossed the threshold into the steam-filled room, he kicked the door closed behind him.

An enormous, frosted glass shower dominated one wall. Steam rose from the top.

The second my feet touched the plush bathroom mat, Enzo turned me around and unzipped my gown.

I grabbed at the corset bodice and spun to face him, confused at the sharp turn of events. "I don't understand."

He towered over me. "I'm not fucking you with the scent of another man's cologne clinging to your skin." He shifted his hand to grasp the front of my dress. "Or with you wearing a whore's dress chosen for him."

He wrenched the dress out of my grasp. It fell to the floor in a useless heap at my feet.

Since the tight corset structure didn't allow for a bra, I was left in only my panties and high heels.

He wrapped his arm around my middle and lifted me off the floor. Taking several steps forward, he carried me into the shower. He fisted my long hair and yanked my head back, forcing my face under the full blast of the hot spray of water as he growled, "And I'm definitely not fucking you with all that makeup covering up your pretty face."

I coughed and sputtered as I struggled in his embrace.

When he finally released me to close the door, sealing us in the enclosed chamber, I plastered myself to the tile wall on the far side of the shower. It quickly filled with more steam, slightly obscuring the sight of him.

I brushed my palms over my face, wiping the water from my eyes.

Enzo stepped close. He removed the now soaked towel from his waist and raised it to my face. "Close your eyes."

I stared at him.

"Do as I say, Bianca."

Not sure what else to do, I obeyed him.

He gently brushed the wet towel over my face, removing the remnants of my makeup, careful to avoid the scratch under my eye.

He tossed the towel over the glass shower wall and flattened his palms on the tile wall over my head. His bright emerald eyes, so different and unique from the rest of his family, studied me. "There's my beautiful girl."

He claimed my mouth. His tongue swept inside as his hand cupped the side of my neck, pulling me closer.

I moaned as my fingers delved into the soft hair on his chest, gripping and twisting it.

Enzo opened his mouth over mine and sucked in a sharp breath at the twinge of pain I caused, before devouring my mouth again, this time with an almost feral intensity.

He reached for my knee and pulled it up over his hip, pushing against my core.

With my high heels still on, his hard cock pressed against my stomach.

I closed my jaw slightly, scraping my teeth against his tongue as he licked and laved. He nipped at my lower lip in return.

Fuck. This man was sweet poison to me.

When he broke the kiss, I leaned against the shower wall, breathless, taking in the absurdity of the situation.

He reached for a bar of soap. It appeared an almost unnatural bright white next to his tan, work-roughened hands. Enzo may be the heir to a billionaire fortune, but it was no secret he worked the grapevines next to his men, side by side with his father and brother. He slowly, methodically flipped the bar over and over in his palm, lathering it.

He looked at me through a lowered brow. "Take off your panties and heels."

I opened my mouth to object.

Before I could, he said, "Don't."

Despite the heat of the water, a shiver ran up my spine. I slipped out of one heel then the other, immediately sinking five inches. It made me feel even smaller and more defenseless against his already superior height.

Enzo kicked the now ruined leather heels to the corner. "Panties. Unless you want me to tear them off."

Slipping my thumbs into the waistband of my panties, I pushed the sodden silk fabric over my hips. They fell to the tiled floor in a sodden heap.

"Good girl," he said as he continued to work the soap into a generous lather. "Now turn around and face the wall."

I frowned.

"Do as you're told."

After another moment's hesitation, I turned and faced the shower wall but immediately twisted my head over my shoulder. Licking my lips, I asked, "What are you going to do?"

He reached past me to set the soap back in the dish.

I couldn't help but flinch at the gesture.

He chuckled.

My shoulders and back muscles tensed.

Everything about the energy surrounding us screamed *too far*!

You pushed this man too far.

And it both terrified and aroused me.

His fingertips touched the center of my back.

Startled, I jumped and cried out in shock at his touch.

Enzo leaned forward, bracing his forearm over my head. "Shhh…." He ran his fingertips up and down my spine, each time inching further down my back. Up, then down to my lower back. Up, then to the top curve of my ass. Up, then to the seam between my ass cheeks, pausing and playing a little.

I tensed again, clenching my cheeks.

He resumed running his soapy fingers up and down my spine, still ending each time a little further down my ass.

He leaned in. "Remember what I told you in the church?"

I leaned my forehead against the warm tiles, my eyes partially closed. My brow furrowed. It was hard to focus with the hypnotizing rhythm of his fingers. "No?"

He continued to caress my skin. "I told you I would no longer hide my dark side from you."

He pressed two fingers between my ass cheeks, teasing my tight hole. He pushed one soapy fingertip inside of me. "I warned you that your last virgin hole would be mine."

My eyes sprang open. I braced my palms against the tiles and tried to shove away from the wall.

Enzo was faster.

He shifted and placed his forearm across my shoulder blades, pinning me.

I seethed through clenched teeth, "Let me go."

He ran his teeth along the outer shell of my ear before

rasping, "You see? That right there is our problem, babygirl. You keep fighting me."

I couldn't deny it. He was right. I fought him, so he would fight *for* me.

It was toxic and twisted and the biggest reason of all why we shouldn't be together.

I tried to push away from the wall again but couldn't move. He was too strong.

He pushed his finger in further.

My mouth opened on a gasp as I rose up on my toes.

"That ends here and now. I was willing to play by your rules because I knew I had hurt you, but clearly that isn't working, so we're going to play by my rules from now on."

Is he serious?

Playing by *my* rules?

At what point was I *ever* in charge of this twisted game between us?

He pulled his finger out and pushed it back in.

"Oh God!" It didn't hurt as much as it felt all kinds of wrong. "I'm not playing games with you, Enzo."

He moved his arm from my back to sweep my hair away from my shoulder. He then stroked my cheek. "Good. This isn't a game to me either. This is about the future. And it's past time you accepted that your future is with me. Not in New York and sure as fuck not with another man. It's with me."

I started to turn. "What if I don't—"

Before I could even finish my objection, he snatched both my wrists and stretched them over my head with one of his hands, pinning my face against the shower wall. He forced a second finger into my ass.

"Ow! Ow!"

The tops of his thighs brushed against the backs of mine.

I tried to turn my head to see over my shoulder, but his large body blocked my view.

His hand parted my cheeks, then something larger than his finger pressed against my hole.

"Wait! No!"

He reached around and flattened his hand on my stomach, pulling my hips back against his as he continued to pin my wrists over my head. "Time to prove who owns you, *tesoro mio.*"

His hips pushed upward.

I tried to clench but couldn't prevent the soapy head of his cock from slipping inside my dark hole. My fingers curled as my thigh muscles tightened and my ass stretched around his girth.

He thrust again, pushing deeper inside.

The air froze in my lungs as a cry died in my throat. I couldn't breathe. I didn't want to move, afraid it would increase the pressure and pain. "Please, take it out," I begged.

He released my wrists and wrapped his hand around my throat, tilting my head back onto his shoulder while his other arm wrapped around my middle. The full length of his body pressed against my back, hot and slick from the shower. He shifted his hips upward again, pressing deeper into my ass.

This time I did cry out.

He kissed my neck. "Don't focus on the pain, baby. Focus on the feeling."

I whimpered. "I don't know what that means."

"Where's my cock?"

I moaned.

He squeezed his fingers tighter around my throat. "Where's my cock?"

"In my ass."

He pulled out slightly and thrust back in. "That's right, babygirl. My cock is inside of you. Filling you. Do you feel that pressure? Do you feel me inside that tight virgin ass of yours?"

"Yes," I breathed.

His hand moved to cup my left breast. He toyed with the rigid nipple, pinching it. "How does it make you feel? Knowing you're submitting to one of my darkest fantasies about you?"

"I don't know."

He thrust harder, deeper. "You're lying. Tell me," he growled in my ear as he pinched my nipple harder.

I arched my back, which only served to push him deeper into my ass. "Vulnerable. I feel vulnerable," I blurted out.

He spread his fingers and slid them over my stomach to cup my pussy. Two of his calloused fingers rubbed between the folds, back and forth, causing the delicious friction that sent me over the edge that first time. "You know why, baby-girl? Because I know your secret. Deny it all you want, but you like it when I overpower you. Dominate you."

The hot water poured down over both of our bodies, adding to the sensitivity of my skin.

He leaned backward, lifting my feet off the shower floor,

driving his cock painfully deep into my ass as his finger flicked my swollen clit.

Lost in the overwhelming sensations, I didn't realize we had shifted back until he set me back down and I was further away from the wall.

He fisted my hair at the base of my skull and bent me at the waist.

I pressed my palms against the wall to stop him from bending me completely over.

Without warning, he spanked my ass.

"Ow!"

He pulled out then thrust back into my ass.

"Oh God! Wait!"

He pounded into me, again and again. From this position, each thrust filled me completely.

He twisted his hand in my hair. "New rules, baby," he ground out with each thrust. "Each time you threaten to leave me, I fuck one of your holes, right then and there. And I promise you, I won't give a damn where we are or who is watching."

His hand moved around my hip to tease my clit.

I was so close. I couldn't believe I was actually going to come with him fucking my ass, but he was right. It went beyond the pain. It was the *idea* of him inside my ass.

The domineering, pornographic *wrongness* of it that was so fucking off-the-charts arousing. It was the church all over again. Everything about this was so dark, twisted, hot. There really was something seriously wrong with me. *With both of us.*

I slammed my palm against the tiles several times. "Fuck. Oh God!"

He pinched my clit and I came so hard my knees buckled.

Enzo pulled out of my ass and turned me around to lift me into his arms, nudging me to wrap my legs around his waist.

I rested my forehead on his shoulder, spent. I could barely whimper when he pressed his cock back into my now stretched asshole from the new angle.

It wasn't long before he roared his own release, spurting his come deep inside my ass.

After gently washing us both with soap, he toweled me off and lifted me back into his arms.

He carried me into the bedroom and tucked me between the sheets in his bed.

I was too worn out emotionally and physically to fight him.

As he climbed in behind me and wrapped his arm around my middle I murmured, "I really hate you, Enzo, you know that?"

He kissed the top of my head. "Actually, babygirl. I know for a fact you don't. That's your problem. Go to sleep. We'll talk in the morning."

He was right. I didn't hate him.

And it *was* a problem.

CHAPTER 22

ENZO

*G*od, she was gorgeous in the morning.

Her dark hair was a tangled mess of curls fanned out over the pillow. Her lips were slightly open as she snored softly. There was the smudged shadow of mascara under her eyes, the remnants of last night's makeup... and she couldn't have looked more beautiful.

My jaw tightened at the faint scratch and slight bruise under her eye, both of which had faded significantly.

I was going to thoroughly enjoy destroying both her parents' lives.

When it had just been me they had wronged through their machinations with Renata, I had been resigned to letting the past be the past as long as I was able to reclaim Bianca as mine.

Now that I knew they were actively trying to keep Bianca from me—no, worse, trying to marry her off to another man — all bets were off.

It was scorched earth time.

It would be tricky since there was still an ongoing investigation into their daughter's death and I was a primary suspect, but I would manage it.

I brushed the hair back from Bianca's cheek. She stirred as her eyes fluttered open. There was one perfect moment when her sleep-hazed eyes stared up at me with pure warmth and tenderness.

Then reality crashed in.

The wall between us slammed down.

Her gaze iced over.

She leaned up on her elbows, clasping the blanket to her naked breasts. She shoved her hair out of her face. "Oh *Dio*! Oh no! *Madonna santa*! What have we done? How could you have let me sleep here last night? Where are my clothes? What am I going to tell my parents?"

I leaned onto my side, propping my head up on my hand. "It's a proper scandal. Father Luca will be especially horrified. I'm sure he will insist we marry immediately for the sake of the sanctity of the church and your reputation."

She swiveled on her torso to glare at me. "You've got a lot of nerve talking about the sanctity of the church!"

With that she shimmied out of the bed, taking the blanket with her. She wrapped it around her middle as she raced into the bathroom. She returned to the bedroom seconds later, holding three pieces of badly wrinkled fabric. "I distinctly remember you *unzipping* this dress."

"I faintly recall something similar."

She marched to the bed and tossed all three pieces at my

head, one by one. "Mind telling me why it's in *three* pieces now?"

I laughed as I caught each piece before they hit me in the face. "Now that you mention it, I also seem to recall, at some point later in the evening while you were sleeping, feeling as though I could *greatly* improve the dress by tearing it to shreds."

"That was *Gucci!*"

"I will buy you a thousand Gucci dresses to replace it."

"I would rather strut naked through the piazza than wear one stitch of clothing bought by you!"

"As much as I can get behind the idea of you walking around naked, it will be difficult as the wife of a Cavalieri to get away with it."

"Wife?"

"Yes, wife."

"We agreed that I *wasn't* marrying you."

"No, we agreed that you *were* marrying me."

"No, we agreed that you were being a *bully.*"

"No, we agreed that I was *protecting* you."

She threw her arms up in the air, which caused her blanket to slip, exposing the tops of her breasts. Unfortunately, she grabbed it before it could drop any lower. "I'm not having this argument with you again."

I laced my fingers behind my head and leaned back onto the pillows. "Good. I'm glad we're in agreement."

"Good." She turned to head back into the bathroom, then pivoted. "Wait."

She pointed a finger at me. "We are in agreement that we are *not* getting married."

"No. We are in agreement that it is useless for you to argue with me. We *are*, in fact, getting married as soon as I can arrange it."

She stormed toward the bed. "You're impossible."

"And you're adorable."

She waved her hand in front of me. "It's not going to work, Enzo. Whatever it is you're planning. I'm warning you. It's not going to work."

I ran my gaze over her. "Are you sure?" I then gave her a wink. "I think it's working pretty well so far."

She balled her hands into cute little fists. "Argh!"

Before she could step back, I snatched her around the waist, pulled her down onto the bed and yanked the blanket from around her body. As I rolled on top of her, I cupped her breast, leaning down to flick her nipple with my tongue. Then cast a glance up at her. "So what do you think is my plan?"

I swirled my tongue around her areole before pulling the nub into my mouth.

Bianca's back arched as she moaned. She was breathless when she answered. "You're trying to bully me into marrying you."

I ran my hand over her hip. "To be fair, you did say you loved me."

She leaned up on her elbows. "I was tied up and you were spanking me with your belt at the time! Confessions under torture are unreliable."

I forced a knee between her thighs, spreading them as I placed my forearms on either side of her head, forcing her to fall back onto the pillows. "Is that a challenge, beautiful?"

She swallowed. The sight of the delicate muscles of her

throat contracting had my cock hardening as I remembered that same sweet throat choking on my shaft. "If you think I'm going to say it again, you're crazy."

I kissed the top of her cheekbone. She really had the greatest cheekbones, sharp and defined. I skimmed my lips to the tip of her nose. "I'll make you a deal. If I can make you say you love me, *without using my belt*, you have to spend the day with me."

"And if I don't?"

"You're free to leave."

It was a lie, of course. I had absolutely no intention of letting her out of my sight. It was now clear, whatever dangerous game Renata had been playing, her parents were also involved up to their fucking eyeballs. Now they were planning on using my girl as a pawn.

They would have to get through me first.

I would do anything to keep Bianca safe. Even the possibility that she could share the same fate as Renata made me want to howl with rage. Renata made her choices and sealed her fate.

My girl was an innocent in all this.

And I would see she stayed that way.

She would not be tainted by this noxious bullshit.

Her eyes narrowed. "Just like that? No more talk of marriage?"

"Oh no. We're still getting married, but I'll at least let you leave this bed."

She smirked. "That's big of you."

I raised one eyebrow and shifted my hip to rub my hard shaft against her thigh.

Her eyes widened.

I trailed my lips along her jaw. "Are you up for the challenge, or are you afraid you'll lose?"

Her lips thinned as she shoved at my shoulders. "Do your worst. I'm not saying it."

I slipped my other knee between her thighs and moved down over her body. Kissing her neck, her collarbone, the top of her breast. I ran the tip of my tongue over her stomach as I caressed her hip.

I ran my hand over her inner thigh, before lifting her knee. Turning my head, I kissed her thigh as I inhaled the warm, intoxicatingly musky scent of her skin.

Bianca chuckled. "If this is your plan, I've already won."

I straightened my arms and planted my fists on either side of her hips as I stared down at her. "Explain."

She stilled. All sense of mirth gone.

Although I had taken her virginity and was the first man to fuck her amazingly tight ass, I was a selfish bastard. I had wanted it all. All her firsts. I had been robbed of her first kiss. That went to some dick back when she was fifteen. I begrudgingly accepted that, but I had always assumed the rest would belong to me.

My own unique treasure.

A treasure money could never buy.

Renata and her parents' Machiavellian plans had ruined that for me.

At least when Bianca sucked my cock, I could assuage my anger at being denied that first by knowing the man who came before me was a milquetoast who didn't know how to handle a real woman and didn't complete the job.

If I was about to learn I wasn't the first man to taste her, then someone was going to die. There were certain things I couldn't get past. Like the idea there was another man walking this earth who knew what my girl's pussy tasted like.

She remained silent.

"Start talking, Bianca. Has another man had his tongue in your cunt?"

She gasped as she sat up and shimmied her hips back until she hit the headboard. "You have no right to ask me something so crude."

I slipped my hands under her knees and pulled.

She slid down on the bed toward me until the juncture of her thighs slammed against my balls.

A haze of red anger blurred my vision.

I wrapped one hand around her throat. It took all my concentration to only hold her gently and not to squeeze my fingers as my other hand cupped her pussy. "Answer me. Now. Has another man tasted your pussy?"

"No. Damn you. I just won't come that way."

I released the breath I had been holding. Staring at her with a furrowed brow, I observed, "You came readily enough when I touched you before."

Her cheeks flushed a bright pink as she avoided my gaze. "That was *different*. I'm not talking about this with you, Enzo!"

I gripped her jaw and forced her head forward. I then leaned down and placed a quick kiss on her tightly closed lips. "Oh my beautiful, amazing girl. You really are an absolute treasure."

I slid down to bury my face between her sleek thighs. Using two fingers of my right hand, I spread her lower lips open. I ran my tongue up the center to tease her already swollen clit.

Bianca pressed her hand against my head to push me away as she tried to wiggle her hips to the side. "I don't like this."

Capturing her gaze, I opened my mouth and released a warm breath over her exposed flesh before saying, "Does that mean you forfeit? If so, then say it, say you love me... and mean it."

Bianca bit her lip.

I watched as indecision played through her dark eyes.

With a resigned huff, she fell back onto the pillows.

I flicked her clit with the tip of my tongue.

Her thigh muscles tightened.

I flicked it again.

Bianca's hips shifted.

I swirled my tongue around and around, applying gently intensifying pressure with each pass.

Bianca fisted the sheets.

I slowly increased the rhythm as I watched her chest rise and fall with her labored breath.

Once again, she tried to object. She attempted to twist her knees to the side. "Enzo, please. I'm not sure..."

I placed my palm on her stomach, steadying her. "I am, baby."

I continued to tongue her clit in a slow and steady rhythm, only gently varying the pressure as I teased her entrance with the tip of my finger.

Her head fell back. "Oh! Oh!"

I pushed my finger inside and twisted it, hooking the tip

to make sure I stimulated all those delicious, delicate nerve endings.

Her hips bucked.

Her pussy clenched around my finger. I added a second one.

This time when she reached her hand to my head, it was to grasp my hair. "That's it, babygirl. You taste so fucking good," I growled against her pussy, knowing she'd feel the vibration of my voice.

I pumped my fingers in and out of her tight passage as I matched the rhythm with my tongue.

"Oh, God! Oh, God! Enzo!"

Her hips bucked again.

I flicked her clit harder. "Say it, baby."

Her back arched.

Knowing she was excruciatingly close, I pulled my mouth away. I added a third finger and thrust in hard as I leaned over her. "Say it," I demanded.

She closed her eyes and rolled her head to the side.

"Eyes on me," I snarled.

Her eyes snapped open.

I jutted my chin up. "Say it. Now."

Her mouth opened as she breathed heavily.

I twisted my fingers inside of her until my thumb was pointing downward. I then slid it close to her tight asshole.

Her eyes widened as I pressed the pad of my thumb against her puckered hole.

I returned to kneel between her thighs. I leaned over her pussy, teasing her with the warmth of my breath. "Say you love me, babygirl."

She licked her lips, then whimpered. "Fine! I love you."

My mouth fell on her. Devouring her sweet pussy as I licked and laved.

Her back arched and stayed suspended in the air as she screamed her release.

The moment she fell back to the mattress, limp and spent, I swept my tongue over her pussy again.

"No," she moaned. "It's too...."

"Shhh."

Keeping my touch light, I coaxed a second orgasm from her.

As her body trembled from the release, I reared up and placed my cock at her entrance. I sank in deep, relishing the feel of her tight, clenching muscles.

Her body jerked from the impact. I knew she was still getting used to the feel of my thick girth stretching her open.

As I increased the pace of my thrusts, I pulled her earlobe into my mouth, sucking on it hard. Whispered harshly into her ear, "I didn't tell you the rest of my plan."

Her half-closed eyes stared up at me.

My hips ground against her core as I brushed her tangled curls away from her forehead. My balls tightened. I ground my teeth, the pleasurable pressure along my shaft increasing. "I'm going to get you pregnant with my child. Then you'll never be able to leave me."

Bianca cried out as she shoved at my chest.

I rolled onto my back, gripping her hips and forcing her to straddle me.

"Pull out, Enzo. I mean it."

"Never."

She pulled on my chest hair as she tried to buck off me.

The pain spurred me on.

I bounced her on my shaft until I came with a roar, filling her with my seed. I then pulled her down on top of me, holding her close, refusing to allow her to dislodge my cock until every drop of my come had melted into her body.

Her head rested against my heart. "Why are you doing this to me?"

I stroked her soft, silky hair. "Because I love you, and you love me."

She sniffed.

I could feel the first drops of her tears against my skin. "I've told you before, I don't consider loving you a good thing."

"I'm aware."

"So why do you want to keep a woman who hates the love she feels for you?"

My hand paused then cupped the back of her head. I leaned up and kissed her forehead. "Life without you is hell. So if the trade-off for a life with you is a love reluctantly given, it will be heaven in comparison."

She tilted her head to look up at me. "That's fine for you, but what about me, Enzo? Is that the life you want for me too?"

I placed my hand on her head and pulled her back down to my chest.

Fuck.

She wasn't wrong.

One solution to protect her was to marry her, but there was another.

I could simply give her the money she needed to be independent of her parents and send her back to New York. She'd be safe there, away from her parents' schemes. It was doubtful the third man would consider her enough of a threat to chase her to America.

The first guaranteed my happiness.

The second hers.

I knew which solution was the right one.

I just wasn't capable of choosing it.

CHAPTER 23

ENZO

I knocked softly on the bedroom door.
No answer.
I knocked again.
Still no answer.
After a third time, the door swung open.

An extremely irate Aunt Gabriella stood before me. She had a silk eye mask pushed up over her forehead and was tying the belt to her robe around her waist. "Do you have any idea what time it is?"

I flinched. The entire household knew never to disturb Aunt Gabriella before noon when she stayed at the villa, especially after a party like last night. That had been an ironclad rule even when I was a boy. "It's early, I know."

"No, early would be ten o'clock." She looked at the Cartier tank watch on her wrist. "Eight o'clock is an ungodly 'anyone who knocks on my door deserves to be shot' hour. Someone had better be maimed or dead."

"I need a favor."

She turned her back and headed deeper into the bedroom. "Come back at noon."

She climbed into bed and pulled her silk eye mask down over her eyes.

"Please, Aunt Gabriella."

She lifted up one side of the eye mask. "What do I get in return?"

I rubbed my jaw. "My *Riva Aquarama*."

She had been lusting after my classic mahogany-hulled runabout yacht since I secured it in an auction for a million euro two years ago.

She threw off the eye mask and sat up. "For keeps?"

"For the season."

She thrust her lower lip out.

I raised a finger. "And you can only take it out if Roberto is piloting it."

"Is he the handsome silver fox crew member or the awkward young one?"

"I refuse to dignify that... but yes, the silver fox. Do we have a deal?"

"Deal." She waved her hand at me like a genie on a throne granting wishes. "What is your favor?"

I braced myself for her laughter. Taking a deep breath, I said, "I need more clothes."

I RETURNED to my bedroom with a handful of designer dresses and three tote bags filled with shoes, purses, scarves, makeup, and jewelry.

As I heeled the door closed behind me, I smirked at Bianca. "You have no idea how much this just cost me."

She smirked back as she took a wooden hanger from my grasp and inspected the Valentino dress. "Serves you right. If you hadn't torn my dress, you wouldn't have had to go begging your aunt for clothes."

"I wanted to ask Amara, but she was... occupied."

Despite being an adult, there was still something wrong about approaching a parent's bedroom door and hearing... sounds.

"You could always just let me go home."

I kissed her bare shoulder. "Out of the question. A deal is a deal."

She grabbed several hangers and headed toward the bathroom as she tossed cheekily over her shoulder, "Well I hope you enjoyed it, because after that stunt about trying to knock me up, that was the last time you're getting anywhere near me."

She slammed the bathroom door shut.

I smiled.

We'll see.

* * *

BIANCA WAS SITTING in the passenger seat of my silver Ferrari GTC4Lusso, tossing the contents of her evening purse into the purse she'd borrowed from Aunt Gabriella. She paused to check her mobile.

"Fuck."

"Language," I growled, tossing her a quick glare as I navigated a sharp turn.

She stuck her tongue out at me.

"Do that again and I'll take it as a sign you want me to lick your sweet pussy again."

She snapped her jaw shut as her cheeks flushed pink.

"My parents called over twenty times. There is also a number I don't recognize. Since it's local I'm assuming it's Nevio wondering what happened to me."

I snatched the phone from her hand and tossed it into the back seat. "They all can keep wondering."

"Hey! I have to at least call my parents back."

"No."

"Enzo."

"The answer is no, Bianca, and that's final. It was your father's business dealings that got Renata killed. The fact that she is a woman is the only fucking reason why your mother is still breathing after I learned she hit you. And don't get me started on her trying to pawn you off on that asshole, Nevio Zettici. I don't know what his involvement in this bullshit is, but trust me, I'll find out."

She crossed her arms. After several moments of silence, she said, "How come you're allowed to curse, but I'm not?"

"Because I'm a big, scary man and you're a beautiful woman with a pretty mouth."

She studied me. "I can't decide if that was meant to be romantic or dirty."

I took my eyes off the road to give her a wink. "Both."

"So what am I supposed to do all day? Just sit around and watch you work?"

"Absolutely not. You are behind on at least two projects, and I need an adjustment on a third."

She frowned.

"The designs you owe me?"

"You mean for the *fake* companies you created just to *spy* on me?"

"The names were fake. The companies are real. And it wasn't to spy on you, it was to watch over you, to keep you safe."

"Semantics."

I pulled in behind Cesare's Alfa Romeo Giulia Quadrifoglio. We were both at the headquarters office today wrapping up a few things, since the next few weeks would be spent at the villa supervising the bottling at the winery.

Bianca moved to open her door.

I stopped her with a look.

I got out of the car and buttoned my wool overcoat as I crossed behind and opened her door while surveying the street. I then offered her my arm and escorted her into the building.

It felt good.

The only thing that would make this moment better was if I were able to introduce her to my staff as my wife.

The receptionist, Liliana, stood as we approached. "Buongiorno, Signor Cavalieri. The items you requested are in your office."

I nodded. "Thank you, Liliana. May I introduce you to Signorina Moretti."

Bianca stretched out her arm. "Call me Bianca, please."

Liliana stared at her hand but didn't take it.

Bianca looked at me, uncertain.

It hadn't occurred to me that it would be awkward having Bianca here. It wasn't like any of the staff knew Renata or liked her. She'd barely come into the office and even then, only to complain.

Liliana recovered and smiled as she took Bianca's hand, easing the momentary tension. "Welcome. Can I get you a caffe or latte?"

Bianca nodded. "Actually, I'd love a caffe, but I can get it myself if you point me in the right direction."

Liliana waved her off. "It's my pleasure. I'll bring it to Signor Cavalieri's office."

I nodded to her. "Thank you, Liliana. She will take hers with two sugars and no cream. The usual for me."

"Yes, sir."

I placed a hand at Bianca's lower back and ushered her past the various desks, nodding greetings to my staff as we went. We climbed the private staircase which led to the private executive level.

When we reached my office, I escorted her inside and closed the door. Taking her coat, I hung it in the closet then took off my own coat, gesturing toward a high-backed oxblood leather chair which had been pulled up to the other side of my executive desk.

The contents on the top of my desk had been pushed aside to make room for a laptop and several files. Even though we had plenty of office space and I could have easily found an empty desk, I wanted her with me.

Bianca wandered over to the drafting desk I kept in the corner.

While I loved working at the winery and my family's other companies, it was no secret my first love was architecture and the restoration of old buildings. It was a passion my money allowed me to indulge. When we dated, I learned Bianca shared my love of old murals and the art which helped inspire my work.

She surveyed my blueprint sketches. Picking up one of the archeology books I had stacked on the corner of the desk, she opened it to the page I had marked with a leather bookmark. It showcased the presumed floorplan of an old Etruscan villa from this region. "What is this for?"

"I'm rebuilding the cottage located in the corner of the vineyard more in the fashion of an authentic Etruscan villa."

She laughed. "It's a great idea, but a little bit of a shame. I really loved your last rebuild. Did you get bored of it already?"

I cleared my throat as I turned away. "It burned down."

She gasped. "I'm so sorry. I hadn't heard."

I picked up a file from my desk. "I wanted to talk to you about the color and font choices on the layout you sent last week."

The last thing I wanted to do was explain to her that I was the one who burned it down.

Or why.

She crossed my office and stood at my shoulder to look at

the file I was holding. Seconds later, she snatched it from my hand. "What is this? This isn't my work?"

Uh oh.

I raised up my palms. "Technically, it is."

She held up the file and jabbed the words "Cavalieri Properties" with her finger. "This font looks like shit because that's not the font I chose because that's not the company name I was given."

"Lang—"

Her nostrils actually flared. "If you say language right now, I swear to God—"

We stood there glaring at one another, ignoring Liliana when she walked in with our caffes. Sensing the bad timing, she hurried to the desk and placed the cups on my desk so quickly coffee sloshed over the rims to pool onto the saucers. She left without a word and closed the door behind her.

We then continued as if uninterrupted.

I ran a hand through my hair. "Of course I had to change the name to the *real* company name."

Bianca tossed the file onto the desk and braced her fists on her hips. "You mean you have altered *all* my hard work this way?"

"I didn't just hire you for the sake of hiring you, Bianca. You're an extremely talented graphic artist and these are real projects... just the company names were fake."

She tossed her purse onto a nearby chair and sat down... in my chair. She unbuttoned the sleeves on her black silk blouse and rolled them up.

She then took a sip of caffe as she tapped the spacebar on *my* computer, not the smaller laptop I had brought in for her use, several times to wake up the screen. "I'm going to need access to *all* the original files and a list of what companies are supposed to go with what project to fix this mess. What's your password?"

I told her the password and then leaned a shoulder against an antique oak file cabinet and observed her.

She was magnificent to watch. The moment the desktop screen glowed to life her entire focus zeroed in on work. Her long, tapered fingers flew over the keys as she opened project file after file and downloaded the software necessary to fix her work.

Never in a hundred million years would I have let Renata sit in my office chair, let alone have given that viper the password to my business computer which contained countless sensitive files, including all the Cavalieri banking information. I didn't hesitate to give it to Bianca.

As she worked, she swept her hair off her shoulders, twisted it into a messy bun and speared one of my pens into the thick twirls, then returned her attention to the keyboard.

I didn't realize it was possible to be jealous of a pen.

Usually I hated long hours at the office, preferring to spend them outside on a building site or at the vineyard. Not today. I had never enjoyed an afternoon in the office more than today with Bianca at my side.

We spent hour after hour arguing over copyedits, fonts, colors, spacing. At times, I thought she deliberately disagreed with me just to be contrary. She even refused to leave for lunch. It had been my plan to show her off by treating her to a nice lunch outside the office, but she insisted on just ordering something in.

I thought my family were workaholics. Her work ethic put us to shame.

Still, I looked forward to a quiet dinner together.

She had been so wrapped up in work, she hadn't even demanded I take her home.

I hoped later to keep her talking about her designs and our upcoming projects all the way back to the villa. I had most of my belongings moved there while we were in the office. I didn't want to take Bianca to the home where Renata had lived. I already had a crew working on removing all the ghastly furnishings Renata purchased and another crew painting over the mural with her face on it.

I would sell the house and buy something special just for Bianca and me.

Something ancient we could restore together. A project we could share.

Until then, we would stay at the villa. It was more secure anyway.

I also texted Amara and asked if she would lend Bianca a few things until I could arrange for a personal shopper to drop off the purchases I'd made on the sly for Bianca from the designer shops in Rome while she was working at my desk.

I thought about having the guard I had watching her house and monitoring her parents' movements pack up her things but thought better of it. I didn't want another man, even an employee, touching my girl's personal items and lingerie.

And yes, I was that jealous and possessive.

We were just wrapping up for the day when Liliana popped her head into the office. Her face looked strained.

"There is someone here to see you. He doesn't have an appointment."

I held up Bianca's coat for her to slip her arms in. "Tell whoever it is to go away and make one for another day."

Before Liliana could respond, an odd-looking man with hanging jowls pushed past her. He had the appearance of someone who'd recently lost a great deal of weight and now his skin and clothes didn't quite fit his new, smaller stature.

He pointed to the silver badge displaying a white cross and red shield and bearing the words *Arma dei Carabinieri* on his black uniform. "I am *Luogotenente Carica Speciale* Longo, and I don't make appointments."

He looked pointedly at my hands on Bianca's shoulders. "I'm investigating the recent death of your wife."

CHAPTER 24

ENZO

Keeping a steady gaze trained on Longo, I said to Bianca, "Wait for me in the executive lounge. I won't be long."

Bianca bristled. "I'm staying."

Without saying a word, I bent and placed my shoulder into her midsection, lifting her high. Wrapping my arm around the backs of her thighs so she couldn't kick, I turned to Longo. "Back in a moment."

I stormed out of my office.

Bianca pounded her small fists on my back. "Put me down! Enzo! How dare you!"

Matteo looked up when we entered his office, leaning back in his chair and steepling his fingers. "I wish I could say this was the first time I've seen a Cavalieri cousin carrying a woman like a sack of potatoes into my office, but surprisingly enough, it's not."

I deposited Bianca onto his soft brown leather sofa.

Pointing a stern finger at her, I ordered, "Stay."

I then turned to Matteo. "Call the villa. An inspector just showed up. And keep *her* here."

Bianca sprang to her feet. "She was my sister. I deserve to hear what he has to say."

"No, you don't. I've already warned you. Your sister was involved with some seriously dangerous people and until I know who all the players are, the less your name is mentioned the better. I don't need this asshole knowing who you are."

She stretched her arms out wide to each side. "He's a freaking *Luogotenente Carica Speciale* with the *Arma dei Carabinieri*. You don't think he already knows who I am?"

I crossed to her in two strides and wrapped my hands around her face, placing a hard kiss on her lips. Leaning in closer to her, I whispered in her ear, "Be a good girl for Matteo or I'll take my belt to that pretty ass of yours later."

She gasped.

I turned and slammed the office door shut behind me.

As I marched back toward my own office, I rapped a sharp knock and then immediately opened Cesare's office door.

He looked up from his computer. "Hey brother, not for nothing but when Milana's back at work you may want to wait for a shout-out before opening that door so quickly," he said with smirk.

"There's an inspector in my office about Renata."

His lips straightened to a thin line. Rising, he grabbed his suit jacket from off the back of his chair and shrugged it on. Buttoning it as he walked, he said, "Game on, brother."

When we entered my office Longo was loitering around the open files on my desk.

I cleared my throat.

He looked up, his loose jowls shaking as he complained, "You rich people think the rules don't apply to you, but the *Arma dei Carabinieri* is not in the habit of being kept waiting."

My brow lowered as I turned to Cesare. "I wasn't aware that was a rule, were you?"

His eyebrows raised. "I wasn't either. Look at that. Learn something new every day."

I tilted my head to the side. "Although to be completely fair, we were aware of the rule that the rules don't apply to obscenely rich people like us."

Cesare smiled and wagged his finger at me. "I have to say, I'm a big fan of that rule."

I returned his smile. "Me too."

Longo yanked up his too-large black uniform trousers, straightening the red stripes along the sides which had bagged when the trousers had slid low on his hips. "This is no laughing matter. A woman is dead," he sputtered, foamy spittle forming at the corner of his mouth.

Jutting his loose-jowled chin up at me, he swiped his hands over his lips. "Your wife, Signor, is dead."

My gaze narrowed. "I'm aware, Longo."

"That's *Luogotenente Carica Speciale* Longo to you."

Cesare placed his hand on the man's shoulder. "Listen, *Longo*. We are all aware of the tragic situation. No one in this room killed her, so why don't you tell us why you're here."

Longo shrugged Cesare's hand off. "I'm not so sure about that."

He reached into his pocket and pulled out a small note-book and pen. Flipping open the cover, he gestured with the tip of his pen and recited, as if quoting from verse, "The coroner has ruled the death of Renata Cavalieri an *Omicidio volontario* according to the Italian Criminal Code, specifically Article 575 which states voluntary homicide is committed when a person intentionally kills another human being. This carries a prison term of not less than twenty-one years. The *Pubblico Ministero* intends to seek the maximum penalty for this egregious offense to such an innocent young woman."

It was frustrating but not unexpected. We had tried to avoid this, of course, but whoever ordered the coroner's report wanted to make sure there was an investigation.

I crossed my arms over my chest. "Who ordered the coroner's report?"

Longo scribbled on his pad. "That seems a very suspicious question. Why would you want to know?"

I shrugged. "Our local police determined her death was the result of a tragic fall. My wife loved the Apennine mountains' hiking trails, but they can get treacherous, especially after a rainfall. I believe I have a right as her husband to know why there is a report conflicting with what I was told."

That was all bullshit of course.

"That information is confidential. Besides, it is the prerogative of the *Arma dei Carabinieri* to investigate any death they please." He checked his notes. "Neither of you have an alibi for her time of death."

It was bad enough I was implicated in this mess. I wouldn't have my brother dragged in as well. "That is not accurate as you well know. Cesare was at the hospital, at the bedside of his intended, Milana Carbone."

"Yes, it seems tragic accidents seem to befall the women of

your acquaintance."

Cesare cupped his right fist in his left hand. "Go ahead, say something else flippant about my girl being in the hospital and almost dying. I dare you."

Longo puffed out his chest. "Are you threatening an officer of the law?"

"You're goddamn right I am. The rules don't apply to me, remember?"

Longo pointed his finger at us both as he seemed to vibrate with righteous anger. "You Cavalieris don't scare me! I will have you both placed in *custodia cautelare!*"

I placed a restraining hand on Cesare's chest. "I'd be very careful about threatening us with preventive custody, Longo. You and I both know you don't have the standing to declare us a danger to society or a flight risk. Our family's roots go back to before Italy was a country."

Cesare smirked. "Not to mention the obscene amounts of money we would donate to the judge's favorite charity to get your request *reconsidered.*"

Longo sputtered. "Your money won't save you from several eyewitness statements. They all state you left the hospital on the night in question and did not return for several hours and when you did"— he checked his notes— "you were in an agitated state with mud on your shoes."

I exchanged a look with Cesare. I turned back to Longo. "What about the security cameras?"

"What about them?"

I sighed. This meeting was getting tiresome. "There must be security footage of him leaving then returning to the hospital?"

Longo yanked up his pants again. "The security footage seems to be missing from that night."

Cesare cracked his knuckles. "Convenient, wouldn't you say?"

Longo wiped his mouth again. "What are you implying?"

Cesare's eyes narrowed. "I wasn't *implying* it."

Longo flipped through the pages of his notebook as he turned his focus on me. "And you have no alibi. In fact, we have several statements that you stormed out of the hospital in an agitated state deliberately in search of your wife."

"That's true."

Out of the corner of my eye, I saw Cesare cast me a concerned look.

I wasn't planning on falling on my sword for her murder unless Cesare continued to be implicated. It was clear whoever was setting us up had enough money and power to tamper with evidence and buy off witnesses.

I would be damned if I let Cesare go down with me or for me.

"So you admit you killed her?"

Cesare stepped forward. "He said nothing of the sort."

Longo put his notebook away. "He doesn't have too. This was just a courtesy visit. There isn't a doubt in my mind that you beat your wife to death. She tricked you into marriage by claiming she was pregnant. When you found out there was no baby, you took your fists to her. You then threw her body off a cliff to make it look like an accident and paid off the local cops to look the other way."

I widened my stance as I stared him down. "I'm hearing a super creepy bedtime story, but no evidence."

"In the days after your wife went missing, you were photographed with bruised and cut knuckles."

"It was harvest time. It's a well-known fact we are hands-on winery owners. I think you'd find that half the men in this village had bruised and cut hands that week. Next."

Of course, their injuries would be from the vines. Mine were from punching a wall.

"Why did your cottage burn?"

"What?"

"The cottage where you and your wife were staying at the vineyard. The night she disappeared. The cottage burned under mysterious circumstances."

Fuck.

I let out a frustrated breath. Since there was really no other excuse, I went with the truth. "I burned it down."

"You burned it down?"

"Yes."

"Why?"

"Because I felt like it."

"You expect me to believe that you burned a perfectly good cottage to the ground... just because?"

Cesare interrupted. "It's one of those funny rich people things."

Longo pulled on the waistband of his trousers. "More like you were getting rid of the evidence of the savage beating you gave your wife." He wrinkled his nose. "Which *bedtime story* do you think is more believable? That you burned it down *just because*... or to hide evidence of a *murder*?"

Before I could answer, my father arrived.

He strolled into the office, his sharp gaze missing nothing.

He nodded to us both. "Boys." He then turned to the inspector. "Jesus Christ, Longo, is that you?"

Longo's mouth thinned. "Don Cavalieri."

"Damn, man. Your wife stop feeding you?"

Longo pointed to the red and silver shoulder epaulettes showing two silver stars and three bars. "It's *Luogotenente Carica Speciale* Longo now."

My father's eyebrows rose. "They actually promoted you? Was there some kind of mass casualty event in the *Arma dei Carabinieri* I wasn't aware of? That's the only way an incompetent, corrupt little shit like you would make *Luogotenente Carica Speciale.*"

Longo's face flushed a mottled red. "We both know you killed Angelina. And now I'm going to put away both your sons for murder! *Like father like son.*"

My father snatched Longo by the front of his uniform and lifted him off the floor.

Longo cried out, "Unhand me! I'm a *Luogotenente Carica Speciale!*"

"Listen to me, you little asshole. I'm going to find out who is paying you to launch this puppet investigation and when I do, I'll personally see to it that you spend the rest of your career cleaning up horse shit from the mounted brigade."

Papà tossed him to the floor.

Longo scurried backward on his ass before rising. He pointed a finger at us before storming out. "You're all going to pay for this."

I looked at my father. "Old friend of yours?"

"He was a civilian recruit in his first six months when your mother died. He suspected I killed her and was trying to impress his superiors."

Cesare laughed. "Bet it really chapped his ass that he was right, and no one would listen."

"You could say that."

I rubbed my eyes. "Whoever is behind this, they are fabricating evidence and buying off witnesses."

My father laid a hand on my shoulder. "Well then, we'll just have to buy off better witnesses."

Cesare smirked. "It really is annoying when someone uses our own toys and tricks against us."

I shook my head. "Yeah, can't say I care for it."

Cesare headed toward the door. "I have a few things to finish up here and then I'll swing by Benito's office on my way home and warn him about Longo sniffing around."

"Maybe we'll get lucky. Maybe that buffoon will actually lead us to the third man. Especially since Bruno Moretti hasn't moved any money or put in for any land permits since this whole mess began. The Agnellos are definitely laying low. They know we are on to their land scheme, but they won't wait forever. They'll get anxious to get moving again soon."

Papà nodded. "Good point. We'll put some of our men on him."

Before we could make any further plans, there was an angry screech, then the sound of shattering glass.

Matteo shouted down the hallway. "Enzo, your presence is required."

Papà and Cesare both turned to look at me.

I inhaled and squared my shoulders as if I were a soldier heading into battle. "I should probably go take care of that."

CHAPTER 25

BIANCA

The moment Matteo opened his office door to call out to Enzo, I shouldered past him and marched down the hallway.

I stormed into Enzo's office, already in mid-sentence. "—another think coming if you—"

I stopped short when I came face to face with his father and brother. I clamped my mouth shut, sucking my lips between my teeth.

I hadn't seen them since the funeral. So many snakes had crawled out from under rocks since then.

One Cavalieri was intimidating enough, but three of them? Forget about it.

They filled the room with dark, male energy.

I had never really interacted with Cesare in school and since Enzo and I had barely started dating when my parents and Renata orchestrated that horrible deception on him, I never had a chance to formally meet his father.

Before that, I had stayed far away whenever my family was at the villa for any social engagements because of all the rumors about him murdering his wife.

My gaze shifted, deliberately avoiding Cesare's questioning gaze.

How could I look him in the eye, knowing what my sister had done?

I then caught Barone's narrowed gaze and my heart stopped.

His was worse, with good reason.

The stench of the inspector's cheap cologne still lingered in the room. Because of my family, his eldest son had been forced into a disastrous marriage and was now suspected of murder.

I opened my mouth to say something, but I couldn't think of a single thing.

How would I even begin to apologize for the actions of my super corrupt, unethical family?

Deciding I couldn't, I turned to leave.

Enzo moved forward and wrapped his arm around my middle.

He placed a kiss on my cheek and gently pulled me back into the room. "Bianca, you remember my father, Barone, and brother, Cesare?"

I swallowed and said nothing, keeping my gaze trained on the floor.

A pair of scuffed, dark brown work boots appeared a few inches from the toes of my polished high heels. I slowly looked up over the denim trousers and hunter green cable knit sweater pulled over a barrel chest to finally meet the stern gaze of Barone Cavalieri.

He placed both his hands on my shoulders before pulling me in for a bear hug.

And that was precisely what it felt like, being hugged by a giant bear.

I didn't know what to do.

Barone said quietly, "There's no need to be scared. We're going to protect you like one of our own."

Protect me? One of our own?

Tears pricked the backs of my eyes.

My father had never been even remotely affectionate, let alone protective of me. Was this what it felt like to have a parent who gave a damn about you?

Barone pulled back. He leaned down to meet my gaze and gave me a warm smile.

I couldn't help but smile back.

"Hey, don't hog my future sister-in-law."

Sister-in-law. They both have me practically married to Enzo and I haven't even said yes.

The walls were closing in on me.

Shocked, I turned to find Cesare standing close, ready to also give me a hug. As he did, he whispered in my ear, "Your sister's actions were her own. Remember that. We do."

Cesare released me and Enzo immediately pulled me into his side.

I was grateful for the extra support, since I wasn't sure my legs would hold me.

Everything was upside down and topsy-turvy.

Where I expected anger, I received kindness.

Where I should have received tenderness, I experienced only cold cruelty.

When I wanted answers, I only got half-truths and more questions.

Around and around and around I spun.

It was like I was being gaslighted by everyone around me.

No one told me the full truth. Not Enzo. Not my parents. No one.

I desperately wanted to ask about the investigation and what the inspector said, but I knew it was pointless, especially with all three of them in the room. There wasn't a chance in hell they'd tell me. I would just get the usual platitudes. *Don't worry. It's being taken care of. It's for your own good.*

Barone and Cesare both said their goodbyes but not before saying they would see me later at the villa for dinner.

Later at the villa. Like one big happy family.

Enzo kissed me on the cheek and crossed to his desk. He gathered the files we had updated throughout the day. Flipping open several of them, he started to sign the top memo with his recognizable sharp, slashing signature, showing his approval of my changes.

I rested my palms on the edge of the desk. Schooling my features, I fought to keep my voice calm. I didn't want another fight. "I didn't want to be rude after your father and brother have been so kind, but they mentioned seeing me later for dinner. Since I'll be at my parents' house, will you give them my excuses?"

Enzo glanced up, but then looked back down at his paperwork. He shifted a finished file to the left stack and opened the next. "You're not going to your parents' house," he said brusquely.

The only sound in the office was the scrape of his pen across paper.

I took a deep breath. *Don't overreact. Not yet.*

I tried again. "I'm really worn out and need some time alone, so I'd rather not go to the villa for dinner. If that's okay? If you could just drop me off at home instead?"

This time he didn't look up. "We don't have to have dinner with them. I'll make something for just the two of us, and we'll eat it in my suite."

I've always found it especially jarring when my heart raced in a calm atmosphere. It was as if being out of sync with the energy in the environment added to the hysteria of the moment.

I licked my dry lips as I dug my thumbnail into the thick varnish of the desk, wondering if my nail would leave a scratch mark. "You're supposed to take me home at the end of the day. We had a deal."

"I lied."

No remorse. No explanation. No groveling. No apology. Just a simple, blunt statement of fact.

My heart raced so fast it was now skipping beats, as if it were tripping over itself.

In my mind's eye, I saw my heart as a battered and bruised object running down a hillside before stumbling and then just free-falling into nothingness. One of the pitfalls of an artist's imagination.

He grabbed the stack of files and tapped the edges of them against the desk to align them before slamming them down.

I jumped at the sudden, loud *thwack*.

I raised my gaze to his and shrugged. "So that's it? You lied?"

Enzo circled around to the front of the desk. He curled a firm hand around my neck and pulled me close. "Don't do this now, Bianca."

I stared at his lips. "Do what?"

He leaned down and grazed my lips with his. His warm breath scorched my lips. "Pretend you thought, for even one moment, I was actually going to let you leave my side."

My eyelids drifted half closed as if weighted down.

He wasn't wrong.

I knew, deep down, he wasn't going to take me back to my parents' house.

It didn't mean I had to accept it. "You promised," I said in a calm, even tone, almost as if in a trance.

He nipped my bottom lip with his teeth. "I'll make it up to you, but first I have to drop these off at marketing and have a final word with Cesare and then we can leave." He pulled away. "I'll be right back."

I didn't move for several seconds.

I just stared at the dark void visible through the open threshold he had just exited.

I then calmly crossed to the closet and put on my coat.

After placing my purse on my forearm, I reached into Enzo's inner coat pocket and palmed his Ferrari car keys.

CHAPTER 26

ENZO

"*I*s that your car?"

Cesare's question brought me up short.

I was halfway out of his office, anxious to get back to Bianca.

With his question, I turned on my heel and headed back inside to gaze out his windows which had a view of the side of our building at the corner of the piazza.

My Ferrari was pulling out of its reserved parking spot. Although from my vantage point I couldn't tell who was behind the wheel, I had a good idea. "Goddammit," I cursed as I rushed toward the door.

I called out to Cesare, "I need your—"

Before I could finish my sentence, he tossed me his car keys. "Here. I'll catch a ride with Papà."

I stretched up my arm and caught the keys midair without breaking stride as I raced out of the office and down the hall.

"Don't scratch my baby!" he called out to my retreating back.

I took the back stairs two at a time. I then shoved at the heavy metal door which led to the alley.

She had a lead on me, but she probably went out through the front office.

This back way shaved off several minutes.

Getting behind the wheel of Cesare's Alfa Romeo Giulia Quadrifoglio, I threw it into gear and pulled out into the lane.

I only caught a glimpse of the Ferrari as it made a right several streets up.

By the time I made my way through the winding, congested street, she was nowhere to be found. I went up a street, reversed and tried another, reversed again, and tried a third before I caught a glimpse of her.

She was headed out of town, curiously, toward the villa.

Soon she would be on one of the more open roads where there would be less traffic and I would be able to gain ground.

The Ferrari swerved, barely missing a roasted chestnut cart before swerving back in the other direction, clipping the right fender on an old metal horse post.

I hissed air through my teeth and gripped the steering wheel harder as Bianca had another near miss with the corner of a building as she navigated a tight turn.

I wasn't worried so much about my car as I was about her.

I loved the woman, but she had always been a terrible driver.

It was one of the reasons why I was relieved she had settled in New York when she left for school in America.

It was well known that very few people drove in New

York. Even the wealthy chose to use public transportation or car services because of the insane traffic and limited space for vehicles. I had already been driven to distraction worried about her every minute of the day.

I didn't think I would have survived the ordeal if I'd had to worry about her behind the wheel of a car as well.

I lost sight of her around a corner as she turned down a narrow cobblestone street but picked up her trail again as the lane cleared. The Ferrari picked up speed.

We were on one of the roads which would lead to the northern portion of the Cavalieri lands.

The Ferrari passed one car, then another, picking up speed as it swerved in and out of the remaining traffic.

I shifted gears and pressed down the gas pedal as I followed suit.

She was driving dangerously fast. Too fast.

These roads were not well maintained. They were marred by loose gravel and holes, not to mention the occasional blind corner and slow-moving farm vehicle. Bianca knew better.

My mobile phone rang. Fortunately, I drove Cesare's car enough that my phone immediately synced with his console. I answered. "Pull over," I growled.

"Stop following me," she fired back.

As we drove deeper into the Abruzzo countryside, we left the rest of the cars behind. I was now directly behind her. Despite the darkness, I could see she was holding the phone to her ear, which meant she didn't have both hands safely on the wheel.

"Put the damn phone down and pull over."

Her silhouette turned to look behind her. The moment she

did, the Ferrari fishtailed. She turned back and got control of the vehicle.

"Stop the fucking car!"

She must have placed the phone on speaker and tossed it onto the passenger seat because I could hear her speak, but she sounded slightly far off. "Stop tailing me!"

"You stole my car!"

"I'll give it back. I just want to be alone."

She raced around another corner. The back end of the car pitched to the left as she took the turn at high speed.

"Dammit, woman. I swear to God if you don't pull that fucking car over this minute—"

"You'll what, Enzo? Dump me? Break my heart? Punish me? Lie to me? Kidnap me?"

As she ranted, the car picked up speed. She hit a patch of loose dirt and the car shimmied, kicking up a massive dust cloud, obscuring my vision. I was forced to tap the brakes, for fear of rear-ending her.

Seeing her taillights a safe distance ahead, I sped up.

We raced past the turnoff to the villa. The road narrowed as we headed higher up into the Apennine mountains. The tree cover became thicker as the vineyard and farmland receded. Sharp, jagged walls of gray rock were on the left where the road had been blasted into the mountain by dynamite generations ago.

On the right was a steep drop to the valley below.

Christ.

"Baby, please. Listen to me. Please, babygirl. Pull the car over. This isn't safe."

"Just stop following me!"

Another car appeared out of the gloom on the left and laid on its horn as the two cars passed within inches of one another without sideswiping.

Bianca jerked the wheel to the right and overcorrected. Her tires came dangerously close to the edge of the cliff.

My heart leapt into my throat as I watched the gravel kick up and then fall into nothingness as a high-pitched screech rent the air from the rubber of her tires scraping along the tarmac.

Horn still blaring, the other car passed me as Bianca moved the Ferrari back onto the road.

The air returned to my lungs in a rush so profound I felt light-headed.

Fuck.

If I stopped following her, she could still get into an accident the way she was driving.

If I continued to follow her, she would just get more agitated, guaranteeing she would get into an accident.

I needed to put a stop to this. Now.

I knew these roads like the back of my hand.

In another two turns there was a small clearing. It was near an Etruscan watchtower ruin.

It would be my only opportunity to put a stop to this madness.

I gave her one last chance. "Baby? Are you still there? Please, pull over. Let's talk."

"Leave me alone, Enzo!"

The line went dead.

"Fuck!" I pounded my fist against the center of the steering wheel.

I backed off and gave her space.

I watched helplessly as she took the next turn at a near catastrophic speed.

One more turn to go.

I tightened my grip on the steering wheel.

Despite my staying back, she entered the final turn at a dangerous rate of speed. The car understeered and drifted too far to the outside of the turn. The back end of the car would have pivoted and continued to drift, pulling her over the edge, if she hadn't swerved directly into a tree.

There was the deafening crunch of metal against wood as the back passenger side of the Ferrari connected with the thick, gnarled, ancient trunk of a beech tree. The metal groaned and crunched as Bianca revved the engine, sending the car lurching forward, dislodging it from the trunk's grip.

Sweat broke out on my brow as I watched her roll back onto the road as if she hadn't just cheated death.

When I got my hands on her, I would see to it she never, ever got behind a wheel ever again for the rest of her life. I would have it written into our marriage vows.

She also wasn't going to be able to sit for a week when I got done whipping her ass with my belt.

Finally, the clearing appeared ahead.

It was beyond time to put a stop to this.

I shifted to the left lane and slammed down on the accelerator. Pulling up alongside the back quarter panel on the driver's side of the Ferrari I banked right. Sharply turning the steering wheel, I slammed the front of my car into the side of hers.

The force of my strike sent her car spinning toward the

left and back in a full one eighty until she was facing the wrong way. I turned my car into the force of her turn, until our cars were side by side, spinning in a yin-yang circle.

Bianca stared at me in shock through the driver's window as she unsuccessfully tried to break the spiral.

Our cars spun around and around in a macabre dance, crashing off the road and through some underbrush until they finally came to a stop only a few feet from one another at the base of the Etruscan ruin.

Wrenching open my car door, I stormed over to her car.

I pulled on the door handle.

Locked.

She stared at me through the window. Eyes wide with terror.

I pounded my fist on the window. "Open this door," I raged.

My blood boiled in my veins. How dare she fucking risk her life like this.

Even seeing her safely stopped was not enough for me.

I needed to have her in my arms.

I needed to touch the warmth of her skin, to feel her heartbeat, to hear her breath to reassure my fevered brain that she was alive and safe. I had never been so fucking scared in my entire life. I didn't think I would ever recover from the sight of her car skidding off the road and almost sliding off the edge of the cliff. I would see that image in my nightmares for years to come.

She shook her head and twisted the key in the ignition. The engine turned over several times, sputtered and then stalled. As I knew it would. She turned the key again. This time the car didn't even turn over.

I pulled on the door handle again. "I'm warning you. Open the fucking door, Bianca."

Her lips thinned. She crossed her arms and stared straight ahead.

I searched the ground, kicking at the dried, fallen leaves. Finding what I was looking for, I picked up the sharp rock, crossed to the car and raised my arm high.

I heard Bianca's muffled scream as she threw her arm over her head, covered her face, and hunched over the center console.

I smashed the window.

It splintered into a green translucent spiderweb of fractured cracks radiating from the hole caused by the jagged point of the rock. Knowing the uneven glass fragments would have blunt edges for safety, I reached my arm through the space caused by the point of impact and unlocked the door. I wrenched it open and reached for her.

Bianca screamed as I pulled her out of the car by the lapels of her coat.

She straightened her arms and pushed at my chest as she leaned back and swung her head from left to right. "No! Let me go!"

I fisted her hair at the back of her skull and pulled her upright at the same time I pivoted to the left, slamming her against the side of the car, pinning her there with the force of my body.

I grabbed her jaw with my free hand. "Stop struggling," I gritted out.

She breathed heavily through her clenched teeth as her gaze traveled wildly over my face.

The temperature had dropped dramatically. There was a cloud of gray, frozen air between us with each excited exhale, the stillness of the mountain forest settling on us like a wet, heavy blanket.

My brow furrowed. "Why would you do something so foolish?"

She refused to answer.

I tightened my grasp on her jaw. "Dammit, answer me. Why would you risk your life like this? You could have died! I could have..." I swallowed the sickening bile which rose in the back of my throat. "I could have lost you," I shouted, unable to control my fear-fueled anger.

She struggled in my grasp. Wedging her forearms between our crushed bodies in an attempt to dislodge me. "I'm not yours to lose! I'm not yours!"

Her denial echoed off the cut rock face behind us, like a demoralizing Roman chorus.

I pressed my hips into hers. "Don't say that. Don't you ever fucking say that."

She threw back her head and screamed so loud the very trees seemed to tremble and shake with her denial. "I'm not yours!"

I slammed my mouth down on hers.

Her body twisted and kicked, but I held firm, forcing my tongue past her lips as I kept a grip on her jaw, pressing my fingers into her cheeks to prevent her from biting down.

It was a kiss. It was a show of ownership. A branding.

She pounded her small fists against my shoulders, but I refused to relent.

I tasted it all.

Her desperation.

Her anger.

Her fear.

Her love.

Her hatred.

I only softened the kiss when she ceased to fight me, submitting to me.

The moment I released her mouth, she leaned her forehead against my shoulder and let out a long, keening wail. She gripped the lapels of my suit jacket. "Please, Enzo. Please, I'm begging you. Please, I can't do this anymore."

She tilted her head back and stared up at me with tear-filled eyes.

"Please, just let me leave."

CHAPTER 27

BIANCA

*H*e was a poisoned wine I was slowly killing myself with…sip by sip.

A delicious dark pain, like the sick pleasure you got from pressing on a bruise.

I had twisted and tangled myself in the chains that now bound me to him.

And I knew if I didn't break free now, at this very minute, there would be no hope.

I could feel each link pressing against my flesh, tightening around me.

Choking me.

Killing off parts of my soul.

Piece by piece.

My independence.

My freedom.

My sense of self.

I could hear the entire *Little Earthquakes* album by Tori

Amos playing in my head. It was the soundtrack to my breakup with him. My pain, confusion, and insecurities put to music.

I could feel myself falling back into that terrifying place again, where I would have done anything, said anything, been anything he wanted... just to get him back... just to get him to choose me.

Rocking back and forth as I listen to "Tear in Your Hand" over and over and over again while I clutch an old sweater of his that still smells of his cologne to my chest.

His gravitational force was too great. He was a dark star pulling in everything around him. He was right, what he had said in the church, I *was* drawn to his intoxicating darkness, to his energy. Drawn to the poetic idea of the tarnished, honorable man, the noble enemy, the tortured romantic hero.

I was falling for it. Head over heels. Again.

There were moments when I fought it, but those moments were becoming fewer and farther between.

And wouldn't that just be a fitting end to our fucked-up fairy tale?

The evil mother and wicked sister getting their comeuppance and the discarded princess and the prince reuniting and living happily ever after?

Except this wasn't some story in a book, this was my *life*.

It had taken me months to claw back my sense of self, my self-respect, my self-worth.

The lonely nights I'd spent gripping an empty wineglass, screaming the final lyrics to the song "Little Earthquakes" at the top of my lungs until the neighbors banged on the walls. Give me... Give me... Give me...

And I wasn't ready to toss it all out for a man, especially one who had hurt me so badly.

He was literally under investigation for the murder of my sister, and it wasn't stopping him from trying to manipulate me into marrying him, by getting me pregnant no less. The very same unforgivable trick my family played on him.

Why was what they had done evil, and what he was doing righteous?

Because they were motivated by money and he was motivated by what? Love?

But was it love?

He caressed my cheeks as he stared intently into my eyes. "You don't mean that. You're just overwrought because of the inspector's visit. You don't need to worry about the investigation. I'm handling it."

Hysterical laughter bubbled up in my throat. "How could I get upset about something I know nothing about?"

He bared his teeth. "Is that what this bullshit is about? Jesus fucking Christ, Bianca. Did you pull this dangerous stunt, *risk your life*, because you're angry I sent you out of the room when the inspector arrived?"

I stayed silent. Let him think that was why.

Let him think this was all just a petulant tantrum. It was safer than the truth.

He pivoted away several steps, running a hand through his hair. He turned back to me. Raised his hand and curled his fingers into a fist, before turning his back on me again. He paced a few steps away, then turned and marched violently back toward me.

He raised his fist and slammed it down on the hood of the

Ferrari so hard he dented it. As he did so, he let out a primal roar, like an anguished beast.

I screamed and ran.

The terrifying, pounding piano cadence of "Precious Things" drummed in my head as I pitched headlong through the forest.

Running in a jagged line between the trees, I headed toward a massive, circular stone structure. It was covered in burnt umber and amber ivy leaves with clusters of dark berries clinging to the ancient ruins like a cloak.

Enzo pursued me, loudly crashing through the underbrush.

My smaller frame gave me the advantage as I easily ducked under bare, low-hanging branches without having to slow my pace.

The heel on one of my shoes snapped just as I reached the tower. Trying to catch my breath, I braced my palm against the worn brown limestone bricks and bent to examine the damage.

And Enzo caught up with me.

He wrapped his hand around my shoulder and pressed my back against the tower wall.

He placed his forearm over my head and leaned over me.

Without preamble he ground out, "We don't know the names of everyone involved so everyone is a suspect, including that inspector. Whether you like it or not, I am not able to tell you the full truth about what is happening. Milana only knows a portion of the truth and it made her a target. She came very close to dying. Your sister knew the full truth and she was brutally killed. So if you think, for one second, that I am going to take that risk with your life, a life that is more precious to me than my own, you are out of your goddamn mind. And I don't give a fuck how pissed you get about it."

This was it.

This was my lifeline.

My out.

If I didn't take it, I would truly be lost.

I placed my hands on his chest, tucking my fingers inside his suit jacket to feel the warmth of his skin through his linen shirt. It was amazing how he managed to radiate so much heat despite the chill in the air, even without a coat on. Everything about him was just so big and powerful.

For a moment, I almost lost my nerve, but I knew I needed to be strong.

I survived losing him once.

I would survive it again. Maybe.

Staring at the knot in his tie, I blurted out, "Send me back to New York."

"What?"

Still refusing to meet his gaze, I rushed on, tripping over my words. "You could lend me the money. You have the connections to get me a new passport. Send me back to New York. We don't need to marry for me to be protected. I could just leave the country like I did before. I could go back to school, back to my life there."

My new anthem song, Tori Amos' "Girl."

It wasn't a particularly happy life without him, but it was a life… and it was simple and uncomplicated and my own. And maybe one day I would meet someone who would help me forget all about Enzo Cavalieri.

People moved on from their first loves all the time. They married and had children and lived fulfilling lives with kind, decent partners. They chose stability over drama and chaos and heartache.

He cupped the back of my head and pressed the side of my face to his heart.

I held my breath so long I thought my lungs would burst.

Over the steady thump of his heart, I heard the rustling of small creatures in the dried leaves as they scurried about the forest floor around us and the forlorn sound of the wind as it whistled through the gaps in the ancient bricks of the tower.

It was hard not to feel the spiritual presence of generations of violent power struggles which took place on this very blood-soaked spot. I guessed it was fitting that I was fighting for my very survival here as well.

His chest expanded as he took a deep breath before responding. "I'm sorry, *tesoro mio*. The answer is no. We will get married as planned."

My knees buckled. I would have collapsed to the ground if he had not pressed his body against mine, pinning me to the tower wall.

How could I make him understand?

That to me, *he* was the real danger.

I clawed at his shirt. "Don't do this to me, Enzo. Please. If you love me, let me go. I can't be yours. Can't you see that? You'll swallow me whole." I pounded my chest with my fist. "There will be nothing left of me."

He lifted his head and turned away, avoiding my gaze.

I placed my hands on his cheeks and turned his head back to face me as I rose on my toes. "Enzo! Look at me."

He stared down at me. His eyes cold emerald shards.

My hands shook as I pressed my palms to his jaw. "You win. Okay? You win. *I love you.* I've always loved you. But I can't *be* with you. Things get too dark... too twisted... too fucked up. Love shouldn't be this hard."

I pressed the top of my head against his chest and held back a sob as I clung to his suit jacket. "Love is supposed to be holding hands and going to the movies and having silly fights over dirty dishes in the sink."

I looked up at his sharp, angular features. His mouth was set in a hard line. His brow lowered. There was a slight tic in his upper cheek as he stared silently down at me. He could have easily been a Roman centurion come to life, standing at the ready, just waiting for the command to strike a spear through my heart.

With his rigid expression, I couldn't tell if I was getting through to him or not. I continued to plead, as if I were a prisoner kneeling on the gallows begging for their life to be spared. "Love isn't murder plots and punishing sex in churches and secrets and lies and forced marriage and endless fights. Everything about us is toxic and messy and complicated."

Now it's "China", the most heartbreaking song of all.

Drained, I fell against the cold bricks, dropping my arms to my sides.

I leaned my head back and squeezed my eyes shut as the tears fell. "Can't you see? The universe is telling us... *begging us...* to run far away from each other, for our own salvation."

My voice was hoarse from the cold air and my desperate

pleading. I could only rasp my final entreaty. "Love isn't always enough. Some things just aren't meant to be."

At first there was just silence.

Then....

My only warning was the crackling crunch of a dead leaf under his shoe.

CHAPTER 28

ENZO

The deep, dark primeval woods were a fit setting.

All I could hear was a pounding battle cry with every beat of my heart.

With each denial she made, a piece of my humanity was ripped from my flesh until all that was left was blood, bone, and sinew.

I was no longer a man.

I was a beast.

A savage force intent on one thing and one thing only... claiming my mate.

Spearing my fingers into her hair, I yanked her body against mine as I pulled her head back.

"You don't mean that, I would lose all hope. There would be no point in taking my next breath, knowing you were in the arms of another man suffering through such a pathetic, vapid excuse of an existence."

Her already bruised lips fell open on a cry, but I didn't want her mouth.

My gaze fell to her pale, vulnerable neck. I could see her rapid pulse, the fluttering of a bird's wing as it beat against a cage.

"You, my sweet, innocent dark angel, were not meant to be loved on such weak terms."

My lips pressed against her skin. I needed to feel the vibrations of her pounding heart. I imagined I could almost smell her fear. I dragged my teeth up the column of her neck, over her jaw, scraping her skin, marking her.

"Real love. True love. Is not fit for poetry. It is vicious and ugly. It is a jealous, possessive, spiteful beast that claws and tears at your insides when separated from its other half. I should know."

I tore at her cashmere wool coat, wrenching it off her shoulders, pinning her arms to her sides.

I pushed her back, slamming her against the brick wall, following with my body. "It is ever wakeful and relentlessly ravenous, waiting for the moment when it will be made whole again."

Fisting the collar of her black silk blouse, I ripped it almost in half, sending buttons scattering, exposing the thin lace chemise she wore underneath. I palmed her breast through the silk while I sank my teeth into the soft flesh of her neck.

She cried out as she twisted her torso and arched her back trying to escape me. "Enzo, stop! You're hurting me."

I ran my tongue over the crescent moon bite mark. "Good,

I want to hurt you. I want to scar you. To ruin you for any other man." I grabbed her face and searched the beautiful terror in her eyes. "I want to break and wound you, so that you have no other option but to curl up in my lap and let me hold you for eternity."

She gasped. "You're mad."

I ran my thumbs over the fresh tears that spilled from her eyes. "Of course I am. That's what happens to a man when he is separated from the woman he knows, deep in his heart, in the very marrow of his bones, that he was put on this earth to love and cherish and protect.

He spends his days in tortured misery thinking about her and his nights howling at the moon like a beast searching for its mate."

I fell on her mouth, thrusting my tongue inside, tasting her horror and confusion. Relishing the soft feel of her face between my hands and her body crushed against mine.

She wrenched free.

Yanking up her coat, she stumbled several feet away as she scrambled along the ancient wall, all the while keeping her wide and frightened gaze on me. "It was *you* who cast me aside. It was *you* who decided that your family name and honor were worth more than the undying love you are professing now. And you want me to sacrifice *everything*... my independence, my career, my freedom... *everything*... for you now? You, who wouldn't sacrifice your *precious* reputation for me? *Vaffanculo!*"

I pulled on the Windsor knot securing my tie.

Yanking it free from my collar, I twisted the expensive silk between my fists as I slowly stalked her. "I am tiring of this argument, Bianca. I made a mistake. I admit it, but I'll be goddamned if I'll let that stand between us now. You're mine. And it's past time we moved forward with the future we were both denied."

She scurried around the wall to the interior of the ruin, placing a large stone altar-looking structure between us. She slammed her palms on its worn, pockmarked marble surface. "That's what I've been desperately trying to tell you since I returned to Italy. *I no longer want that future with you.* I don't want to marry you. I don't want to carry your child. It's too much, Enzo. All of it. *You're* too much."

Each word was like a body blow.

My vision blurred in a smoky haze of red smoke, as if I were viewing her from the middle of a stormy battlefield. '

That was what this felt like, like I was battling for my life, for my soul, for my love. I knew without a doubt if I lost this fight with her, this battle, then I would lose the war.

For there was no life for me without her.

I knew that with absolute clarity.

She was my everything.

My brother's words came back to me.

See the hurt not the hate.

Focus on the hurt.

Focus on us.

At my silence, she let out a resigned sigh and turned her back on me. She had only taken a few steps toward a jagged opening in the tower wall caused by several collapsed rocks when I said, soft and low, "I'll kill him."

She turned her head but kept her back to me. "What?"

I took several steps toward her. "I *will* kill him," I repeated more decisively.

She slowly turned to face me, a crease between her brows. "Kill who?"

I cocked my head to the side as I gazed at her. With absolutely no remorse, I said calmly, "Whoever dares to take my place."

She shook her head. "I told you, that was a lie. There is no one."

"No, but eventually there will be. You're too talented and beautiful and smart. Eventually there will be. And when there is… I'll kill him."

Her mouth opened and closed several times before she finally said, "You're not serious. You're just saying this to scare me."

I stepped closer. She was so stunned by my admission, she didn't think to move out of my reach. I caressed her cheek with the backs of my knuckles. "I don't make idle threats. I have the money, power, and resources. Any man who dares to even look at you. I'll kill him. And the next one and the one after that."

She swallowed and shook her head rigidly from side to side. "No. You didn't kill my sister. I know you didn't. You said so and I believe you. You're not capable of murder."

I cupped her cheek as the side of my thumb rubbed her lower lip. "I said I didn't kill your sister. I never said I wasn't capable of murder."

She stumbled backward. Her steps uneven on her broken heel.

I followed until I had her cornered against the wall. I lifted my arms, caging her in.

She lowered her head. Her voice was barely above a whisper. "Don't you want me to be happy, Enzo?"

I curved a finger under her chin and raised her face to capture her gaze. I leaned down and kissed her forehead. Closing my eyes as I inhaled the familiar scent of her perfume. "My precious babygirl, I want that more than anything on this earth."

"Then why are you doing this?"

I slipped my hands inside her coat and slid it off her shoulders and down her arms. Catching it before it fell to the ground, I spread it out on a pile of dried leaves and moss to the right of where we were standing. I then reached for the few buttons that remained on her black silk blouse. One by one I undid them. She watched me as if in a trance.

Keeping a watchful eye on her reaction, I said, "I wish things could be different. I wish I could tell you I loved you enough to let you go if I had to...."

I slipped the blouse off her shoulders and let it fall to the forest floor, leaving her in only the black lace chemise and skirt. I then knelt before her. Caressing the back of her calf, I lifted her leg and slipped the broken heel off her foot. "And that I was deeply sorry for the part I played in hurting you."

I took off her other shoe and rose. "And that I hoped you would give me a second chance. And that I would wait until you were ready, for however long it took, for us to get married and start a family, on your terms."

I wrapped my arm around her waist. "I wish I could tell you that if you couldn't find it in your heart to forgive me, that I hoped you could find love and happiness with another man who knew how amazingly wonderful and beautiful and sweet and kind and passionate and creative and talented you are." I lowered the back zipper to her skirt.

It was at that moment she seemed to come out of her stupor.

She reached behind her and raised the zipper. "I would wish all those things for you too, Enzo. I would want you to be happy as well."

I lowered the zipper again. "You're not listening, *tesoro mio*. I said I *wished* I could tell you those things. I *wish* I was the type of man who would want those things for you."

She raised the zipper. "I don't understand."

I forced the zipper down.

This time tearing the fabric.

Before she could react, I pushed the skirt off her hips.

I placed my hands on her narrow waist and lifted her off the ground.

I spun to the right and placed her bare feet on her splayed coat. Releasing her, I watched her intently as I shrugged out of my suit jacket and tossed it over the marble altar. I then undid the first few buttons of my dress shirt before reaching to untuck it.

"The problem is, babygirl, I'm not that kind of man. I'm an arrogant, selfish bastard. I'm a Cavalieri."

I pulled my shirt off and tossed it aside, before reaching for my belt buckle. "And you were right, my family's name and reputation are extremely important to me. Like our reputation for claiming what we want and not letting anything—or anyone—stand in our way."

Despite her lack of clothing, she turned to run.

I caught her from behind.

With my arm securely around her waist, I used my free hand to pull off my belt.

I wrapped the soft leather around her throat and threaded the end through the metal buckle loop.

She was lucky I was wearing a suit today and not my usual denim or this would be my much thicker, heavier leather belt.

I pulled it just tight enough to subdue her struggles.

She reached up to pull the strap away from her neck.

I rasped against her ear, "Letting you walk out of my life is not a mistake I plan to make twice."

Keeping one hand on the belt, I shoved my other hand between her thighs. I pushed my two center fingers between her pussy lips. I wasn't the least bit surprised to feel that she was already wet. I knew my girl even better than she knew herself.

"Enzo, don't you dare!"

I chuckled. "Too late, baby."

I pushed my fingers inside of her. "Remember what I said last night about obeying my rules? I warned you what would happen if you tried to leave me again."

She rose on her toes. Her back arched and her head pushed onto my shoulder as she moaned.

I kept her in place with my grip on the belt around her throat.

Keeping her small frame bowed before me, I played her like a treasured instrument. Pushing my fingers in and out of her tight hole with perfect rhythmic timing, tuned to her body's every tremor.

As her breathing increased and became more erratic, I tightened the belt around her throat and increased the pace and pressure of my hand, driving it more forcefully into her sweet cunt.

Both her arms reached up to clasp the belt around her throat as her body arched and swayed on the tips of her toes, unbalanced, relying on the strength of my arms to keep her upright. I knew the chokehold on her throat and the precarious position of her body would only add to the weightless, lightheaded feeling she was experiencing from my touch on her clit.

Her body jerked in my grasp.

She was close. So close.

I pulled on the belt, cutting off her air as I rammed a third finger deep inside of her, knowing it would increase the powerful intensity of her release by adding a tantalizing shadow of death to her *little death*.

Her body spasmed with her orgasm.

I loosened the belt, allowing oxygen to flood back into her lungs.

Her chest expanded as she sucked in air.

With the belt still dangling from her neck, I turned her around.

Wrapping my hands around the backs of her thighs, I spread her legs and lifted her high, forcing her to straddle my hips.

I placed one arm under her ass and the other across her back as I fell to my knees onto her splayed coat. I then laid her onto the ground, covering her with my weight, pushing my hips into her core.

Her eyes were dazed and unfocused, shimmering with unshed tears.

She weakly reached up to press against my chest with her palms.

I leaned down and pulled one erect nipple into my mouth, swirling my tongue around the sensitive tip.

Bianca rolled her head to the side and moaned.

I flicked my tongue back and forth before gently biting the nub. I drew back and laved at the areole before pursing my lips and blowing on it. "What's the matter, baby? Didn't you like coming for me?"

She kept her face averted and her eyes closed as she whimpered, "It's not right."

I moved to her other nipple and flicked it with my tongue. "It felt right to me. You were so nice and wet. You moaned so sweetly as I stretched your pussy with my fingers."

Her brow furrowed. "No. It's wrong. You're twisting things. I shouldn't want this."

I breathed against her flesh. "Want what baby? The darkness? The pain? Me?" I bit down on her nipple.

Her eyes flew open as she cried out. She tried to shimmy out from under me, but I had her pinned. I latched onto her nipple. As she squirmed, I sucked harder. Her hips bucked.

As I released her, I pushed my hand between our bodies and pressed the heel of my palm against her pussy. "Admit you want this. Admit I'm the only man for you."

I was absolutely certain she loved me as I loved her.

We were meant for one another, and I would be damned if I let our past define our future.

She was scared and confused and hurt and overwhelmed.

It was why she wanted to run from me.

From us.

I wasn't going to let her.

And if there had been time to allow for all those emotions to play out, I would have given it to her.

But there wasn't.

I needed her to have the protection of my name. Now.

The whole village knew Renata was my wife in name only, and that it had been a sham marriage.

It was why the third man dared to kill her.

I would make sure they damn well knew differently with Bianca.

No one would dare touch her.

If they did, they died.

I looked down at her. Christ, she was beautiful when she was in thrall. It was like watching pleasure personified. It was almost too gratuitous, like watching a heavenly angel get off.

Bianca moaned as she rolled her head back and forth and refused to speak.

Having enough of her refusal to submit, I sat up and shifted to the side. I grabbed her ankles and lifted her legs high into the air, securing them with one hand. Pulling my arm back, I smacked her bare ass with my open palm.

Bianca screamed.

She bent her knees and tried to dislodge my grip, to no avail. "Stop! It hurts!"

I ruthlessly spanked her ass and the backs of her thighs over and over again. Her sensitive skin turned a beautiful, bright pink.

Her small fists beat at my back and shoulders as she leaned

up and tried to stop the relentless punishment. "Please! No more!"

From her vulnerable position with her legs in the air, there was nothing she could do.

I paused with my arm in midair. "Do you want me to stop?"

She sniffed. "Yes."

"Then I want the truth."

"Haven't you done enough? Please don't make me say it."

The beast in me wanted to press forward.

It wanted to toss her onto all fours and fuck her from behind. It wanted to feel the burn of her punished skin with each thrust. It wanted to hear her screams. It wanted to give in to the animalistic pleasures the setting inspired.

But the sanity of the man was returning.

It didn't mean I would settle for less than her complete submission.

I slowly lowered her legs.

She immediately turned onto her side. I curled my body behind her, resting her head on my forearm as I pulled her into my embrace.

Closing my eyes and stifling a groan of pure pleasure as I was rewarded with the hot press of her punished skin against the tops of my thighs.

I reached down and lowered the zipper to my trousers. I pulled out my shaft and fisted it. "You know what is going to happen next?"

She slowly nodded.

I placed the head of my cock at her entrance. It was slick with her arousal.

I pushed into her tight heat and kissed the top of her head, as I tightened my hold on her.

We both knew what this meant.

I thrust harder, anticipating the moment I would release my seed deep inside her womb.

There was no turning back now.

CHAPTER 29

BIANCA

*H*e pressed in deep.
Filling me.

Possessing me.

Taking over.

I closed my eyes. Warm tears stung my wind-chapped cheeks.

There would be no chance of escape for me now. I wasn't sure if there had ever really been one.

With each thrust, I could feel him not only driving deeper into my body, but deeper into my mind, my thoughts, my heart. I could imagine the in sync pounding of our hearts as the beating of a hammer against a blacksmith's forge hammering the links of the chains that now irretrievably bound me to Enzo.

He was too powerful.

And I didn't mean his money or his influence or his family.

I meant him.

There was something deeply sick and twisted about wanting to run to the protection of your tormentor's arms. I was like a moth drawn to a shimmering light, captivated by its radiant beauty, despite knowing that death lingered behind its warm glow.

I couldn't help myself.

I loved him. I loved him so much it hurt.

I loved him beyond reason or rational thought.

He was no good for me.

I knew I could do better.

I could find a kinder, gentler man, one who would treat me well and give me a normal, stable life. Someone who was easier, simpler to love.

But I would never find someone who *consumed* me like Enzo.

I yearned for him.

I accused him of being mad, but it was only because I recognized the same madness in myself.

There were times where I just wanted to spread open his ribcage and crawl inside of him.

That wasn't normal thinking!

The only place I'd ever felt truly safe was in his arms.

When he enclosed me in his embrace...when those big strong arms wrapped around me and I rested my head against his chest and listened to his heartbeat...it was like I ceased to exist.

My mind regressed to a primal state where all that mattered was my complete submission to his will.

And that is why I'm desperately trying to run as far away from him as possible.

A love like that wasn't healthy.

It wasn't sustainable. It burned too hot, too bright, until there was nothing left of the person but ash.

He tightened his arms around me as he grasped my right thigh and shifted it high. He then leaned his hips in, deepening his thrusts.

I cried out as my hand fisted the silk lining of my borrowed coat. "Oh God!"

He slipped his arm out from under my head and propped his forearm just above my head.

He was now prowling over me, caging me in, like an animal standing over its latest trophy capture.

He slammed into me harder, quickening his thrusts. "That's it, babygirl. Take my cock," he growled.

I reached back and clasped my ass just under the cheek where it met my upper thigh and pulled it open, hoping it would ease the pressure on my pussy as his thick shaft pounded into me. "You're too big," I breathed. "It hurts."

He pulled out and sat back, taking me with him. He opened my legs and forced me to straddle his hips. His intense, dark green gaze captured mine. "Be a good girl and"—he slowly impaled me with his cock— "bite me again."

My eyes widened.

His hands spanned my hips as he violently thrust upward. He clenched his jaw and ground out, "Do it, Bianca. Bite me. Harder this time."

My heart raced. I licked my lips.

He lowered his brow as he bared his teeth and literally growled at me. "Now."

He thrust so hard and so painfully deep, I momentarily saw stars.

I grabbed his shoulders, leaned forward, and sank my teeth into his flesh, latching onto his neck, just above his collarbone. Deep.

Enzo's fingers squeezed my hips as he thrust several more times before throwing his head back and unleashing an almost unholy roar that sent the winter birds scattering from the bare tree branches above us.

He pressed his hand to the base of my skull, holding my mouth to his neck as I continued to bite him as he spasmed inside my body, filling me with his come.

I actually had to pry my teeth from his flesh, shocked to see the deep, crescent-shaped mark I had made. Breathless, I collapsed.

He gently lifted me up. Closing my legs, he curled me onto his lap and held me.

We stayed that way for I didn't know how long.

Finally, the darkness and chill forced us to move.

FIGHTS WERE LIKE STORMS.

Usually afterward there was this strange, weightless feeling, all the negative energy dissipating to leave the air clean and refreshed. A new beginning.

Unless that storm was a hurricane.

Then nothing felt clean and new afterward, just damaged and worn out.

We both stood.

Enzo gently unbuckled his belt that was still around my neck.

I had actually forgotten it was still there, having gotten used to the weight and feel of its restraint.

If that wasn't a scarily symbolic, screeching warning from the universe, I didn't know what was.

Enzo then retrieved my coat, brushed the dead leaves off it, and silently put it on me as if I were a child, lifting one arm then the other, then closing the front and buttoning it over my now wrinkled lace chemise. He knelt and lifted up my left foot, brushed off the dirt and put on my broken shoe. He broke the heel off the right one and put it on my other foot.

He then shrugged on his dress shirt, but didn't button it, and stuffed his tie into his trousers.

We faced each other awkwardly in the center of the watchtower ruin.

Without warning, I burst into tears.

Not cute little tears streaking down my cheeks.

Sobs.

I didn't even know why.

Well, I did know why, but I didn't.

I was just so overwhelmed and just so....

Enzo wrapped his hand around my neck and pulled me into his embrace. Enclosing his strong arms around me, he pressed my head against his chest, close to his heart.

He kissed the top of my head. "Don't cry, babygirl. I swear

to God, I will spend every waking moment of my life making sure you don't regret staying with me."

I sniffed, then grumbled, "It's not like you're giving me much of a choice."

His chest vibrated as he chuckled. "My vow stands."

"I'm scared," I whispered against his shirt.

I was scared of getting hurt again. Scared I wouldn't survive the pain. Scared I was making a mistake by staying. Scared I would be making a bigger mistake if I left. Scared of loving someone like him. Scared of the future. Scared of what people would say. Scared of the scandal. Scared of what my parents would do.

He squeezed me tighter. "I'm not." He leaned back, clasped his hands around my face and tilted my head back. "There is nothing to be scared of. I will never... ever... hurt you like that again, *tesoro mio*. From now on, it's you and me. Nothing is going to come between us, not your parents, not this bull-shit investigation, not what anyone thinks, nothing, because none of that matters. All that matters is us. Understood?"

I never doubted he would protect me from the world.

The problem was... who would protect me from him?

CHAPTER 30

ENZO

I could still feel the sting from her bite mark on my shoulder.

If I had my flask with me, I would splash it with alcohol to prolong the delicious ache.

There was something so darkly erotic about knowing my flesh bore the mark of my girl's mouth. If my life wasn't such a cocked-up mess right now, I'd head to Rome to get it tattooed over, just so every time I looked in the mirror, I would see the red crescent marks from her sharp teeth and remember this moment.

I raised my arm and ran the palm of my hand over the back of her head, smoothing her soft curls as I held her tight.

The damp night air had caused her usually wavy hair to tangle and curl into a sexy, tousled mess. I gently pulled a small twig free from her locks and tossed it aside. I then placed my coat over her shoulders.

She whimpered slightly.

I tightened my hold on her as I leaned down and kissed the top of her head. "Not much longer, baby." I rubbed her upper arms to keep her warm

We were waiting for Alfonso. Our little stunt had knocked both cars out of commission. Neither would start. Fortunately we were not that far from the villa.

After a few more minutes, I saw headlights through the forest gloom.

Alfonso rolled up in my father's Fiat 124 Spider Lusso. He pulled to the side and jumped out. Crossing behind the car, he pulled open the passenger side door.

I rose from the log where I had been sitting with Bianca tucked on my lap and carried her to the car. A warm blast of air hit my face as I bent down to place her on the seat. I was pleased Alfonso remembered my request to jack up the heat and turn on the leather heated seats.

Bianca opened her eyes briefly, but then closed them again.

I stroked her cheek. I hated her seeing this exhausted and worn out, knowing I was the cause.

I pulled on the seat belt strap and leaned over her to buckle it, then closed the car door as softly as I could.

I stared at Bianca through the car window. "If you could take her back to the villa, I'll—"

Alfonso interrupted me. "None of that." He popped the Fiat's trunk and handed me the keys. "I brought my tools. By the sound of it, I'll at least get Cesare's car running."

"I can't do that to you, Alfonso."

He waved me off. "Take care of your woman. It's a simple stall. It will only take me a few minutes and I'll be right behind you. Vito's working late at the winery if I can't get it running. He'll come get me."

I rubbed my eyes. "I owe you one."

He smirked. "Don't worry. I'll collect."

I patted him on the shoulder and circled around to the driver's side. We both knew he wouldn't.

Alfonso was good people.

He was like a second father to me and loyal to the family to a fault. Although none of us were under any illusion as to why he had stuck around all these years, refusing to leave despite the many offers he had received from our competitors.

It had nothing to do with my father's charm or his affection for Cesare and me.

And everything to do with my Aunt Gabriella.

After the hell I'd been through with Bianca, the man had my sympathy *and* empathy.

I CARRIED Bianca over the threshold to my suite of rooms and kicked the door shut behind me.

The living room area was piled high with neatly stacked boxes. The personal items I had requested be moved up here from my piazza house. The rest of my belongings would be put in storage.

I glanced around the room until my gaze fell on a small

bookcase centered under the arched window. I was pleased to see the most important item of all my belongings had been unpacked by the household staff, per my careful instructions.

On the three shelves, twenty leather-bound books with gilt lettering on the spines were lined up: landscapes volumes one through five, portraits volumes one through three, flowers, volumes one through six, and so on.

Holding Bianca close, I crossed the living space, through to the bedroom. I laid her on the bed and folded the top comforter over her shoulders before heading into the bathroom.

After running a bath, I returned to the bedroom.

Walking to the opposite side, I opened the door to the changing room, turned on the light and left the door open so I could hear Bianca if she called out. Relieved to be getting out of these clothes, I pulled off my wrinkled shirt and slipped out of my shoes and trousers.

Tossing on a silk robe, I tied the belt around my waist and crossed to the bed.

Bianca was curled up on the bed, clutching a pillow tightly. Her beautiful dark eyes were open, watching me.

I went down on my haunches before her. Using the tips of my fingers, I pushed her hair away from her face. "I'm running a bath."

She just stared at me.

My stomach tightened with worry.

Had I pushed her too far today?

After removing her broken shoes, I carefully pulled her up to a sitting position and gently set the pillow to the side.

Standing over her, I pulled my coat off her shoulders, then helped her out of her ruined jacket. I lifted her arms and pulled the lace chemise over her head.

She lowered her arms and crossed them over her breasts.

Sensing her vulnerability, I used the bed coverlet to gather her back into my arms and carried her into the bathroom. I had adjusted the lighting to the lowest setting, so there was only a soft glow. Letting the blanket fall away, I carefully lowered her into the freestanding, oblong black marble soaking tub.

I removed my robe and slipped in behind her, settling my legs on either side of her hips. I drew her back, so her shoulders rested against my chest.

I picked up the natural sponge from the nearby table. The hot, soapy bathwater gleamed on her skin in the room's soft light when I ran the sponge along her left arm and across her front, then down her right arm. I dipped it into the water again and repeated the motion the opposite way.

It had been close to an hour since she had said a word.

"Would you like me to wash your hair?"

She didn't respond.

I turned on the sterling silver spigot and lifted the hand shower. Careful to avoid her face and eyes, I directed the warm spray of water over her long, thick hair, soaking it. Setting the hand shower aside, I poured shampoo into the center of my palm and lathered it into a silky foam before spearing my fingers into her hair, massaging her scalp.

My cock stirred to life against the curve of her ass. I would never get enough of this woman.

It wasn't just that she was sexy as hell sitting in front of me in this tub, with the soft curve of her back glistening from the sparkling sheen of the soap. Even the simple, domestic act of washing her hair did it for me. It was something so intimate and pure. A genuine show of affection and care.

I hoped she let me wash her hair every day of our lives.

I wanted more moments like this.

Craved them.

She may not realize it now, but I couldn't wait to hold her hand and go to a movie. I looked forward to the day we fought over dirty dishes in the sink. I wanted that sweet, domestic bliss with her.

I wanted a married life with her.

I wanted chaotic mornings filled with messy kitchens, a barking dog, children late for school, and my beautiful wife standing in the middle of it all staring at me with love in her eyes, wanting it no other way.

I may have the money for a large house with a full live-in staff, but I'd never really felt comfortable with that lifestyle and my short marriage to Renata had proved it. I had been miserable in that large house on the piazza. I preferred life at the villa, where the small household staff had their own homes on the vineyard property and were more like family than employees.

My real dream was to rebuild the cottage. I had already started construction. Since it would be a simple design and we were headed into the winter season at the winery, I would have it built in a very short time. Then I would move Bianca in, and we would be happy.

She would be happy. I would make sure of it.

I lifted the hand shower and rinsed her hair.

She tilted her head back as the spray turned her hair into a silky black waterfall down her back.

I set the hand shower back in its cradle and wrapped my arms around her, pulling her against my chest.

She sighed. "Tell me the truth, Enzo."

Her voice was still a little hoarse from being exposed to the elements earlier.

I pressed my right cheek to the left side of her head. "Always, babygirl."

She lifted her hands and rested them on my crossed arms where I held her. "Do you honestly think it's possible for two people like us to have a happily ever after?"

I answered without hesitation. "Yes."

She twisted to look up at me. "Truly?"

I looked down at her. Her full lips were a dark pink, bruised from my harsh kisses. "I love you too much to accept anything less for you."

She turned back around.

I held her close. "You said the universe is telling us this won't work. I don't see it that way. Although the circumstances are tragic, I think the universe has given us a second chance, and I'll be damned if I'm going to waste it."

"I never really thought of it that way."

She was quiet for some time. Then she spoke again. "I just can't help *aspettare l'altro chiodo*. It just seems wrong. Like we stepped through to the other side of the mirror and will pay a price."

"It's been a long day. You're just tired."

I wanted to tell her that she was wrong, but I had just promised not to lie to her.

I lifted her out of the tub and dried her off. Raising her arms, I slipped one of my softest, thinnest cashmere sweaters over her head. It reached down to her knees. She wandered into the bedroom as I drained the tub.

When I entered the bedroom, I caught her looking at one of the leather-bound volumes from my bookcase. Her brow was furrowed. "Where did you get these?"

I stood silently.

She removed a second volume and flipped it open.

Then a third. And a fourth. A fifth. A sixth.

Tossing them on the floor in her haste to open the next book.

She held a seventh volume open and crossed to me. "Answer me, Enzo. How do you have these?" She shook her head. "I threw all these away."

I looked at the book of her carefully preserved sketch drawings. The volume she held was of her portraits. She had always been particularly good at portraits.

After Renata sprung her trap, things had unraveled very quickly.

Within days, my relationship with Bianca was over and two weeks later there were hints of Renata being pregnant.

Soon after, I learned Bianca was leaving for America.

She refused to see me and like a fucking idiot I respected her decision, but fortunately I'd had someone watching the house, which was how I'd found out she had thrown out all of her artwork before leaving. I collected every scrap of paper I could find and had them bound up in these cherished leather volumes.

I had often flipped through them over these last few months.

I took the book from her and carefully closed it before bending to pick up the books from the floor and return them to the shelves in order. "I retrieved them," I said simply.

"Why?"

I slid the last volume into place. "Because it was my fault you were throwing them away. I couldn't stand the thought of you destroying this part of yourself because of me. So I saved them."

She gestured toward the shelves. "You know, some of those sketches are really old and not very good."

I snatched her around the waist and spun her around as I lifted her high. "Bite your tongue, woman. Each one of those drawings is a masterpiece."

She wrapped her arms around my neck. "You're biased."

I kissed the tip of her nose. "Damn straight, I am."

She tilted her head to the side and stared at me.

I cocked one eyebrow up as I carried her to the bed and set her down in the center, pulling the blanket up to her chin. I then leaned over her. "What?"

Her lips quirked up in a smile. "I'm just trying to imagine the great Enzo Cavalieri digging through my garbage bins."

"I'm glad the thought amuses you. Get some sleep. I need to talk with Papà and Cesare. I'll be up later."

I kissed her on the forehead and crossed to the door.

Just as I turned off the light switch, Bianca's soft voice called out through the darkness. "Enzo?"

"Yes, babygirl?"

She sighed. "This was a really strange day."

I paused. "It was."

I could hear the hesitation in her voice. "I'm not sure how I feel about everything that happened."

It was too much to hope that I could decree that I loved her then fuck her senseless, and that would make everything final. "I know. Get some sleep. I'll be up soon."

CHAPTER 31

ENZO

I paused as I walked through the dark kitchen and lifted the cloth napkin covering a large wooden tray, knowing it covered fresh-baked fennel *taralli* left to cool by Rosa.

I looped several of the twisted breadstick snacks over my fingers and popped one in my mouth, before returning the cloth and continuing on my way to the armory.

As I bit into the still warm, crispy yet chewy cracker and savored the buttery herbal flavor, I thought of my girl tucked under the covers in my bed.

The only way I was going to get Bianca to stop fighting being with me was if I put a stop to this bullshit investigation and dealt with her parents. The sooner the better.

I left the kitchen and crossed through the small antechamber into the armory. I was pleased to see Alfonso relaxing before the roaring fire in a tufted, tan leather chair with brass nail head trims.

Above him over the mantle hung the stuffed ten-point red deer stag's head my father shot fifteen years ago the first time he took me out hunting. Alfonso nodded in greeting before leaning his head back and closing his eyes.

The massive walnut and glass gun display case which took up a good portion of the back wall was unlocked and open.

Cesare and my father stood nearby over a sturdy rectangular workbench with four Beretta 686 Silver Pigeon shotguns in various stages of assembly strewn before them.

Now that it was November, we were preparing for the wild boar hunts.

Papà looked up as I entered.

He set aside his cleaning rod and picked up the brown glass growler of *Birrificio Italiano Tipopils* pilsner Uncle Benedict had brought us when he visited for the funeral. Ever the family black sheep, my uncle preferred beer to wine and never missed an opportunity to try and change our tastes as well. Papà poured me a glass and slid it across the workbench.

He picked up his cleaning rod and attached the bore brush. After placing a few drops of solvent on the end, he inserted the brush into the chamber end of the barrel and ran it back and forth. "Everything all settled? I heard there was an issue."

I picked up my own shotgun and ensured it was unloaded before I began to fieldstrip it. "Nothing I couldn't handle."

He nodded and returned to cleaning his gun.

Cesare glanced up from his own task of oiling the hinge pins and action bars. "Benito ran those checks we asked for on Nevio Zettici."

I separated the forend from the barrel. "And?"

He reached for one of the *taralli* I had brought in. "Nothing." He crunched down on a bite.

Before I could express my annoyance, he continued, talking around his bite. "Like, strangely nothing."

I frowned as I picked up a brass cleaning brush. "How so?"

"There's nothing there. Not so much as a parking ticket. We then checked with the *Central Rischi* and the CRIF credit bureau. The guy has no credit or financial history."

Our father looked up. "Think Nevio could be an alias?"

"He supposedly went to our school so on Monday we're going to check the school records. That will tell us."

I applied a small amount of gun oil to a soft, clean cloth and rubbed down the barrel. "What did Benito say about Longo?"

Cesare took a sip of his beer. "Oh, fun fact. He doesn't think Longo is here in an official capacity. He's definitely not the inspector Benito heard might be coming down."

Papà scoffed and shook his head. "Fucking little asshole. I knew it."

Cesare gestured with his beer glass. "That doesn't mean it wouldn't become official if he fabricates enough fake evidence."

I reassembled my shotgun. "I don't know about you two, but I've had enough of standing around holding my dick waiting for something to happen. I think we should start kicking over some rocks."

Papà clicked his barrel and stock into place. "Agreed. I'll call your uncle tomorrow. We'll make arrangements to send the girls up north until the dust settles. They'll be safe there. No one will get within two hundred kilometers of your uncle's mountain *rifugio* without him spotting them through a riflescope."

Cesare and I nodded. We knew the family secret about Uncle Benedict.

The girls would be safe with him.

Alfonso snorted.

We all turned.

He was still sitting by the fire with his eyes closed.

Papà raised an eyebrow. "You disagree?"

"About your crazy as fuck brother? No."

"Then what is so amusing?"

Alfonso sat up straighter and stretched his arms over his head with a groan. "I was just thinking how it was going to take all three of you and a lot of rope, because you're going to need to hogtie Gabriella to get her up to the godforsaken wilds of northern Italy when the winter fashion shows are about to begin in Milan."

The three of us exchanged concerned looks.

Papà said, "Alfonso, maybe you could—"

Alfonso stood, reached for his beer and drained it, then set aside the empty glass before heading toward the outside door. "Not for a million euro."

I tried to reason with him. "Come on, Alfonso. You're the only one she listens to."

He paused with his hand on the doorknob. "Nice try. I like my testicles attached to my body, thank you very much."

He settled his cap on his head. "I'm headed to the stables to see what I can do about repairing the body damage to Cesare's car. *Buonanotte.*"

I looked to Papà. "She's already got my *Riva Aquarama*. I have nothing left she wants that I could bribe her with."

He rolled his eyes. "Dammit. I'm going to have to give her the property in Sardinia, aren't I?"

Cesare stared at me, frowning. "What the fuck did Alfonso mean—'repair the body damage to Cesare's car'?"

I reached under the workbench for the whiskey bottle hidden there, pulled out the cork with my teeth, and pushed it toward him. "Yeah… about that…."

CHAPTER 32

BIANCA

"*G*et your hands off me!"

I glanced up and looked through the marbled glass window to search for the source of the raised voices.

I was tucked up on a settee in a quiet corner of the library, in the older part of the villa.

The windows were smaller, some with old glass panes that resembled thick, melting sugar. I raised up on my knees to look through the windowpanes with modern glass.

My view was blocked by an ancient chestnut tree. Its massive canopy of copper leaves, heavily laden with mahogany clusters of nuts, obscured anything beyond. I settled back into my cushion against the armrest. It was just as well.

It sounded as if the voices were coming from the front courtyard and my view was from around the back.

I balanced the sketch pad on my knees and reached for a charcoal stick.

I drew a faint line, then smudged it with my middle finger. I cocked my head to the side, surveying my work before drawing another line to shadow the first. It was a realistic portrait of Enzo in profile. Well, mostly realistic. I had added a stylistic Roman Centurion helmet.

After the events of yesterday, I had woken feeling worn out, with a slight sore throat.

Enzo said it was because I had been working too hard and had burned myself out on the various side projects I had taken on as well as finishing my midterm schoolwork right before the funeral.

It was far more likely because I had screamed myself hoarse and then been stripped naked and fucked sideways in the middle of an ancient ruin in a primeval forest in November, but I didn't want to start a fight.

Not when he was so concerned and being so nice... and boyfriend-y.

I still couldn't believe he had kept all my drawings. *All* of them. Even the crappy ones.

After I agreed to take it easy and rest today, I assumed he would just head off to the winery. Instead, he had lingered all morning taking care of me. He had even driven into town to pick up fresh art supplies for me to keep me entertained while he reluctantly spent a few necessary hours at the winery.

Now I was tucked under a cozy quilt with a steaming cup of linden flower and honey tea, quietly drawing after promising not to move an inch until he returned.

Amara Beneventi breezed in.

Her cheeks were bright red. She carried with her the cool autumn scent of the outside, that crisp mix of burning wood, dried leaves, and apple.

She was slightly out of breath. She pushed her hair away from her face and placed her hands on her hips. "I really hope you're not going to get mad, but I just turned your mother away."

I sat up straighter. "Claudia was here?"

My stomach twisted as I braced for whatever humiliating thing Amara said next.

Amara crossed the room to me.

I tucked my feet up and she sat on the end of the settee. She leaned her head back and looked at me. She wrinkled her nose. "You won't take offense if I say your mother is a real piece of work?"

I slumped back against the armrest as I rolled my eyes. "I used to think I was adopted."

"Are you sure you're not?"

"What did she want?"

I had turned off my mobile and avoided all communication with my parents since the night of the engagement party.

I wasn't resigned to cutting them completely out of my life, but I did agree with Enzo that something wasn't right about their behavior regarding Renata's death. I hadn't even told him outright about my mother burning my passport and birth certificate. It was enough he knew they were trying to marry me off to Nevio Zettici. It was just for the best if I avoided them until things calmed down a bit.

"She was demanding to see you. Claiming we were

305

keeping you hostage and as a mother she had a right to see her daughter."

My arm paused as I lifted my teacup halfway to my mouth. I looked at Amara and cocked an eyebrow. "She didn't."

Amara nodded. "Laid it on real thick. She may have missed her calling. That woman belongs on the stage."

I grimaced. "Sorry."

She shrugged. "Don't be. You're not the only one with embarrassing family connections. Trust me."

Before we could say anything more, Barone Cavalieri burst into the room.

His brow was lowered as he stormed straight to Amara, like a bull toward a red flag.

He grabbed her by the shoulders and lifted her to her feet. He tore off his work gloves and placed his hand under her chin as he stared intently into her eyes. "Are you okay, dolcezza?"

Despite the imposing man's fierce demeanor that would have scared the crap out of anyone else, Amara smiled warmly, rose on her toes, and kissed him on the cheek. "I'm fine. Just a little drama. She's gone."

"She should have never made it this far onto the grounds. There's going to be hell to pay when I find out who let her through the main gate."

He looked over at me. "Bianca, are you okay?"

I raised up both palms and rushed to assure him. "I'm fine! I didn't even know she was here."

He nodded. "That will be small comfort to Enzo when he finds out. He rode out on horseback to inspect a downed fence in the north field. He should be back shortly."

I raised my eyebrows. "We could always not tell him?"

Barone laughed. "Nice try."

He kissed Amara on the forehead and left.

Amara slumped back onto the settee. She gave me a conciliatory look. "You get used to it."

"The insanely over-the-top protective intensity?"

"Yeah, that."

"At least I know where Enzo gets it from."

Amara pulled the sketch pad from my lap. "This is really good."

"Thank you."

She sat up straighter and flipped through a few more pages. "Like really, really good." Closing the cover and handing the sketch pad back, she studied me consideringly.

I narrowed my eyes. "What? What is that look?"

She held up her hand. "Wait right here! Don't go anywhere!"

A few minutes later she returned with a stack of files.

I crossed my legs, and she dumped them on the quilt on the settee between us.

She grabbed a hairband and twisted her hair into a messy bun on the top of her head. "I need your help. Barone has given me until the end of this week to come up with a new design for the wine labels or he's going to run with the old one."

She flipped the first file open and handed it to me. "This is the old one."

I looked over the familiar image. Everyone in Italy was familiar with the Cavalieri wine label.

She then started opening the rest of the files and pulling out drawings. "Here are the submitted design samples."

I frowned. "This one is terrible. The colors are all wrong. Light blue? Apparently, this designer isn't aware that Donatella Cinelli Colombini, the famous Italian winemaker, has declared that a light blue wine label means the wine was made on land confiscated from the mafia."

Amara's mouth dropped open. She took the design from my hand and tore it in half without saying anything.

I smiled. "Smart choice."

I cocked my head to the left as I studied the next design. "And this one. *Proxima Nova* as a font choice? For a wine label? Are they serious?"

Amara groaned. "I know! Help me! I'm desperate."

I grabbed my sketch pad and opened the package of colored pencils Enzo bought me. "Your main concern is the current label is iconic, so you need to do something that looks new but still feels familiar."

"Yes! Exactly!"

She scooted closer to me, to see what I was drawing.

We spent the next hour coming up with designs. We barely even looked up when Rosa entered with a fresh pot of linden flower tea and some fresh pastries and fruit.

We only took a break when Gabriella arrived in her usual dramatic fashion.

She was followed by a tall man I recognized as the one who'd helped us out, and who Enzo had chatted with about the wrecked Ferrari after we got back to the villa last night. Alfonso was his name, I thought.

I lowered my head, more than a little embarrassed.

He had been the soul of discretion and an absolute gentleman who'd acted like there was nothing amiss about me standing there in a wrinkled coat, leaves sticking out of my hair, as Enzo nonchalantly avoided any explanation as to how we managed to trash two insanely expensive cars in the middle of a deserted road in the Apennine mountains on a cold autumn night.

Still, it was beyond humiliating.

Alfonso's arms were piled high with flat white boxes and several round hat boxes.

Gabriella held several garment bags aloft as she clung to Alfonso's elbow and steered him toward the lounge setting across the room. "Right over here, Alfonso."

She guided him straight into a table. "Oops. Watch the table, darling."

He cast her a dark look before maneuvering around the table and dropping the boxes on the closest marble table at the exact moment Gabriella pulled an expensive looking vase filled with dried flowers out of the way.

Milana followed in their wake, carrying two garment bags.

The moment I saw her, I gathered my things to leave. I knew I should have stayed in Enzo's rooms or a hotel.

Milana tossed the garment bags over the back of a chair and crossed over to me. "Fuck. Are you leaving because you're mad at me?"

Caught off guard, I shook my head. "What? No. I'm leaving because I figured *you* were mad at *me*. Why would I be mad at you?"

She bit her lip. "I told Cesare what you said about Enzo,

and he told Enzo. I'm sorry. I couldn't keep something like that from him."

I played with the spiral wire on my sketch pad. "You were right to tell him."

She put her hand to her chest. "That's a relief. Amara will warn you. I tend to speak my mind. You'll get used to it."

I frowned and averted my gaze.

She caught the look. "You are going to stay, right?"

"I don't know. This feels kind of awkward. Enzo told me what...happened...between you...I mean...what my sister...."

How do you tell someone you're sorry your dead sister tried to kill them?

She leaned in close. "Remember all those nasty stories about my mother in school?"

I nodded. The kids we went to school with had always been really cruel to Milana about her mother.

She continued. "I know we weren't super close, but we were friends. You were always so nice to me. And you never judged me because of something my family did."

I held my hand to my chest. "I would never do that."

She winked. "Neither would I."

The knots in my stomach eased.

She threw a hand over my shoulder. "Besides, we're the same size so I'm planning on us becoming besties so I can borrow some of these clothes," she said as she gestured toward all the boxes and garment bags.

"These are for me?"

She nodded. "Enzo sent for them from Rome yesterday."

Gabriella gestured for us to approach. "Come on, dears. We have lots to unpack and decide on. Thank you, Alfonso."

Alfonso tipped his hat and quietly left.

Gabriella started untying the ribbons on the top boxes. She cast me a sardonic look. "Since you owe me a silk blouse and skirt, I get first pick."

My cheeks flamed. Apparently, she had already learned about the damage to the outfit I borrowed yesterday.

Amara leaned in close. "Welcome to the club. I think we each owe clothes to Aunt Gabriella."

There were boxes and bags from all the major Italian fashion houses.

I responded, "Of course, Gabriella. Anything you want."

She waved her hand dismissively. "I've seen your tits, darling. I think you can call me Aunt Gabriella."

I opened and closed my mouth several times, having no idea how to respond as my cheeks flamed hotter.

Milana laughed. "Look at her face! Don't worry, Bianca. Aunt Gabriella seeing you naked is part of the club initiation!"

Gabriella unzipped a garment bag and pulled out several dresses. "Oh no! This won't do at all." She unzipped another bag and pulled out four more dresses and shook her head, making a *tsk tsk tsk* sound. "These are even worse!"

I had no idea what she was talking about, each seemed more stunning than the last.

She held up a black Valentino cocktail dress. "Does the man think you are entering a convent?"

Amara, Milana, and I all leaned in and took a closer look.

Each dress Enzo had purchased, every single one, was long-sleeved with a high collar and a hem that ended below the knee. We continued to unpack and critique the clothes, trying to decide what could be salvaged and what was hope-lessly too "nun-like."

Aunt Gabriella sighed. "Well, we'll just have to go to Rome ourselves."

I opened my mouth to object.

After all, I technically had my own clothes at my parents' house and regardless of their protests, it wasn't like we were destitute. And despite his insistence, I hadn't actually agreed to marry Enzo yet, and secretly still hoped to put him off, at least for a little while until I was surer about us.

Before I could say anything, Amara patted me on the shoulder. "Don't even try. Aunt Gabriella's infamous shop-ping trips are another one of those things you're just going to have to get used to. The men expect it."

Aunt Gabriella shook her head as she examined more of Enzo's fashion choices. "What could the man have been thinking?"

I sighed. "This might be my fault. It has to do with your engagement party, Milana."

Milana's eyes widened. "Don't tell me he objected to that adorable Gucci corset number you were wearing? You looked hot!"

Amara smirked. "I think it had more to do with how she *accessorized* it."

I raised my palms. "He was my parents' idea. They were trying to set me up."

Trying to force me into marriage to help secure a shady business deal and line their pockets was more like it, but why air my family's dirty laundry when we were all having a nice afternoon?

Amara asked, "Who was he? He looked familiar."

There were fewer things I wanted to talk less about than Nevio, but I didn't want to seem rude when they were all being so sweet.

It was nice hanging out with the women.

I never had a close relationship with my own mother or sister. And being a painfully shy art nerd in school, who was teased as a result of my sister's bullying, meant I never really had many girlfriends.

I pretended to examine the beadwork on one of the longer dresses to hide my discomfort. "He went to school with us. His name is Nevio Zettici. Apparently, he used to have a crush on me. He left a valentine in my desk once, but I thought it was a prank, so I ignored it."

I held the dress up to my chest and turned to face them. "This one isn't so bad. If I wore it with...what? What's the matter? What's happened?"

All three of them were staring at me as if I had suddenly sprouted horns.

CHAPTER 33

ENZO

I slammed my fist on the table. "It's out of the fucking question. I forbid it."

Bianca reared back. "You forbid it? You *forbid* it?"

"That's right. I forbid it."

She leaned her palms on the table. "You are not allowed to fucking forbid anything."

"Watch your fucking language," I growled. "Or I'll put you over my knee and spank your ass."

Her cheeks flamed at my suggestive language in front of my family. Still, it didn't prevent her from firing back. "*You* watch *your* fucking language. Need I remind you that we are not married yet? *If* we get married at all?"

"What the hell is that supposed to mean?"

She crossed her arms. "It means you don't get to tell me what to do, and if this is a sneak peek of what it would be like to be married to you, then I think I'll pass."

I didn't give a shit that my entire family was assembled around us.

At hearing that, I vaulted over the dining room table and snatched her around the waist.

I pushed her backward, pinning her against the wall. "Say that again," I snarled.

Papà tried to interject. "Son—"

Without taking my eyes off Bianca, I said, "Stay out of this, Papà."

I focused on Bianca as I braced my forearm over her head. "You think having these people here will save you from any consequences? Go ahead. Try me. Say you won't marry me again."

I knew this was difficult for her. This entire situation was difficult for us all.

Finding out that the third man, the piece of shit who had been taunting my family from the shadows for months, had actually been in our home, under our noses this whole time, rattled us all.

When I thought about how that man had laid his filthy hands on my woman, I wanted to rip his throat out with my bare hands. And that was nothing compared to what Cesare wanted to do with him for what he'd done to Milana back in school.

We all wanted our pound of flesh.

But that didn't mean I was prepared to use Bianca as bait.

I knew she was stressed and overwrought. I knew I had put her through hell and back these last few days. I was a bastard for putting her through more. If I were a better man, a different man, I would be holding her and whispering soft words of endearment in her ear... but I wasn't that man, and she might as well accept that fact now.

And I wasn't about to relent and back off from claiming her as my wife just because she was upset.

The revelation that the third man was Nevio Rettici, the man her parents were trying to force her into marriage with, made it all the more pressing that we marry and soon.

There was obviously a reason why they wanted their last remaining daughter to marry such a bloodthirsty psychopath.

Especially since there was very little chance that Bruno and Claudia didn't at least suspect that he was responsible for Renata's death.

So to literally sacrifice Bianca to him meant that a great deal of money, or perhaps their own miserable lives, were on the line.

Either way, we were going to find out... but not until I had Bianca safely tucked away on Cavalieri land in Northern Italy with my Uncle Benedict.

One of my family's closest-held secrets was Benedict Cavalieri.

We liked to say that he shunned society and preferred the wilds of Northern Italy because he was the black sheep of the family who hated wine and preferred to raise champion horses instead, but that was only half the truth.

The whole truth was that society was *safer* with Uncle Benedict in the north.

It wasn't a fluke he was the one with the connections and plan to get me out of Italy completely under the radar to avoid serious murder charges if things went south with the Renata investigation.

Bianca's full lips tightened into a flat line. "I'm tired of everyone around me trying to bully me! First my parents and now you. I wasn't going to be bullied into marrying Nevio, and I won't be bullied into marrying you!"

I leaned in and whispered, for her ears only, "I will drag you down to that church, lay you on the altar like a pagan sacrifice, spread your legs, and fuck you so savagely that Christ himself will hear your cries for mercy. The priest will have no choice but to take your screams of pleasure as an 'I do.'"

She inhaled sharply.

I looked down and saw the sharp peaks of her nipples through my soft cashmere sweater that she still wore over a pair of leggings.

The muscles of her throat contracted and released around a swallow. Her cheeks flushed a beautiful pink as she stared up at me, defiance still glittering in the depths of her dark eyes. "You wouldn't dar—"

I raised an eyebrow.

She didn't even finish the sentence.

Before I could say anything further, Rosa entered, followed by two members of the household staff. She let out a furious exclamation. "Why are there scuff marks on my nice, polished table?"

The entire room pointed to me.

She wagged her finger at me. "You and I will discuss this in my kitchen after everyone has eaten, mister." She then ordered my father into the kitchen to fetch the risotto.

Her gentle, motherly scolding diffused the tension in the room.

Bianca smirked. "I think *if* we get married, I'm going to take a few lessons from Rosa on how to deal with you."

I kissed her forehead. "*When* we get married, the only thing you need to know about dealing with me is...." I shifted my body so the others couldn't see and pulled her hand between my legs so her palm would brush my hard cock.

She batted my chest with her hand. "You're impossible!"

Amara and Milana sidled up to Bianca, one on each side of her like a pair of self-appointed bodyguards, and ushered her to the other side of the table.

Cesare and I were forced to take seats on the opposite side as we faced off from our significant others.

As Rosa directed the staff in laying out the silver place settings, cloth napkins, and glassware, she placed a massive, carved wooden bowl filled with radicchio, endive, arugula and frisée salad tossed in a simple olive oil and lemon dressing off to the side of the center of the table.

Another staff member placed a smaller bowl of freshly roasted chestnuts on the table, their rich earthy yet sweet aroma filling the room with the scent of autumn.

Gabriella entered cradling four bottles of *Giuseppe Quintarelli Valpolicella Classico Superiore* she had retrieved from the wine cellar.

I jumped up to help her, setting the bottles at the end of the table. Picking up a bottle opener, I used the foil cutter to breach the foil wrapper before uncorking each one.

Gabriella grabbed the first bottle and circled the table. "This really should breathe first but who cares, drink up!"

Papà entered carrying a massive wheel of parmesan cheese.

He was followed by Alfonso who held a steaming cast-iron pot. Although it wasn't usually done at the dining room table, my family had always enjoyed the pageantry of watching the risotto slowly melt the parmesan.

Papà placed the heavy wheel on a cloth and stepped back as Alfonso dipped the steaming rice directly into the hollowed-out center of the cheese wheel. Papà then picked up a wooden spoon and slowly stirred. Soon the risotto melted the sides of the wheel and was coated in the perfect amount of rich, creamy cheese.

We passed our *coupe* plates up to each be filled with a generous spoonful of risotto. When Papà was finished dishing it out to everyone, he returned the wheel to the kitchen and took his rightful place at the head of the table.

For several minutes we ate in silence, enjoying the simple yet hearty autumn meal.

Then conversation returned to the problem at hand.

It was Papà who broached the topic. "Enzo, I'm sure you can appreciate how much I hate to say this, but Bianca makes a fair point. Her parents will not be lured into a meeting unless she is present."

I put down my fork and steepled my fingers over my plate. "We've only just learned Nevio is the third man. We haven't even tried to take him out without involving her or her parents."

Cesare played with the stem of his wineglass. "Yeah, but we suspected something was shady about him. Maybe not that he was the third man, but we knew something was wrong. We've already tried to get background information

320

about him and he's a ghost. Knowing he's the third man doesn't change that."

I leveled a look at him. "If it were you, would you allow Milana to go?"

Milana lowered her brow. "What's with this *allow me* shit?"

At the same time, Cesare said, "Hell no."

Milana turned to him. "Hey!"

Papà stretched his arms over the table. "We're not going to start that again."

Bianca spoke up. "Can I say something?"

The whole table quieted and turned to her.

She took a deep breath. "You've all been very kind to accept me into your family after what... well... after everything. And I want to show how much I appreciate it—"

I interrupted. "No one is expecting you to risk your safety out of some archaic loyalty test, baby."

She nodded. "I know that, but it would make a difference to me." She turned in her chair to face me. "If we are going to have the slightest chance of a happily ever after, I can't always feel like there is this shadow over my presence here."

Papà cleared his throat. "Bianca, I sincerely hope none of us has—"

She shook her head. "You've all been wonderful. Truly. But your family isn't the only one who puts stock in honor and reputation. I want a chance to redeem my family's reputation, even if it's only me doing it. Here's my thought. If we strike quickly and pick a location we control, my parents will not have the advantage. I would be there for the beginning of the meeting so they see me, and then leave soon after, before it is finished."

I exchanged looks with Cesare, Papà, and Alfonso.

Dammit, it was a reasonable solution.

They continued to look at me. I knew they were waiting for me to voice my opinion since Bianca was my responsibility. I let out a frustrated sigh. "Fine, but if we do this, you listen to everything I say, no arguments."

She nodded. "Done."

We then proceeded to discuss the logistics of arranging a meeting as soon as possible with Bianca's parents. It was time to learn their exact involvement with the Agnello crime family and how to find Nevio Zettici.

At some point, Bianca tugged on my sleeve.

When I leaned down, she whispered in my ear, "For future reference, since you don't seem to be familiar with the concept, that was called a *compromise.*"

I gave one long, wavy curl a playful tug. Fuck, I couldn't wait for this mess to be over so I could marry this amazing woman and settle down into a long, wonderfully boring life of domestic bliss with her.

But first, I needed to murder the man she was supposed to marry instead of me.

CHAPTER 34

ENZO

*T*he acrid sent of fresh paint, stale air, and dust hit me the moment I pried open the front door of the house I had shared with Renata.

Although "shared" was painting it on a bit thick.

Cohabited, or perhaps endured, would be closer to the truth.

As I entered the hall, I turned and craned my neck up, relieved to see the workmen had finished painting over the ghastly mural of Renata.

Although Bianca's idea of having the summit with her parents here was an inspired one, I found being in this place unsettling.

It wasn't the shadows of Renata's ghost which disturbed me. My conscience was clear where she was concerned. She and she alone was responsible for the decisions she'd made which led to her downfall.

If she had only come to me and let me know she was in

trouble, I would have protected her. I knew that deep down in my soul. Even knowing there was no baby, that it had all been a lie, I would not have left her to her fate. Especially since I would have had the grounds for an annulment.

With no baby, and evidence I never slept with her, I would have been granted an annulment and been able to marry Bianca in the Catholic Church.

All would have been as it should from the beginning.

No, it wasn't Renata's ghost which haunted me.

It was the pain I caused Bianca from my own actions.

She left for America so soon after, I never witnessed the heartache.

Through the lens of all the surveillance I had on her, all those photos and videos, all those emails when she thought she was communicating with a client, I thought she had moved on from me.

I thought I was the only one suffering from the loss of our relationship.

Returning to this house felt like returning to the scene of the crime. I guessed it was fitting for this to be the location for the beginning of the end. Today we would learn how to find Nevio. We would learn the truth of Bianca's parents' involvement and finally put an end to this mess.

I surveilled the place before opening the double doors wider and signaling to Cesare and Matteo who were waiting outside with Bianca.

They followed me back inside, through the hallway to the main dining room space which we would use as a conference room.

Cesare grimaced. "I see we still have the fancy, clear acrylic chairs."

I grimaced. "Yeah, sorry. I had the men move everything back in since I didn't have another table and chairs to replace them with."

Bianca shook her head as she stared at the ghastly dining set. "My mother and sister always did have a unique sense of style."

Cesare raised an eyebrow. "Unique. Is that the word?"

Matteo held his fingers up in the shape of an "L" and pretended to view the furniture as if through a lens. "I don't know. It has a certain Psychotic Barbie Dreamhouse quality."

Bianca smiled.

Matteo announced he was going to check the kitchen to see if there was anything to eat, while Cesare mumbled about searching for a different chair to sit in for the meeting.

I crossed to her and wrapped my arm around her waist. Pulling her close, I kissed the top of her head. I appreciated my brother and cousin's attempts at levity to relieve the tense atmosphere. I knew Bianca was nervous about facing off with her parents.

I tilted her chin up to face me. "When this is over, I will take you wherever you want to go. Just you and me."

She wrapped her arms around my waist. "There is this Artist's Residency program in Upstate New York this winter. You live in rustic cabins with no electricity or running water. You're meant to silence the modern world so you can tap into your inner muse through communing with nature. They even teach you how to make your own pigments with natural ingredients."

I raised an eyebrow. "A luxury suite at the Chalet Edelweiss in Courchevel, France for a week of skiing, award-winning dining, and spa treatments you say? You read my mind, babygirl."

She rolled her eyes. "Is this how it's going to be if we get married? You always getting your way?"

"*When* we get married and probably yes." I kissed her on the tip of her nose. "But I'll soften the blow with lots of orgasms."

There was a knock on the main door. I checked my watch. "That must be Papà."

I left Bianca in the dining room and crossed the main hall.

When I opened the door, I was surprised to see Liliana standing on the threshold. Hooked over her arm was a large picnic basket and, in each hand, she held a silver electric kettle. "Buongiorno, Signor Cavalieri."

I looked behind her before responding. "Buongiorno, Liliana. What are you doing here?"

"Signor Cavalieri, that is, Matteo, called the office and asked me to bring coffee and pastries over for a meeting you are having?"

He hadn't mentioned anything to me.

This wasn't exactly a business meeting, but I supposed it wouldn't hurt to grease the wheels a bit by having a hospitable atmosphere.

I stepped aside and ushered her in just as Papà walked up.

He gestured to Liliana. "Coffee and pastries. Good idea."

"It was Matteo's."

We both stepped inside.

As Liliana set the coffee up on the sideboard, Cesare carried a leather chair in from the study.

Matteo appeared from the kitchen. Seeing the pastries, he tossed aside the slightly bruised apple he was holding. "Thank God. Coffee and a brioche! You are an angel, Liliana!"

Just then, there was a knock on the door.

We all exchanged a look.

Bianca took a deep breath. "Showtime."

*　*　*

CLAUDIA WALTZED into the villa like a queen surveying her subjects. She gave Bianca a scathing once-over and announced, "That rag you are wearing is not flattering."

I took a step forward. It wasn't hard to see where Renata had learned her craft.

Not to mention it wasn't the least bit true.

Bianca laid a restraining hand on my chest and shook her head slightly. With a calm smile and in a resigned voice, she responded, "Nice to see you as well, *Mother*."

The woman bristled.

Bruno Moretti grabbed her by the elbow and ushered her into the dining room. He checked his watch and looked at the door. He then mopped his forehead. "Let's get this over with. I'm a busy man."

After most of those who wanted something got a coffee and brioche, we took our seats.

Liliana tapped Bianca on the shoulder. "Here you go, Bianca," she offered as she slid a caffe in front of Bianca, who was already seated. "Two sugars and no cream, right? I remembered."

Bianca looked up at her. "Oh, this was sweet of you. Yes, thank you, Liliana."

I placed a hand over Bianca's and squeezed hers to reassure her. I knew she was nervous. This would be over soon. I nodded to Liliana. "That will be all, Liliana. Thank you. You can head back to the office. We'll clean up."

She looked around the table anxiously before nodding. "Of course." After another glance around the table, she left.

Papà folded his hands before him. "There's no point in wasting time. As you said, Bruno, we're all busy. We know you are laundering money for the Agnello crime family."

Claudia stopped with an unlit cigarette raised halfway to her lips. "How dare you!"

Bruno stood, his mouth opening and closing several times as his flushed, bloated face turned a mottled purple.

I was unimpressed. "Sit the fuck down."

Bruno looked to the door and checked his watch before mopping his brow and sitting.

Claudia straightened her shoulders. "Are you going to let them speak to your parents this way, Bianca?"

Bianca shrugged. "You're the one who insisted on a relationship with the Cavalieris, *Mother*, for the benefit of the family."

Claudia's upper lip curled. "Drink your caffe before it gets cold."

As if reminded it was in front of her, Bianca reached for her cup and took several sips.

Papà continued. "It's over, Bruno. How well you survive

the coming storm is up to you. You can cooperate and tell us what we want to know, in which case I will let you crawl away with a modicum of dignity and enough to survive on."

Bruno wiped his handkerchief across his mouth. "And if I don't?"

Cesare smiled. "Well, and I have to be honest, this is my personal favorite out of the options, *we crush you*. We take your fortune, your reputation, and you leave Italy."

Claudia blew out a cloud of blue smoke as she faced off with me. "Why are you doing this? We are your mother- and father-in-law. We just lost our daughter!"

"It's your own fault you lost your daughter. What happened? Did Renata push Nevio too far? Did she ask for a bigger cut to launder the money? Did she threaten to expose him as the third man we were looking for in Milana's attack unless he paid her more?"

Bruno and Claudia flinched at the name Nevio. They then both looked at the doorway.

I stood and pounded my fist on the table. "Don't look at the door. You're not leaving until we get some answers. I want to know how we find Nevio. What's the matter? Am I hitting too close to the truth? You knew all along that piece of shit was responsible for killing Renata and yet you let him put his bloodstained hands on Bianca?"

I knew the first rule in any enemy engagement was never to show emotion, it gave them the upper hand, but god fucking dammit. How could they have allowed that man in the same room with Bianca, let alone force her on a date with him? Force her to consider marrying him? A fucking murderer. They were her parents. They were supposed to protect her from monsters like Nevio, not offer her up like she was worth nothing to them.

Fuck, I needed to rein it in for Bianca.

I glanced down at her.

The moment I did, I frowned.

She had this faraway expression on her face, almost as if she were in a trance.

Her eyes were unfocused and glassy.

I looked from her to the caffe cup and back.

Fuck.

She'd been drugged.

I looked up at her parents.

Claudia was staring intently at Bianca.

Her sharp eyes flicked up to meet my gaze.

I could see the truth in her sneer.

I snarled, "You bitch!"

Just as I lunged, the doors to the dining room were kicked open.

A small army of *Arma dei Carabinieri* officers stormed in, guns raised.

All hell broke loose.

CHAPTER 35

ENZO

*L*ongo was at the forefront. "Enzo Cavalieri, *accusato di omicidio. Ha il diritto di rimanere in silenzio. Tutto quello che dirà potrà essere usato contro di lei in sede di processo. Ha il diritto di essere assistito da un avvocato e, se non ne ha uno, uno gli sarà fornito gratuitamente.*"

Two guards tried to grab my wrists. I easily shrugged them off.

Papà's voice roared over the din. "Longo, you little asshole. You are not arresting my son on murder charges."

Longo puffed out his chest. "You're right, Don Cavalieri. I'm arresting *both* of your sons." He gestured to the guards to grab Cesare. "Cesare Cavalieri, *accusato di omicidio. Ha il diritto di rimanere in silenzio. Tutto quello che dirà potrà essere usato contro di lei in sede di processo. Ha il diritto di essere assistito da un avvocato e, se non ne ha uno, uno gli sarà fornito gratuitamente.*"

Matteo grabbed the shoulder of one of the men trying to handcuff Cesare.

Longo shouted, "Leave off, Matteo Cavalieri, unless you want to face charges too."

Something wasn't right.

My conscious mind raced to catch up with what my subconscious mind was trying to tell me.

Something was off.

The *Arma dei Carabinieri* officers.

The way they stood.

The way they were behaving.

Something wasn't right.

It was their uniforms.

They were wearing red-striped, black trousers with a white cross-shoulder belt, but instead of the standard cap and gilded frieze, they were wearing dark blue berets and cap badges with blue neckerchiefs, and their boots were all wrong. It was like they were dressed in a mashup of the standard uniform and the operational uniform, usually worn only for public order and riot situations. And the fabric didn't look right. Almost like a cheap knock-off. A costume.

A fucking costume.

I remembered what Benito told us about Longo's investigation not being sanctioned.

This wasn't an arrest raid.

It was a setup.

I grabbed the first guardsman near me. Twisting my hand into the front of his coat, I pulled back my arm and drove my fist into his face. "They aren't *Arma dei Carabinieri* officers! It's a setup!"

Cesare twisted his torso and drove his elbow up and back, breaking the nose of the man standing behind him. Blood gushed from his face as he screamed in agony. Cesare ducked as the next man threw a sweeping punch, throwing his arm wide. Cesare punched him in the kidneys before sweeping his leg. He then kicked him in the face, breaking the man's jaw.

I called out, "Bianca, get behind me!"

I blocked her from view as I squared my feet and raised my fists.

The first man raised his Beretta 92FS pistol. Before he could even get off one shot, I grabbed his wrist, yanked him forward, and flipped him onto his back, breaking his wrist. I pulled the gun from his hand, turning it on him and firing. Killing him.

These were Agnello's men.

Sent by Nevio. I was sure of it.

This was a trap.

All bets were off.

I turned to check on Bianca.

She had a dazed look on her face, as if she wasn't taking in what was happening.

I needed to get her to safety, but there was no way out of this room without first neutralizing the threat.

I grabbed her and tucked her to the side of the sideboard in the corner. "Stay right here, baby. Keep your head down."

I turned over the leather chair Cesare had thankfully brought into the room and blocked everyone's view of her.

I then turned to face off with anyone who dared approach. I was forced to duck for cover myself as another of Agnello's men opened fire. Hitting the floor with my shoulder, I returned fire, striking him square in the chest.

From the floor, I watched as Matteo took out another man

with his bare hands, twisting the man's neck like it was nothing more than a bottle cap.

I wasn't surprised. Uncle Benedict was his father, after all.

Cesare was thrown against the wall as a bullet tore through his shoulder.

I called out his name.

He raised his injured arm and fired at the shooter. Killing the man. He called back, "It's just a graze."

Before I could respond, I was thrown forward as a heavy weight nearly knocked me to the floor. I shifted to the right and the weight rolled off me.

It was Bruno Moretti. His heavy body thudded to the floor. I kicked him onto his back. His sightless eyes stared back at me. Good riddance.

I looked up to see Papà standing a few feet away, gun drawn.

A hard look on his face. Under his other arm, he had a struggling Longo in a headlock.

Benito burst in with two of his men, guns drawn.

Cesare fell into one of the bullet-cracked acrylic chairs. "You missed all the fun, Benito."

Benito pushed his cap back as he surveyed the damage. "Guess it was too much to ask that it be your television turned up too loud."

I crossed to the leather chair and lifted it out of the way, prepared to help Bianca out of her hiding place. All I wanted to do was get her to safety. I would return to help clean up the mess and interrogate Longo later.

She wasn't there.

I stared at the empty corner as if expecting her to materialize.

For a moment, I didn't want to shift my gaze beyond the spot where I'd left her, paralyzed with fear I would see her bloody body.

I forced myself to move.

I spun in a circle.

She was gone.

Papà had shoved Longo into a chair and was leaning over him, shouting questions about the setup and who was involved.

"She's gone," I forced out through a stiff jaw.

No one heard me.

"She's gone," I said louder.

The room quieted. Everyone turned.

"She's gone!" I raged. "Bianca! Bianca!"

I began turning over bodies and moving around the room, searching for her. I raced up to Benito and grabbed him by the shoulders. "Did you see her leave?"

"Who?"

"Bianca Moretti."

"Your sister-in-law?"

I never...ever... wanted to hear her referred to as such ever again. "My fiancée. My future wife. My woman," I raged through clenched teeth. My vision was turning black along the edges as blind panic and rage were taking over.

Finally realizing the situation, Benito's eyes widened. "Yes! Yes! I saw her with her mother, Claudia! They got into a car and drove off. Her mother was holding her around the shoulders. She looked unwell."

"They drugged her. The bastards drugged her."

My father ran his hand through his hair. "They had this planned from the start."

Cesare frowned. "That must be why Bruno could barely sit still and kept checking his watch and looking at the door. He knew they were coming."

Papà shook his head. "How did they manage to drug her?"

Matteo picked up Bianca's cup. "Her caffe, which would mean... Liliana? No. Who instructed Liliana to bring coffee?"

I frowned. "She said you did."

Matteo shook his head. "No. It wasn't me. She must have been a spy for the Agnellos this whole time."

Christ. We were surrounded by vipers.

I stormed over to Longo.

Grabbing his jaw, I forced his mouth open and shoved the barrel of the Beretta I took off of one of Agnello's men into his mouth. "Where are they taking her?"

Longo's eyes widened as snot spilled from his nose. He cried as he shook his head and tried to speak around the barrel.

Matteo looked at Benito. "You should probably make yourself scarce for this part. We'll call you when it's over."

Benito squared his shoulders. "Fuck that. I'm tired of looking the other way. Cavalieri village is my village, my responsibility. I'm staying."

He looked at his men, who nodded in agreement. "We're staying."

He told one of his men to go secure the front entrance to make sure none of the villagers got curious about the loud noises.

Fortunately, Italians were historically prosaic about minding their own business when hearing gunfire, especially when it came from a property owned by the Cavalieri family.

I pulled the gun out of Longo's mouth. "Speak and you better make it good or I'm going to blow your miserable head off."

Longo raised his arms, palms up. "Nevio Zettici paid me to make trouble for you. He wanted me to buy off witnesses and fake some evidence. That's all I know."

I pressed the gun against his kneecap and fired. The man pitched forward and back, screaming as he grabbed his leg. Cesare and Matteo snatched his shoulders and forced him to sit back in the chair.

Papà crossed his arms over his chest as he squared off in front of Longo. He cocked his head in my direction. "Listen, Longo. That was your one and only warning."

Longo blubbered. "That wasn't a warning! A warning is words! You shot me! You shot me!"

Cesare shrugged. "He's not wrong."

Papà nodded. "Fair enough."

I tapped the barrel of my gun against Longo's forehead. "You're right, Longo. Words matter. So I'll be very clear. That was the last time I am going to give you a survivable wound. The next time I put a bullet in your flesh, it will definitely cause your extremely painful death."

Matteo stepped forward. "If it helps, Longo, he'll probably shoot you in the stomach."

I straightened. "I was thinking more of the bowel. That way he'll die covered in his own blood and shit."

Benito groaned. "Dammit."

Cesare looked at him as he was knotting off a rag around his shoulder wound. "What's your problem?"

He took off his cap and fished out the pack of smokes he had tucked inside. "I'm the one who's going to have to deal with the cleanup. There is nothing more putrid than a bloody, shit-stained corpse." He pulled a cigarette out of the pack with his mouth and lit it.

Papà grinned. "You think we're giving you his body to bury? His family doesn't deserve closure like that. I'm going to feed him to the pigs." He then placed his hands on the armrests of Longo's chair and leaned in. "They'll crunch on your worthless bones and shit out your crushed skull."

Longo's head bobbed from one person to the next like a bobblehead as he took in our macabre conversation. Finally he cracked. "Stop! Stop! You people are fucked up! I'll tell you what I know."

I tapped his forehead again with my gun. "Start talking."

Cesare nudged Benito who took out his phone. We all backed up and allowed Benito to frame the shot to avoid Longo's bullet wound or anything that identified us or the location.

Longo whined, "The Morettis fucked up. They got greedy. Started demanding a bigger cut to launder money for the Agnellos. So Nevio... you know... sent them a message with Renata."

We didn't want any of our voices on the recording, so I raised my gun and pointed it at Longo. He got the point.

He grimaced as he placed a hand on his thigh but continued talking. "But it backfired. Nevio wasn't expecting the Morettis to be so dense or greedy. They wouldn't shut up about losing the Cavalieri money connection. They started complaining about money again to the wrong people. Started talking about how they were going to set up Bianca to marry some Cavalieri cousin. Nevio wanted to kill them all, but Dante Agnello didn't want any more attention, so he ordered Nevio to step in and marry the chick instead, to quiet them."

Papà frowned. Lowering his voice to disguise it, he said, "I didn't take Dante Agnello as the romantic type."

Longo shifted his gaze away. "He's not. It's a stall. He wanted the Morettis to think they were trading off a Cavalieri connection for a closer Agnello one. Marrying a top lieutenant in the Agnello crime family would be no small change. Their daughter would be a mafia princess. That meant plenty of money and new connections. Once they shut up and started laundering money again and a few crucial land permit deals went through, Nevio was going to take care of things... like he does."

He was going to kill Bianca, like he killed her sister.

I motioned for Benito to stop filming.

I placed the gun to Longo's head. "Where are they taking her?"

Longo lowered his head. "A small church in Chieti. There's a priest there with a bad gambling habit who'll sign a shady marriage certificate."

I tucked the gun into my waistband.

It was time to stop my bride from marrying the wrong groom.

CHAPTER 36

BIANCA

I heard the chaos around me as if I were underwater.

Everything was muffled and hazy.

I tried to focus on Enzo and what he was saying but he was talking too fast. I slumped against the wall and closed my eyes. A rush of dizziness made my head spin the moment I did, but when I opened my eyes again it only seemed to make things worse.

My body lurched to the side.

With a huge effort, I forced my head to turn. I saw my mother pulling on someone's arm.

Wait. It was my arm. Why was she pulling on my arm? Her lips were moving. I narrowed my gaze and leaned forward, focusing on her wide lips. They looked like two misshapen bright red slugs slipping over her chin.

She yanked me up and hooked an arm under mine.

One word got through the gibberish the two slippery slugs on her face were saying. "Walk."

I dragged one foot in front of the other.

The cold wind outside brought a small amount of lucidity. Just enough for me to pull back. My tongue was heavy as I pushed it around in my mouth. "Wait. Enzo."

Something in the back of my mind told me Enzo wouldn't like me moving.

"Enzo said to follow me."

She pushed me into the back seat of a car. It was warm and quiet. I liked that there weren't any of those loud noises.

I closed my eyes and gave in to the darkness.

* * *

"I DON'T GIVE a fuck what she wears!"

I kept my eyes closed.

"It's still a wedding," my mother whined.

"Are you fucking kidding me with this?" fired back Nevio.

I forced myself to keep my breathing still and even, as I kept not only my eyes closed but my eyeballs still. I didn't want them to see them move behind my eyelids as a sign I was awake and aware.

Thank God I had only taken a few sips of my caffe. Liliana must have drugged it.

I risked a peek under my eyelashes.

Slightly blurred jewel tones. Stained glass.

I must be in a church.

If the stained glass was bright then the sun was still out,

which meant that not much time had passed. I slowly rolled my wrists and ankles. I wasn't tied up. Another good sign.

A voice I didn't recognize interjected. "Can we get on with this, betting for the Breeder's Cup race is about to open in America."

Nevio snarled, "Shut up, priest. We're finished when I say we're finished."

Okay. My mother. Nevio. A church and a priest.

Even my drug-hazed mind could figure out what was happening.

I just needed to stall for time until Enzo arrived.

And there wasn't a doubt in my mind he would arrive.

Claudia spoke up. "I just need to get her changed. I won't have my last remaining daughter married in that black rag."

"Fine, but make it quick."

My mother pulled me to a sitting position. I pretended to come awake, fluttering my eyelids. "Moth—" Oops. Best not upset her. "Claudia?"

She smiled. "Yes, dear."

"Have you rescued me from the Cavalieris?"

She blinked. "What?"

Careful, don't oversell it.

"I assume you heard me yelling your name the other day when you came to visit? I so wanted to see you, but they wouldn't allow it."

"I knew they were keeping you from me," she hissed.

I bit the inside of my cheek. "Of course."

She gave me an awkward half hug, catching my hair in her gold bangles as she patted my cheek. "Don't worry, Mother is here now."

So it's Mother now?

Hoping I wasn't pushing too hard, I asked, "Where is here? And where is Father?"

"Your father," she cleared her throat, "couldn't make it. Here is church and look, sweetie, Nevio is here!"

I forced a smile. Fortunately, Nevio didn't turn around. He continued to talk animatedly on his mobile.

My mother waved her hand dismissively. "He's been very worried about you." She patted my thigh. "We need to get you ready."

I swallowed past the dryness in my throat. "Ready for what?"

She smiled, a smear of red lipstick dotting her front, slightly tobacco-stained teeth. "Your wedding, silly. I told you, Nevio has been worried."

My cheeks hurt as I kept my smile. "Of course."

She gathered a garment bag under one arm as she sank the long, lacquered claws of her other hand into the soft flesh of my upper arm. She pulled me to my feet. I had to brace my hand on the back of a pew as we made our way to the restrooms.

We pushed inside the dimly lit small bathroom. The linoleum was chipped and missing in some spots on the floor. On the walls was a tile pattern of pale yellow and white squares. In the center of every ten or so tiles was a faded daisy.

My mother spun me around.

I flattened my palm against the metal stall door as a wave of nausea hit me at the sudden movement. I still hadn't completely shaken off the drug.

She unzipped the back of my dress. Yanking on the fabric, she said, "Get this rag off."

I rolled my eyes. This *rag* was this season's Valentino. And I actually liked it quite a bit. Despite my mother's critique it was an extremely flattering and classic A-line black dress.

She unzipped the garment bag and pulled out a white wedding dress. As she pulled it off the hanger, my eyes widened with horror.

It was Renata's wedding gown.

I recognized it from the photos my mother had been cruel enough to send me.

I opened my mouth to refuse to allow the fabric to so much as touch my skin but thought better of it. Reminding myself I needed to buy Enzo time, I pushed back the bitter bile in the back of my throat and stepped into the gown, turning around to let her zip it up.

"Suck in your stomach," she commanded.

I pulled in my stomach.

"Suck in your stomach," she said louder.

"I can't pull it in any further! Ow!" I turned my head over my shoulder as my mother caught my skin in the zipper.

"Face forward."

I turned forward.

She zipped the obscenely tight gown the rest of the way and turned me to face her.

She stepped back and dug in her purse for a cigarette. She shook her head as she lit it. She blew smoke in my face before saying, "Well, I knew you wouldn't look as good as your sister. No one would look as beautiful as Renata in this dress, but I thought you'd at least fit in it. You look like a sausage. What did I tell you about eating?"

I bit the inside of my cheek again. "Not to do it."

"Exactly! You should smoke like I do. How do you think I've kept so slim all these years?"

I refused to give in to my mother's body shaming. I was a normal size. I ate normal meals.

Of course I wouldn't fit into Renata's gown.

Like my mother, she had smoked like a fiend and existed on honey, cayenne pepper and lemon water most days, with a side of laxatives.

I refused to live my life that way. It was part of the reason why my own mother rejected me as the daughter who would never measure up to her extreme beauty standards.

I caught a glimpse of myself in the mirror. I was almost glad there was still a lingering haze from the drug. I was wearing my murdered sister's wedding gown.

This was beyond sick and twisted.

If I hadn't already numbed myself to the fucked-up things my mother said and did to mentally attack me most of my life, this definitely would have sent me straight into therapy for a very long time.

Claudia took a step back. Her overly rouged and artificially plumped lips curled as she picked a nonexistent flake of tobacco leaf off her lips. I resisted the urge to remind her that no one but me was watching.

"You look too pale."

Before I could stop her, she slapped me.

I cried out.

As I straightened, she slapped my other cheek.

"There. That's better."

She smoothed her hair and turned. "It's time to *finally* marry you off."

My stomach twisted. I took a deep breath. Everything was going to be okay.

Enzo was on his way.

He had to be.

* * *

THE MOMENT we exited the bathroom, Nevio was there, pacing.

He gestured with his gun. "Let's get this over with."

If I were a fictional heroine in an action-adventure film, I'd fire back a sassy "how romantic," but this was real life and that was a real fucking gun.

I had to yank up the super tight wedding dress and bunch it at my thighs in order to walk in it, and even then, I could only really shuffle down the aisle.

Nevio huffed. "Can't you walk any faster?"

"Why are you doing this?"

"It's nothing personal, just following orders."

I looked over my shoulder at my mother following a few steps behind. She was distracted as she dug in her purse for another cigarette. "My mother is that powerful?"

He also glanced over his shoulder, then looked down at me, a look of disgust on his face. "No. Dante Agnello."

"Oh. Was he the one who wanted my sister killed?"

Nevio pulled on his tie. "Your sister talked too much."

I nodded, pulling my lips between my teeth.

347

We got to the altar.

I looked down the main aisle between the pews to the doors.

Where the hell was Enzo?

The priest was checking his phone and didn't look up.

Nevio cleared his throat.

The priest held up a finger. "Just one second." He put his phone up to his ear. "Joey? Yeah, I need to place a bet. Make it quick."

While our priest was distracted, I looked up at Nevio. "Can I ask you one more question?"

He frowned. "Didn't I just tell you your sister talked too much and it got her killed?"

My stomach twisted. "This has nothing to do with your... your boss."

He rubbed his finger under his nose and looked away. "Fine. Last one."

"Back in school. The valentine. Did my sister say why she wanted me to be attacked along with Milana?"

I knew my sister saw Milana as a romantic rival for Cesare's affections, but why me? Enzo and I weren't dating at the time. We didn't start dating until years later. Did she think I could become one?

Nevio shrugged one shoulder. "She thought it would be funny."

I blinked. "Funny?"

My sister was going to orchestrate a traumatic sexual attack against me for...laughs?

"Yeah. She said it was funny to make you cry." He leaned in and gave my boobs, which were practically pushed up to my chin by the tight dress, a sleazy look. "Maybe I'll make you cry later and see if it's true."

I smiled. "You know what will be really funny?"

He licked his lips. "What's that?"

I turned my head, drawing his attention to the outside doors to the church, which had just opened as Enzo, Cesare, and Barone Cavalieri menacingly filed in. "Watching you cry instead."

CHAPTER 37

ENZO

*N*evio wrapped his arm around Bianca's throat and held his gun to her head. "Stand back!"

Claudia screamed.

Not at Nevio holding her daughter hostage.

No, she screamed at us. "You're ruining everything!"

Papà pointed a finger at her. "Shut the fuck up and sit down."

Claudia shut her mouth and staggered back into a seated position in a pew.

I pointed my gun at Nevio's head. Keeping a steady gaze on him, I asked Bianca, "You okay, babygirl?"

"I'm wearing my dead sister's horrible wedding gown and have a gun pointed at my head, Enzo."

I winced. "Yeah, besides that."

She forced a smile. "Oh, then I'm fine."

"That's my girl. Now Nevio, you and I both know this doesn't end well for you."

Nevio loosened his grip on Bianca's throat and lowered his arm to grasp her around the shoulders.

He pulled the gun away from her head. "Look, Enzo. I don't want any trouble with you or your family. Me killing your wife, it wasn't personal. It was just business."

I nodded. "I can respect that, Nevio. I really can. And I want to apologize. We got off on the wrong foot at my brother's engagement party. You and I aren't that different. And to be honest, you did me a solid killing her."

Nevio's shoulders relaxed. "See? That's what I kept telling Dante! He wouldn't believe me. I told him he didn't have to listen to the bitch go on and on and on about money this and the Cavalieris that. And look, sorry about trying to pin the murder on you."

I shrugged one shoulder. "You had to do what you had to do. Self-preservation. I get it. I would have done the same."

Bianca's eyes widened as if to say, *what the fuck?*

I gave her a quick wink.

Hold on, baby.

I gestured between us with my gun. "So, Nevio, now that we have that sorted, what are we going to do about this?"

Nevio shook his head. "Can't help you there. Orders are orders. Dante needs her father to toe the line, and this is how he wants it done."

I gave Bianca a sympathetic look. I knew she wasn't close to her family, but this wasn't how I'd wanted her to find out. I took a deep breath. "Bruno Moretti is dead. Longo's men killed him when they were firing at us."

Bianca frowned and lowered her head. She didn't look

that surprised or upset. I didn't blame her. By all accounts her father was a cruel and cold man.

Claudia started screaming all over again. My father grabbed her and dragged her out of the church.

Nevio lowered his gun. "Well, I guess that changes things. A dead man can't sign a land permit or bank transfer."

He released Bianca.

She hiked up her dress and ran into my arms.

I grabbed her around the waist with one arm, still keeping my gun hand free, and hugged her to me.

The tightness in my chest eased.

Fuck, that had been close.

Nevio smirked. "So we're good?"

I looked up at him. "Us? Yeah, we're square. There's just one problem."

"Yeah, what's that?"

Cesare, who had used my conversation with Nevio as a distraction to circle around and approach him on the right, stood within an arm's length.

Cesare pressed the barrel tip of his gun to Nevio's temple. "Me."

Nevio stilled. "What the fuck?"

Cesare ground out, "This is for Milana," and pulled the trigger.

* * *

I GRASPED Bianca's head and turned her into my shoulder to shield her from the sight.

I tucked my gun into the back of my waistband and hugged her tight.

She tilted her head back and looked up at me.

I braced myself for her sobs, her trauma, her fear and horror. I would be there for her. I would be strong. I would be her rock.

Her brow furrowed. "It took you long enough."

My mouth dropped open. "Took me...? We got here as soon as we could. You know we were taking on gunfire when you left, right?"

"Did you figure out it was Liliana who drugged me?"

"Matteo went to her place, but it was cleared out. We'll find her."

I cupped her jaw with my hands and searched her face. "Did he hurt you?"

She raised her eyebrows. "Besides the whole gun to my head and trying to make me marry him thing?"

I nodded. "Besides that."

"No."

I leaned in and kissed her forehead gently. "Good. It would have been messy to try and kill him twice."

She smiled.

She was in shock, that much was clear.

All the bravado and dark humor were coping mechanisms.

Soon, probably in a few hours, the adrenalin would wear off, and the reality of all that happened today would settle in. All the drama and loss. How close she came to dying. The death of her father.

And I would be there to hold her when it hit her body like a physical punch.

Because it would hit me too, how close I came to losing her.

We would be there for each other.

But for now, I would pretend with her, and crack inappropriate jokes, because that was what she needed.

The priest interrupted our conversation. "How the fuck am I supposed to explain another dead body on the altar to the Bishop?"

We looked at the priest and then each other.

Bianca mouthed, "Another?"

I shrugged.

Cesare rested his hand on the priest's shoulder as he shook his head in sympathy. "Sorry, Father. Had to be done."

I gestured toward the priest with my head as I looked at Bianca. "You know, since we're here...."

She narrowed her eyes. "Enzo. I'm not getting married wearing my sister's whorish wedding gown by a degenerate gambler priest who was willing to marry me at gunpoint to another man! Sorry, Father."

The priest nodded. "It's a fair point."

I swung my arm out in the direction of the altar. "Just because the man is a lowlife who clearly has no business being a man of the cloth doesn't mean the marriage wouldn't be legal. Sorry, Father."

The priest sniffed and raised his nose in the air. "That one stung a little."

I continued. "And I've obviously proved my point that you would be safer married to me."

Bianca hiked up her gown and stormed down the aisle.

"When we get married it will be with me wearing a *proper* gown, in a *proper* church, by a *proper* priest!"

I pointed to Cesare and the priest. "She said *when* we get married this time, not if. You both are my witnesses!"

I then ran down the aisle and caught up with Bianca to swoop her into my arms and carry her out of the church into the bright sunshine.

CHAPTER 38

BIANCA

ne month later

I TILTED my head to the right as I pushed the diamond cascade earring through my earlobe. "Enzo, hurry up! We're going to be late!"

He called out from the shower, "You could join me in here! Help me hold the soap."

I smoothed the wavy curl in my hair. "Nice try. I know what happens when you play *hold the soap*."

A ripple of pleasure pooled in my stomach at his deep, masculine chuckle.

Although the cottage was a bit of a construction zone mess, we had spent most nights over the last three weeks here. Preferring the quiet solitude of each other's company to the often-boisterous atmosphere of the main villa, which always seemed to be a hive of activity.

During the day, I headed to work at the Cavalieri head-quarters to work on graphic design projects or stayed at the villa office fine-tuning the wine label designs with Amara.

Enzo, meanwhile, worked at the winery supervising the wine bottling with his father and Cesare.

In the evenings, we took pleasure in working at the cottage, adding all the finishing touches that would give it that authentic yet artistic character we both craved.

We wanted the cottage to be a home we helped build ourselves with pieces we found around Italy. So on the weekends we traveled around searching through dusty attics, markets, and old shops, looking for authentic tiles and fixtures to give the cottage character.

In the solarium, we installed ceramic tile with a fabulous Roman motif that we found in Teramo, and stained the beautiful oak fireplace mantle we bought from a medieval monastery in Lanciano. In the courtyard, two bronze lion figurines we found at an estate auction in Santo Stefano di Sessanio flanked the door.

I also couldn't wait to paint the walls so I could hang up the montage of charcoal portraits I had drawn of everyone: Cesare and Milana, Amara and Barone, Gabriella, Alfonso, Rosa, Matteo, the staff at the villa and winery. With Enzo, I was creating a new family and I wanted to be surrounded by their faces.

I looked down at the diamond engagement ring on my hand.

The past was the past.

He finally helped me realize that I wasn't going to lose myself by loving him.

I was, in a way, reinventing myself through his love, in a good way.

Love didn't have to be a winner takes all battle of wills.

Once I stopped fighting my feelings for him, it became more about us.

It became about him supporting my decision not to become an employee of Cavalieri Enterprises, but rather to set up my own graphic design business—with Cavalieri as my number one client—so I still had my own independence.

And me agreeing to move in together, and finally saying yes to marrying him... as long as he agreed to a six-month engagement to give me time to plan a *proper* wedding.

I pulled off my robe and slipped into my dress. Smoothed the black silk over my hips before carefully lifting the hem to step into my heels. I kept the hem lifted to avoid the construction dust in the hallway as I crossed back into the en suite bathroom.

The steam from his shower had dissipated. The air was rich with the scent of spicy sandalwood and just a hint of pine and mint from his cologne and shaving foam. His back was turned to me as he shrugged into his tuxedo jacket.

I stepped behind him and lifted the collar, then smoothed the shoulders of his jacket.

He turned his head and kissed the tips of my fingers. "Thank you, baby."

I peeked at him over his shoulder in the mirror. "You look very handsome."

He winked before turning. He lifted my hands in his,

holding them out wide, and surveyed me. His dark gaze raked over my body, sending a shiver up my spine. "Damn, how did I get so lucky as to have a woman as beautiful as you on my arm?"

My lips quirked in a crooked smile. "I'm pretty sure *luck* had nothing to do with it."

I turned to get the diamond cuff bracelet I needed his help putting on.

"What the fuck, Bianca?"

I turned, feigning innocence. I was prepared for this.

Aunt Gabriella prepared me for this.

I licked my lips and opened them slightly as I blinked my heavily mascaraed lashes several times. "What?" I asked, slightly breathless like she taught me.

Enzo stepped close. He snaked his arm around my waist and pulled me against his hard body. "Don't you *what* me, babygirl. Where the fuck is the rest of your dress?" he growled.

I lowered my gaze and drew a circle on his chest with the tip of my finger. "Now Enzo, we agreed. You said it had to be floor-length and it couldn't show *any* cleavage."

He lowered his brow. "Yes, but...."

I squirmed out of his embrace and stepped back. I swept my arms over my hips, gesturing to my elegant black Valentino Cady Couture evening gown. "My gown actually goes beyond floor length into a small train." I then swept my hand over my collarbone. "And has a high, straight neckline showing *no* cleavage whatsoever, per your instructions."

He grabbed my shoulders and spun me around, so my

back was to the mirror. "Your entire back and the top of your ass are naked!"

It was true, the gown did have a rather daring cut-out back. "You didn't say anything about the back of the dress, darling," I responded, smiling sweetly.

It was how Aunt Gabriella had cheekily gotten around what she called Enzo's Mother Superior restrictions on my wardrobe choices.

Enzo stood before me, cupping his chin as he rubbed his lower lip with his finger.

The silence stretched.

Just when I was about to crack and offer to put on a different dress, Enzo let out a long breath.

He reached past me to pick up my bracelet. He then lifted my wrist and secured the diamond cuff around it. The whole time he had a rather sinister smile on his lips.

Uh oh. I didn't trust his easy acquiescence.

My gaze narrowed. "Why are you smiling like that?"

He checked his watch. "We're going to be late."

He strolled out of the bathroom's dressing area.

I followed him. "Enzo?"

He was shrugging into his black wool coat. He then held up my own coat for me to slip my arms into.

I turned and slipped in the left then the right.

He closed the coat and wrapped his arms around me tightly. As he did so he leaned in to whisper in my ear, "With your pretty little pert ass on display, I'm never leaving your side. Which is going to give me *all night long...* to think of countless creative ways to punish that same cute ass later."

I gasped as my cheeks warmed. I swallowed. "On second thought, maybe I should change...."

Enzo chuckled. "You can't. As you said, we don't want to be late to Papà and Amara's Christmas party." With that he gave me a playful spank through my coat.

Butterflies fluttered in my stomach. I had a feeling we'd be leaving the party early.

As he offered his arm to escort me out, I held up my hand. "Wait, my purse. I left it on the kitchen counter."

I walked down the hall into the kitchen and picked up the small black silk clutch. Just as I turned to leave, my eye caught the plates in the sink. I called out, "Enzo?"

He followed me into the kitchen. "Yes?"

"You didn't wash the plates from dinner?"

He raised his palms. "You said we were going to be late, and I had to get a shower."

"You were the one who said you didn't want any staff here helping with the chores. That you wanted the place to ourselves."

"And you said you were fine with that."

I pointed to my chest. "I am fine with that, as long as I'm not the only one doing all the work!"

He pointed to the sink. "You're not. I promise. It's just a couple of dirty dishes. I'll wash them when we get home."

"I don't want to go to a nice party and come home to dirty dishes."

"Do you want me to wash them now?"

I threw my hands up in frustration. "Of course not! We're late!"

He ran his hand through his hair. "Bianca, babygirl, how do I fix this? How do I make you happy?"

I looked at him, then at the dishes, then back at him… and burst into tears.

"Fuck! Baby! Don't cry!" He threw off his coat. "I'll do them now. Super quick. I promise we won't be late."

I waved my hands. "No, that's not it." I laughed and cried as I wiped under my eyes, worried I was going to ruin my makeup with my silly tears. "We're fighting over dirty dishes."

Enzo shook his head. "No, we're not, because I'm cleaning them right now."

I stepped within his arms and placed my hands on his cheeks. "Enzo, *we're fighting over dirty dishes.*"

I had a flashback to standing in this exact position just over a month ago, begging him to let me go, pleading with him to give up on us, and him stubbornly refusing.

My eyes filled with tears again as my lower lip trembled. "We did it. We're a normal couple in love."

Against fate and all the odds, we'd made it past the little earthquakes.

"I love you, Enzo."

He wrapped his hand around my neck as he leaned down, breathing against my lips before he claimed my mouth, "I love you, *tesoro mio.*"

CHAPTER 39

BARONE

J was in the study with Cesare when Enzo arrived for the party.

I lifted my arm holding the crystal Scotch decanter. He nodded and I poured him a glass.

Once we all had one in hand, Cesare said, "So, let's see it."

I smiled and reached into my inside tuxedo jacket pocket. "Sebastian's courier dropped it off a few hours ago."

I opened the small, black leather box. Nestled inside the black velvet interior was a five-carat pear-shaped yellow-diamond engagement ring.

Sebastian Diamanti had to secure it in a private auction from deep inside Russia for me. I was determined to get a diamond that captured the sunshine warmth Amara had brought to my life.

Enzo slapped me on the back. "So Amara finally agreed to let you propose to her?"

I snapped the ring box closed and returned it to my pocket. "I may have had to gently persuade her."

Cesare threw his head back and barked with laughter. "*Gently persuade?* When he heard Bianca said yes to you, he marched straight into Amara's office and told her that if she didn't agree to let him propose at the Christmas party, he would hogtie her, throw her over his shoulder, and carry her through the village to Santa Maria Church where he would bribe Father Luca with *two* new roofs, if he would marry them on the spot."

I frowned at Cesare as I raised my glass to my lips. "Like I said, *gently persuaded.*"

Enzo finished his drink and buttoned his tuxedo jacket. "We should join the girls. The guests will be arriving soon, and I can't leave Bianca alone for too long in the dress she is wearing."

He gave me a hug as he slapped me on the back. "I'm happy for you, Papà. Amara is a good girl."

I hugged him in return. "Same, son. I'm happy things worked out between you and Bianca."

Cesare hugged me as well. "*Buon Natale*, Papà."

I clasped him tightly. "*Buon Natale*, son."

He stood back and squeezed my upper arm. "I love you, Papà. Thanks for being a randy old goat and going after Amara. If it hadn't been for you, I might not have convinced Milana to give me a second chance."

I laughed. "What are fathers for?"

He headed toward the door. "Are you coming?"

I nodded. "Soon."

When he left, I pulled out the ring a second time. I opened the lid and stared down at its bright, shimmering depths.

My heart swelled.

Life was good.

My sons were happy. They had found amazing women who loved them.

Women who would carry on the Cavalieri family legacy with pride and honor.

And against all expectations for myself, I had also found a woman I loved and cherished.

I couldn't wait to see the look in Amara's eyes when I finally proposed, and she said yes.

At the sound of a scuff of a shoe, I finished my Scotch and turned, expecting to see either Enzo or Cesare urging me to join the guests. "I know, I'm coming—"

A dark figure stood on the threshold. "Dante Agnello sends his regards."

There was a bright muzzle flash in the dimly lit room.

An exploding fiery pain in my chest.

Then only darkness.

EPILOGUE

LILIANA

*T*he news was all over the Italian newspapers.
Barone Cavalieri Shot.

I needed to get out of here.

Out of Rome.

Out of the country.

I thought fleeing Cavalieri village would be far enough, but not now.

Not after this.

I knew too much.

They knew I was involved.

It would only be a matter of time before they found me.

They may have stopped looking after Bianca was returned safely, but that would change now.

I looked down at my phone again at the headline.

Barone Cavalieri Shot.

My hand shook as I tried to put the key in my apartment lock.

I dropped the keychain.

As I bent to pick it up, my shoulder bumped the door.

It swung open.

I stayed low on my haunches.

There wasn't a doubt in my mind that I had locked the door earlier.

Rising, my heart beat a wild cadence in my chest as I surveyed the quiet, dark interior of my small studio apartment.

I swallowed past the suffocating fear drying my throat. "Hello? Is anyone in here?"

Doubtful a homicidal mafia assassin would shout out *here*, but you never knew.

I listened for any sounds coming from inside.

All I could hear was the incessant drip from the leaking kitchen/bathroom faucet the landlord refused to fix.

Someone in the hall behind me cleared their throat.

I jumped and clutched at my chest.

They waved their hand impatiently in front of them. *"Mi scusi!"*

I nodded. *"Sì!* Of course! *Scusa!"*

The hallways were so narrow in the cheap apartment building that two people couldn't pass, so I hurried inside and shut the door so my neighbor could continue on. I leaned against the door and tried to calm my racing heart.

Just then a light in the corner turned on.

Fear strangled the scream in my throat.

Sitting at my tiny dinette table was a large, handsome man who looked just like Barone Cavalieri, but I knew that was impossible.

Barone Cavalieri was in surgery with a bullet in his chest.
I turned to run.

I stopped when I heard the sickeningly familiar sound of a gun being cocked.

Slowly turning back, I faced the intruder.

He kicked out the only remaining chair. "Have a seat. You and I are going to have a little chat."

On shaking legs, I crept over to the chair and sat down. Smashing my legs together to keep them from trembling, I gripped the worn edges of the seat, digging my nails in. "Who are you?"

"Benedict Cavalieri."

STAY TUNED FOR...

Seduction of the Patriarch
Cavalieri Billionaire Legacy, Book Four

ABOUT THE AUTHOR

Zoe Blake is the USA Today Bestselling Author of the romantic suspense sagas *The Diamanti Billionaire Dynasty* & *The Cavalieri Billionaire Legacy* inspired by her own heritage as well as her obsession with jewelry, travel, and the salacious gossip of history's most infamous families.

She delights in writing Dark Romance books filled with overly possessive billionaires, taboo scenes, and unexpected twists. She usually spends her ill-gotten gains on martinis, travels, and red lipstick. Since she can barely boil water, she's lucky enough to be married to a sexy Chef.
www.zblakebooks.com

ALSO BY ZOE BLAKE

CAVALIERI BILLIONAIRE LEGACY

A Dark Enemies to Lovers Romance

Scandals of the Father

Cavalieri Billionaire Legacy, Book One

Being attracted to her wasn't wrong... but acting on it would be.

As the patriarch of the powerful and wealthy Cavalieri family, my choices came with consequences for everyone around me.

The roots of my ancestral, billionaire-dollar winery stretch deep into the rich, Italian soil, as does our legacy for ruthlessness and scandal.

It wasn't the fact she was half my age that made her off limits.

Nothing was off limits for me.

A wounded bird, caught in a trap not of her own making, she posed no risk to me.

My obsessive desire to possess her was the real problem.

For both of us.

But now that I've seen her, tasted her lips, I can't let her go.

Whether she likes it or not, she needs my protection.

I'm doing this for her own good, yet, she fights me at every turn.

Refusing the luxury I offer, desperately trying to escape my grasp.

I need to teach her to obey before the dark rumors of my past reach her.

Ruin her.

She cannot find out what I've done, not before I make her mine.

Sins of the Son

Cavalieri Billionaire Legacy, Book Two

She's hated me for years... now it's past time to give her a reason to.

When you are a son, and one of the heirs, to the legacy of the Cavalieri name, you need to be more vicious than your enemies.

And sometimes, the lines get blurred.

Years ago, they tried to use her as a pawn in a revenge scheme against me.

Even though I cared about her, I let them treat her as if she were nothing.

I was too arrogant and self-involved to protect her then.

But I'm here now. Ready to risk my life tracking down every single one of them.

They'll pay for what they've done as surely as I'll pay for my sins against her.

Too bad it won't be enough for her to let go of her hatred of me,

To get her to stop fighting me.

Because whether she likes it or not, I have the power, wealth, and connections to keep her by my side

And every intention of ruthlessly using all three to make her mine.

Secrets of the Brother

Cavalieri Billionaire Legacy, Book Three

We were not meant to be together... then a dark twist of fate stepped in, and we're the ones who will pay for it.

As the eldest son and heir of the Cavalieri name, I inherit a great deal more than a billion dollar empire.

I receive a legacy of secrets, lies, and scandal.

After enduring a childhood filled with malicious rumors about my father, I have fallen prey to his very same sin.

I married a woman I didn't love out of a false sense of family honor.

Now she has died under mysterious circumstances.

And I am left to play the widowed groom.

For no one can know the truth about my wife...

Especially her sister.

The only way to protect her from danger is to keep her close, and yet, her very nearness tortures me.

She is my sister in name only, but I have no right to desire her.

Not after what I have done.

It's too much to hope she would understand that it was all for her.

It's always been about her.

Only her.

I am, after all, my father's son.

And there is nothing on this earth more ruthless than a Cavalieri man in love.

Seduction of the Patriarch

Cavalieri Billionaire Legacy, Book Four

I had buried the secrets of my past... now they were the lethal

weapons I would use to strike at our enemies.

I'd been indispensable in forging the billion-dollar Cavalieri empire, but always from the shadows.

My power and wealth were only rivaled by my reputation for ruthlessness.

Beneath it all, I'd been waging a war to keep the truth of my past hidden.

A past so dangerous, it threatened to shatter the very family I'd strived to safeguard.

Years ago, I handed over the mantle of patriarch to my younger brother, while I retreated to the north of Italy.

At the time, it was the best decision to protect the family from the stain of my sins.

But it put my brother in the line of fire of a vengeful mafia syndicate.

He thinks this is revenge for his actions in the present.

My brother is wrong.

He wasn't the target... I was.

They used her as a pawn to threaten my family.

I would use her to destroy them.

Her youth and sweet innocence meant nothing to me.

She would become an instrument of my revenge.

Whether it took seduction, punishment, or both, I intended to exploit her as a means to an end.

Yet, the more my little kitten showed her claws, the more I wanted to make her purr.

My plan had been to manipulate her into helping me topple the mafia syndicate, and then to retreat back into my dark past.

But if she keeps fighting me... I may just have to take her with me.

Scorn of the Betrothed

Cavalieri Billionaire Legacy, Book Five

A union forged in vengeance, bound by hate... and beneath it all, a twisted game of desire and deception.

In the heart of the Cavalieri family, I am the son destined for a loveless marriage.

The true legacy of my family, my birthright ties me to a woman I despise.

The daughter of the mafia boss who nearly ended my family.

She is my future wife, and I am her unwelcome groom.

The looming wedding is a beacon of hope for our families.

A promise of peace in a world fraught with danger and deception.

We were meant to be the bridge between two powerful legacies.

The only thing we share is a mutual hatred.

She is a prisoner to her families' ambitions, desperate for a way out.

My duty is to guard her, to ensure she doesn't escape her gilded cage.

But every moment spent with her, every spark of anger, adds fuel to the growing fire of desire between us.

We're trapped in a dangerous duel of passion and fury.

The more I try to tame her, the more she ignites me.

Hatred and desire become blurred.

Our impending marriage becomes a twisted game.

But as the wedding draws near, my suspicions grow.

My bride is not who she claims to be.

IVANOV CRIME FAMILY TRILOGY

A Dark Mafia Romance

Savage Vow

Gregor & Samara's story

I took her innocence as payment.

She was far too young and naïve to be betrothed to a monster like me.

I would bring only pain and darkness into her sheltered world.

That's why she ran.

I should've just let her go…

She never asked to marry into a powerful Russian mafia family.

None of this was her choice.

Unfortunately for her, I don't care.

I own her… and after three years of searching… I've found her.

My runaway bride was about to learn disobedience has consequences… punishing ones.

Having her in my arms and under my control had become an obsession.

Nothing was going to keep me from claiming her before the eyes of God and man.

She's finally mine… and I'm never letting her go.

Vicious Oath

Damien & Yelena's story

When I give an order, I expect it to be obeyed.

She's too smart for her own good, and it's going to get her killed.

Against my better judgement, I put her under the protection of my powerful Russian mafia family.

So imagine my anger when the little minx ran.

For three long years I've been on her trail, always one step behind.

Finding and claiming her had become an obsession.

It was getting harder to rein in my driving need to possess her... to own her.

But now the chase is over.

I've found her.

Soon she will be mine.

And I plan to make it official, even if I have to drag her kicking and screaming to the altar.

This time... there will be no escape from me.

Betrayed Honor

Mikhail & Nadia's story

Her innocence was going to get her killed.

That was if I didn't get to her first.

She's the protected little sister of the powerful Ivanov Russian mafia family - the very definition of forbidden.

It's always been my job, as their Head of Security, to watch over her but never to touch.

That ends today.

She disobeyed me and put herself in danger.

It was time to take her in hand.

I'm the only one who can save her and I will fight anyone who tries to stop me, including her brothers.

Honor and loyalty be damned.

She's mine now.

RUTHLESS OBSESSION SERIES

A Dark Mafia Romance

Sweet Cruelty

Dimitri & Emma's story

It was an innocent mistake.

She knocked on the wrong door.

Mine.

If I were a better man, I would've just let her go.

But I'm not.

I'm a cruel bastard.

I ruthlessly claimed her virtue for my own.

It should have been enough.

But it wasn't.

I needed more.

Craved it.

She became my obsession.

Her sweetness and purity taunted my dark soul.

The need to possess her nearly drove me mad.

A Russian arms dealer had no business pursuing a naive librarian student.

She didn't belong in my world.

I would bring her only pain.

But it was too late…

She was mine and I was keeping her.

Sweet Depravity

Vaska & Mary's story

The moment she opened those gorgeous red lips to tell me no, she was mine.

I was a powerful Russian arms dealer and she was an innocent schoolteacher.

If she had a choice, she'd run as far away from me as possible.

Unfortunately for her, I wasn't giving her one.

I wasn't just going to take her; I was going to take over her entire world.

Where she lived.

What she ate.

Where she worked.

All would be under my control.

Call it obsession.

Call it depravity.

I don't give a damn… as long as you call her mine.

Sweet Savagery

Ivan & Dylan's Story

I was a savage bent on claiming her as punishment for her family's mistakes.

As a powerful Russian Arms dealer, no one steals from me and gets away with it.

She was an innocent pawn in a dangerous game.

She had no idea the package her uncle sent her from Russia contained my stolen money.

If I were a good man, I would let her return the money and leave.

If I were a gentleman, I might even let her keep some of it just for frightening her.

As I stared down at the beautiful living doll stretched out before me like a virgin sacrifice,

I thanked God for every sin and misdeed that had blackened my cold heart.

I was not a good man.

I sure as hell wasn't a gentleman… and I had no intention of letting her go.

She was mine now.

And no one takes what's mine.

Sweet Brutality

Maxim & Carinna's story

The more she fights me, the more I want her.

It's that beautiful, sassy mouth of hers.

It makes me want to push her to her knees and dominate her, like the brutal savage I am.

As a Russian Arms dealer, I should not be ruthlessly pursuing an innocent college student like her, but that would not stop me.

A twist of fate may have brought us together, but it is my twisted obsession that will hold her captive as my own treasured possession.

She is mine now.

I dare you to try and take her from me.

Sweet Ferocity

Luka & Katie's Story

I was a mafia mercenary only hired to find her, but now I'm going to keep her.

She is a Russian mafia princess, kidnapped to be used as a pawn in a dangerous territory war.

Saving her was my job. Keeping her safe had become my obsession.

Every move she makes, I am in the shadows, watching.

I was like a feral animal: cruel, violent, and selfishly out for my own needs. Until her.

Now, I will make her mine by any means necessary.

I am her protector, but no one is going to protect her from me.

Sweet Intensity

Anton & Brynn's Story

She couldn't possibly have known the danger she would be in the moment she innocently accepted the job.

She was too young for a man my age, barely in her twenties. Far too pure and untouched.

Too bad that wasn't going to stop me.

The moment I laid eyes on her, I claimed her.

She would be mine… by any means necessary.

I owned the most elite Gambling Club in Chicago, which was a secret front for my true business as a powerful crime boss for the Russian Mafia.

And she was a fragile little bird, who had just flown straight into my open jaws.

Naïve and sweet, she was a tasty morsel I couldn't resist biting.

My intense drive to dominate and control her had become an obsession.

I would ruthlessly use my superior strength and connections to take over her life.

The harder she resisted, the more feral and savage I would become.

She needed to understand… she was mine now.

Mine.

Printed in Great Britain
by Amazon

26452400R00218